“I’m glad
Not the s
but all he could think of.

Marybeth looked startled. Frightened almost. The long trip from Boston must have worn her down. “Where can I find a place to stay?” The way her gaze darted around the room, she reminded him of a rabbit trying to escape a dog pack.

Hadn’t she heard his remark about lodging? Did she see something in him to cause her concern? Rand swallowed hard. If he didn’t have such faith in his parents’ choice, he would think this was all a mistake. Instead of being happy or even interested in being in his company, Marybeth almost seemed afraid.

Then it struck him. She knew. Someone, probably Maisie, had told her the one thing Dad had insisted was Rand’s responsibility to tell her. Now she was frightened of him, and he had no idea how to go about soothing away her fears and assuring her of his constant efforts to live for the Lord.

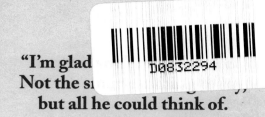

Books by Louise M. Gouge

Love Inspired Historical

Love Thine Enemy
The Captain's Lady
At the Captain's Command
**A Proper Companion*
**A Suitable Wife*
**A Lady of Quality*
†*Cowboy to the Rescue*
†*Cowboy Seeks a Bride*

*Ladies in Waiting
†Four Stones Ranch

LOUISE M. GOUGE

has been married to her husband, David, for fifty years. They have four children and eight grandchildren. Louise always had an active imagination, thinking up stories for her friends, classmates and family but seldom writing them down. At a friend's insistence, she finally began to type up her latest idea. Before trying to find a publisher, Louise returned to college, earning a BA in English/creative writing and a master's degree in liberal studies. She reworked that first novel based on what she had learned and sold it to a major Christian publisher. Louise then worked in television marketing for a short time before becoming a college English/humanities instructor. She has had fifteen novels published, several of which have earned multiple awards, including the Inspirational Reader's Choice Award and the Laurel Wreath Award. Please visit her website at blog.louisemgouge.com.

Cowboy Seeks a Bride

LOUISE M. GOUGE

HARLEQUIN® LOVE INSPIRED® HISTORICAL

™ LOVE INSPIRED BOOKS

ISBN-13: 978-0-373-28295-1

Cowboy Seeks a Bride

This edition published by arrangement with Love Inspired Books.

www.Harlequin.com

Printed in U.S.A.

What time I am afraid, I will trust in Thee.
— *Psalms* 56:3

This book is dedicated to the intrepid pioneers who settled the San Luis Valley of Colorado in the mid to late 1800s. They could not have found a more beautiful place to make their homes than in this vast 7500 ft. high valley situated between the majestic Sangre de Cristo and San Juan Mountain ranges. It has been many years since I lived in the San Luis Valley, so my thanks go to Pam Williams of Hooper, Colorado, for her extensive on-site research on my behalf. With their permission, I named two of my characters after her and her husband, Charlie. These dear old friends are every bit as kind and wise as their namesakes. I also want to thank my dear husband of fifty years, David Gouge, for his loving support as I pursue my dream of writing love stories to honor the Lord.

Chapter One

July 1881

Randall Northam is a gambler. Randall Northam is a killer.

The words pulsed through Marybeth O'Brien's head, keeping time with the clatter of the iron wheels on the railroad track as the train propelled her inescapably toward her prospective husband. Until a few moments ago she'd thought his most notable quality was being the second son of a wealthy Colorado ranching family. But the lively young woman seated across from her had just imparted a vital bit of information Randall Northam's parents had left out when they'd arranged this marriage. And from the enthusiasm brightening Maisie Henshaw's face, Marybeth could see her story wasn't finished.

"Yep, he shot that thieving varmint right in the heart. Why, Rand can outdraw anybody." The red-haired girl elbowed her handsome young husband in the ribs. "Even me."

Dr. Henshaw chuckled indulgently, his expression

utterly devoid of censure, but rather, exuding only devotion for his wife. "You may have heard stories about how wild the West is, Miss O'Brien, but you will certainly feel safe with Rand protecting you."

"Just like me protecting you." Maisie chortled in a decidedly unladylike manner.

Her more refined husband nodded his agreement with a grin. "Well, we all have our talents."

Marybeth returned a weak smile while gulping down a terror she'd never felt as she'd made her plans to go to Colorado. She'd had some concern, yes. A great deal of doubt, of course. But never fear. In fact, the farther she'd traveled from Boston and the closer to her destination, she'd actually begun to look forward to meeting her prospective husband. If he turned out to be all that his parents and his own letters stated, she would reconsider her lifelong vow never to marry. But this disclosure about her intended changed everything and reaffirmed her determination never to be trapped in a miserable marriage, as her mother had been. She lifted a silent prayer of thanks for this encounter with the Henshaws and for finding out the truth about Mr. Randall Northam before meeting him.

Even as she prayed, guilt teased at the corners of her mind. She'd accepted her train fare from Colonel and Mrs. Northam, arguing with herself that perhaps Randall would turn out to be as kind, handsome and noble as his father, a former Union officer. If so, perhaps she could convince him to postpone the wedding until she found Jimmy. Surely, with two brothers of his own, he would understand her desperate desire to find her only brother who'd fled to Colorado eight long years ago to escape their abusive father. Finding Jimmy would not only reunite her with her only living relative, it would provide a means for her not to marry at all. That was, if Jimmy still had Mam's silver locket. With the key to a great treasure tucked inside, the locket would mean she could repay the Northams for her train fare.

"Don't you think so?" Maisie reached across and patted Marybeth's gloved hand.

"Wha—?" Marybeth felt an unaccustomed blush rush to her cheeks. How rude of her not to pay attention to her companions. "Forgive me. Would you repeat the question?"

"Now, Maisie, dear." John Henshaw bent his head toward his wife in a sweet, familiar way. "Miss O'Brien must be tired from her travels. We should give her time to rest so she will be at her best when she meets her future husband."

"Oh, I'm sorry." Maisie's pretty face crinkled with worry. "Would you like a pillow? A blanket?" She nudged her husband and pointed to the bag beneath his seat. "Honey, dig out that pillow I packed."

"Thank you. You're too kind." Marybeth accepted the small cushion, placed it against the window and rested her head, not because she wanted to sleep, but because she needed time to think. Although she hated missing the beautiful mountain scenery as the train descended the western side of La Veta Pass, she closed her eyes to keep Maisie from further talking. Again guilt pinched her conscience. This was no way to treat such kind people.

When they'd first met early this morning, the Henshaws had recognized their social duty to an unattached young woman traveling alone, just as several matrons and couples had all the way from Boston. Due to their protecting presence, Marybeth hadn't been accosted by a single man on the entire trip, although one well-dressed man in particular had stared at her rather boldly today when the doctor wasn't looking. He would have been more careful if he'd known Maisie was the one to watch out for. Marybeth wanted to laugh thinking about her new friend being a sharpshooter. If anything, she looked like a perfect lady in her fashionable brown traveling suit and elegant matching hat.

The moment the conductor had escorted her to the seat across from the Henshaws, Marybeth could see they were decent Christian people. Because they lived in the town where she would soon reside, she'd gradually told them more about herself, at last telling them she was Randall Northam's intended bride. Maisie had hooted with joy, announcing she'd known "Rand" all her life, and his sister, Rosamond, was her best friend. As if unfolding a great yarn, she told Marybeth about Rand's shoot-out over a card game in a saloon.

A gambler, a killer and, no doubt, a drunkard. This was the man she was expected to marry? Indeed she would not marry him, not in a hundred years.

Rand checked his pocket watch and then glanced down the railroad line toward Alamosa searching for the telltale black cloud of smoke from the Denver and Rio Grande engine. The wind was up today, so maybe tumbleweed or sand had blown over the tracks, slowing the train. Maybe a tree had fallen somewhere up on La Veta Pass and they'd had to stop to remove it before proceeding down into the San Luis Valley.

Rand chewed his lip and paced the boardwalk outside the small station, his boots thudding against the wood in time with his pounding heart. How much longer must he wait before the train arrived? Before his bride arrived?

He glanced down at his new black boots, dismayed at the unavoidable dust covering the toes. Hoping to look his best for his new bride, he brushed each boot over the back of the opposite pant leg and then wiped a hand over the gray marks that ill-advised action left. So much for looking his best. Where was that train anyway?

"Settle down, Rand." His younger brother, Tolley, half reclined on the bench set against the station's dull yellow outside wall. "If the train's going to be late, Charlie'll let you know." He jutted his chin toward the open window above him. Inside, Charlie Williams manned the telegraph, but at the moment no syncopated clickety-click indicated an incoming message. Tolley shook his head and smirked. "Man, if this is what it's like to get married, I don't want any part of it. Where's my cocksure brother today?" He patted the gun strapped to his side, clearly referencing the worst day of Rand's life.

"Could you just keep quiet about that?" He shot Tolley a cross look. After three years his brother still wouldn't let him forget the time Rand had been forced to kill a horse thief. Instead of understanding how guilty Rand felt about the incident, Tolley idolized him, even wanted to emulate his gun-fighting skills. "Don't say anything to Miss O'Brien except 'how do you do' and 'welcome to Esperanza.' Let me take care of the rest, understand?"

"Yes, boss." Tolley touched his hat in a mock salute. He glanced down the tracks. "Looks like your wait is over."

Rand followed his gaze. Sure enough, there came the massive Denver and Rio Grande engine, its black smoke almost invisible in the crosswinds, its cars tucked in a row behind it. Now his pulse pounded in his chest and ears, and his mouth became dry, just as it had before that fateful gunfight. Cocksure? Not in the least. Just able to hide his emotions under stress better than most people. At least most of the time. Today he couldn't quite subdue his nerves.

The engine chugged to a stop and sent out a blast of gray-white steam from its undercarriage. Porters jumped out, set stools in front of the doors and gave a hand to the disembarking passengers.

"Rand! Hey, Rand." Emerging from the second passenger car, Maisie Henshaw ignored the porter, practically leaped from the last step and ran toward him. Behind her, Doc Henshaw, toting a valise and his black doctoring bag, stretched out his long legs to keep up with his bride. Rand would never understand how these two very different people had gotten together, but it sure wasn't any of his business. Besides, anybody could see how happy they were.

Rand hoped his own imminent marriage would be just as happy. That would be an extra blessing on his road to redeeming his past. For three years he'd worked hard to live a perfect life by following every order, every wish of his parents, and taking on more than his share of chores to gain his older brother's respect. Now, if Miss O'Brien would have him, he would be marrying the young lady his parents had chosen for him. It made him feel as if he'd almost arrived at redemption. Almost.

Maisie dashed up and gave him a sisterly hug. "My, you're looking handsome. Any special reason you're all gussied up and out here waiting for the train?" She elbowed Doc in the ribs and chortled.

"Now, honey." His hands full, Doc gently bumped her shoulder with his own. "Let the man be."

"All right, all right." Maisie sniffed in mock annoyance. "But I'm in no hurry to go home." She marched over to the bench and plunked herself down beside Tolley. "Move over, kid."

Doc just chuckled at her antics. "Hello, Rand. It's good to see you." He sat next to Maisie.

Rand had only a moment to give his impromptu audience a scowl of irritation before their eyes all turned toward the train car. Maisie giggled and Tolley let out a low whistle. Rand followed their gaze. And nearly fell onto the bench beside them.

Slender and of medium height, the young lady had thick auburn hair piled high on her head, with a cute little brown-and-blue hat perched at the summit. Her sandy-colored dress—well, more suit than dress, and trimmed with dark blue bits of ribbon and such—hugged well-formed curves that he wouldn't let himself dwell on until after they were married. But it was her face that held his attention. Like a classical Roman statue of *Venus* he'd once seen in a magazine, her elegant beauty was flawless and her porcelain cheeks glowed with a hint of roses. He couldn't make out the color of her eyes, but she'd said in a letter that they were hazel.

Oh, mercy, she's even more beautiful than her picture. What did I ever do to deserve this prize? Nothing, that's what. It was all a matter of grace.

Thank You, Lord, for sending me such a lovely bride.

That was, if Miss O'Brien would have him once he told her the truth about his past.

Foolishly putting off the inevitable, Marybeth had offered a silly excuse to the Henshaws for not following them right away. Maisie had teased about her shyness but hadn't forced the issue. The last passenger in the car, Marybeth had slowly moved toward the door where the conductor had given her a patient smile.

At last she emerged from the darkness, shielding her eyes from both the sun and the wind. A porter offered a hand and helped her to the ground. She pressed a dime—her last one—into his hand for the services he'd so diligently rendered during the trip. "Thank you."

As he bowed to her, a sharp whistle split the air. She located Maisie seated by the train station and pointing enthusiastically at a tall, broad-shouldered cowboy. He was dressed in a dark green plaid shirt, spotless black trousers and shiny black boots. While she couldn't see his face due to the broad brim of his light brown hat, his physique was certainly attractive, the sort that girls at her school always gushed over when the matrons weren't in the room.

Her gaze lit on the gun strapped to his belt and a shudder went through her. In traveling across the country, she'd noticed more than one cowboy wearing a gun. Another traveler had told her the weapons were necessary because of wild animals and maybe even train robbers. Yet how many of those cowboys had killed a man, as this one had?

He strode toward her with a firm gait and her heart pounded with fear…and a very odd thrill. What was wrong with her? She'd never been one to court danger. Indeed, she avoided confrontation at all cost.

"Miss O'Brien?" He tipped his hat to her.

Now she could see his face and her breath left her. When he hadn't sent a picture, she'd wondered if his looks were not particularly appealing. That was far from the case. In all of her twenty years, she had never seen a more handsome man, from his bright green eyes to his tanned, well-formed cheekbones and slender nose to his attractive, slightly crooked smile that revealed even white teeth. He even smelled good; a woody fragrance she couldn't quite identify. But it was those eyes, emerald green and reflecting the darker shade of his shirt, that held her attention, that mesmerized her.

"Yes, I'm Marybeth O'Brien." Her voice squeaked, but he had the good manners not to laugh. "Mr. Northam?"

"Yes, ma'am." He reached out to take her gloved hand. "Please call me Rand. We mostly go by first names out here. That is, if it's all right with you."

At his touch, a hot spark shot up her arm, turning to ice as it reached her neck. She couldn't stop a shudder, but again he didn't react. "Yes, that's fine." Somehow she managed to say the words. Somehow she managed to keep her knees from buckling.

For countless seconds they stood staring at each other. Marybeth tried to reconcile the idea of this young, incredibly handsome man being a killer, a gambler, a man exactly like her father. That thought shook her loose from her hypnotic state. Hadn't Da looked every bit the gentleman when he was sober? For the first time in her life she understood how Mam had been swept off her feet and right into a tragic, abusive marriage.

"Well—" She broke away from Rand's hold. "I have a trunk someplace." She looked around and spied it being unloaded from the baggage car. "There it is. Shall we?" She took a step in that direction.

"Yes, ma'am." Rand nonetheless gently touched her upper arm to stop her. "I brought my brother along to take care of that." He motioned to a younger version of himself. "Tolley, get yourself over here and meet Miss O'Brien… Marybeth, this is my brother Tolley."

The brothers' good relationship was evident in the boy's teasing smirk and overly polite address to her. "How do you do, Miss O'Brien? Welcome to Esperanza." From his singsong tone, she guessed he'd been coached.

"Very well, thank you, Tolley. I understand first names are the rule here, so please call me Marybeth." For some reason she felt no fear of him, despite the gun he wore. Did his easy smile and wide-eyed innocence hide a murderous spirit, too?

"Yes, ma'am." He shot a look at Rand almost as if seeking approval. "I'll take care of that trunk and see you later."

"Oh." Marybeth's heart sank as he strode away. She'd hoped the boy's presence would serve as a buffer between her and Rand. She looked up at Rand. "I—I was thinking…"

Again he touched her upper arm. Again a shiver raced up to her neck. "If you don't mind, I'd like for us to go over to Mrs. Williams's café for a bite to eat before I take you to your lodgings. That way we can start getting acquainted."

Marybeth's stomach answered for her with a slight

rumbling. Heat flooded her cheeks. "Oh, dear. I guess you have your answer."

His smile held no censure. "Good. She has the reputation of being the best cook in Esperanza."

Marybeth accepted his offered arm—his very muscular arm—and they began their trek down the rutted street toward the center of town. Maybe this was best. She could break with him in public rather than in private. That way, if he was like Da, he wouldn't dare strike her. Da had always kept the abuse to the privacy of their shabby house so no one would see his true nature. Her only dilemma would be finding a place to stay afterward. Maybe that Mrs. Williams would help her. Maybe someone would. One thing was certain. Dr. and Mrs. Henshaw would be no help. From the admiring looks on their faces, it was obvious they thought Rand was nothing short of a hero.

Feeling the warmth of Marybeth's hand on his arm, smelling the fragrance of her lavender perfume, Rand adjusted his usual long stride to suit her shorter one. She had a dainty way about her that filled him with admiration. Most young ladies he knew tended to have a sturdier manner, although few were as tomboyish as Maisie and her sisters. He'd have to take particular care of this little gal until she became accustomed to Western ways. Pampering her would be his new favorite activity.

People along the street acknowledged him with a nod, a tipped hat or a wave, but no one interrupted their journey to the café. He knew they'd gossip about Marybeth and him, just as they had Nate and Susanna when his older brother was courting the Southern belle. He hoped their respect for the Northam name would inspire townsfolk to give him a wide berth so he and his prospective bride could get acquainted.

Prospective bride. That was how he'd thought of Marybeth ever since Mother had first written to him about her six months ago. Now that she was by his side, he was pretty close to dispensing with the "prospective" part. With his parents and sister extolling her character in their letters and saying they all agreed she was just the right gal to suit him, he felt as if he already knew her. They'd also written to say she would help to bring that element of refinement Dad hoped to add to the community.

Marybeth's letters had informed him that she liked music, liked to read, enjoyed cooking and housekeeping; the usual feminine qualities to make a man eager to go home at the end of the day. Her beauty was just a bonus. Not that he deserved any of it, of course. But maybe this was another example of God's grace toward an unworthy sinner.

"Here we are." He steered her toward Williams's Café and swung the door inward to let her enter first. The aroma of simmering chicken and freshly baked bread poured over them, whetting his appetite.

Before stepping over the threshold, Marybeth gave him a tremulous smile, causing his heart to bounce around inside his chest. The sweet little thing was skittish, bless her heart. Of course, he felt a bit nervous, too. Maybe by the time they finished dinner, they'd feel more comfortable with each other. Sharing a meal could have that effect on a person.

"Hello, Rand." Mrs. Williams, proprietor and chief cook, gave him a wave from the kitchen door. "Take any seat you like."

"Thanks, Miss Pam. Come over and meet my…meet Miss O'Brien." Stopping short of calling Marybeth his bride, Rand paused to hang his hat on the wall peg. He led her to a table beside the wide front window where both of them would be able to watch the passersby. It was also far enough away from the half dozen other customers to keep their conversation fairly private.

"Welcome to Esperanza, honey." Miss Pam walked across the recently enlarged dining room and held a floured hand out to Marybeth. Seeming to think better of it, she brushed the hand on her white apron and chuckled. "Oops. I just finished making dumplings to go with the stewed chicken, so let's not get any flour on those nice gloves."

"How do you do, Miss Pam?" Her smile warm and friendly, Marybeth seemed to catch on real quick to the casual way things were done out here, another attractive quality in Rand's mind. "Chicken and dumplings sounds wonderful."

"Miss Pam's are the best," Rand said. "Make that two."

"Coming right up." Miss Pam signaled Lucy, her waitress, before returning to her kitchen.

Lucy took their order for coffee. When she brought it, she gave Rand a surreptitious wink and then went about serving the other customers. Rand doubted the wink held any other meaning than teasing because Lucy and his best friend, Seamus, were courting.

As Marybeth removed her tan kid gloves, she glanced around the room and out the window, her shyness apparent. Rand gently captured one hand across the narrow table, hoping to likewise capture her gaze. Her long, slender fingers felt just right in his grasp, except for the tiny tremor in them. He gave her a reassuring squeeze.

"I'm glad you're finally here." Not the smartest thing to say, but all he could think of.

She looked startled. Frightened almost. The long trip from Boston must have worn her down. "Where can I find a place to stay?" The way her gaze darted around the room, she reminded him of a rabbit trying to escape a dog pack.

Hadn't she heard his remark about lodging? Did she see something in him to cause her concern? Rand swallowed hard. If he didn't have such faith in his parents' choice, he would think this was all a mistake. Instead of being happy or even interested in being in his company, Marybeth almost seemed afraid.

Then it struck him. She knew. Someone, probably Maisie, had told her the one thing Dad had insisted was Rand's responsibility to tell her. Now she was frightened of him, and he had no idea how to go about soothing away her fears and assuring her of his constant efforts to live for the Lord.

There it was, the tiny hardening in Rand's expression that signaled the beginning of his anger. Oh, he'd find a way to cover it until they were alone. Then she'd pay. Just as Mam never knew exactly what had displeased Da, Marybeth had no idea what she'd done to anger Rand. Now his perfectly formed face was lined with a winsome sort of sadness, just like Da when he sobered up and felt ashamed for his brutality.

Rand cleared his throat. "We planned to have you stay with my brother and his wife, but Susanna's expecting her second— Uh-oh, sorry. Maybe where you come from, folks don't talk about such things."

Marybeth hid her surprise at his comment. Indeed, such matters were never discussed at Fairfield Young Ladies' Academy. However, in the lower class neighborhood where she'd grown up, people never held back when discussing the hows and whys of childbirth. Rand's concern for her sensibilities spoke well of him. It was a quality more in keeping with the man his parents had recommended to her so highly.

"I certainly understand why Susanna doesn't need company right now." She offered a little shrug to indicate a lack of concern, just the opposite of what she felt. Being in another woman's house could provide protection. "Perhaps a hotel?" She would have to take a job to pay for it, but she'd planned to do so anyway. Her purse was empty, and traveling to Wagon Wheel Gap to search for her brother, Jimmy, would require another season of earning the funds to do so.

"Another uh-oh." He smiled and grimaced at the same time, a wickedly attractive expression. *Oh, Lord, guard my heart against this man's charms.* "We don't have a hotel. My father plans to bring in a hotelier from back East, maybe even England. He's working on that and a lot of other things to build up the town. Of course that doesn't help us right now."

Before alarm could take hold of Marybeth, Lucy arrived with two bowls of steaming chicken and dumplings. Once again Rand took her hand. This time he bowed his head and lifted a short, sincere-sounding prayer of thanks for the food. Emotion churned through Marybeth's chest like a roiling sea. Da had prayed, too. Magnificent prayers in his lilting Irish brogue, prayers

God would surely hear for their beauty. Yet he never changed, never improved his ways. She set aside the memories but would never permit herself to forget them, lest she end up like Mam.

"Can I bring you anything else?" The waitress gave Rand a simpering smile at odds with her tomboyish swagger. She was flirting with him, but from his friendly, "No, thank you," Marybeth could see he was oblivious to her attempts to get his attention. An odd sort of jealousy smote Marybeth. No, that was just silly. Not jealousy at all. Simply an awareness of the girl's bad manners in flirting with a man when he was in the company of another woman.

They wordlessly began to eat and Marybeth's appetite roared into command. If not for the two years spent at Fairfield Young Ladies' Academy, paid for by the ladies of her Boston church, she would shovel the delicious food into her mouth just as she had as a child.

"About where you're going to stay..." Lifting the shaker next to the salt, Rand added a healthy dash of pepper to his dinner. "Mrs. Foster is the local piano teacher and church organist, and she's got an extra room. She'll be mighty glad for the company because her husband died last year and she's still at loose ends. She's an older lady and a bit talkative, but kind as can be. I hope that meets with your approval."

The doubt and apology in his voice, along with his sorrowful wince as he mentioned the husband's death, gave Marybeth pause. He possessed all the outward trappings of a gentle, thoughtful man. But so had Da.

"It's very kind of you to arrange that, Rand." She offered a polite smile that hid her relief over not having to worry about lodging.

Confusion clouded his expression. "Did you think I wouldn't find proper lodging for you?" His tone held a note of injury.

"W-well." Her chest tightened into a familiar knot. Had she touched a nerve? Was he angry? "No, of course not. I mean, yes, of course you would."

He shook his head and chuckled. "Now that I think of it, when we were writing, I don't believe we addressed the topic of where you would stay." He gave his head a little shake. "An unfortunate oversight."

"Yes, that's it." The knot in her chest eased. "Just an oversight."

They'd almost finished their meal, so she'd best tackle the difficult subject hanging over them. That way, if he became angry, she could look for help. Perhaps Miss Pam. Or the plump older couple seated at a table in the corner. No, they were leaving. In fact, they were coming this way.

"Howdy, Rand." The man clapped him on the shoulder. "Who's this pretty newcomer?"

Rand introduced Marybeth to the Archers and said they lived south of town in the Bowen community.

"You've got yourself a fine catch, missy," said the woman. "Lots of girls around here have tried to lasso this boy since the day he first started shaving."

While the Archers laughed, Rand rolled his eyes in a charming way. "You folks have a nice day."

They took their dismissal in good humor and left. Once again the situation gave Marybeth pause. They obviously didn't fear Rand. Miss Pam and Lucy didn't, either. When had Marybeth decided he was her father come back to life? Maybe she didn't have to be afraid of him. Maybe she should dismiss her fears and give him a chance to prove himself.

"Are you ready to go?" Rand started to push back from the table.

"No." Trying to gather her thoughts, Marybeth took another sip of coffee.

"Oh." Rand settled back down. "You want dessert? Apple pie? Or Miss Pam's special elderberry pie?"

His sudden eagerness to please made Marybeth want to laugh, but what she must tell him was too serious for her to indulge in any such levity.

"No, thank you." She glanced out the window, where people walked to and fro on their daily errands. On the way here, she'd noticed many people giving Rand friendly waves. Like Miss Pam and Lucy, every single one appeared to admire him. Still, she must proceed with caution. "I have to tell you something." She lifted her coffee cup for another bracing sip.

"I was afraid of that." His face fell and his shoulders drooped with disappointment. "You won't marry me because I'm too ugly. There was a reason I didn't send a picture, you know."

Marybeth almost spewed coffee all over him, barely catching the liquid before it escaped her lips. Now she could see the mischief in his eyes that bespoke an awareness of his good looks without being excessively prideful, a rare quality. Most handsome men of her acquaintance strutted about, clearly proud of their appearance.

Once she regained her composure, she shook her head. "I'm afraid it's a bit more serious than that."

"Ah." The humor left his face but a gentle twinkle remained in his eyes. "Go on. You can tell me anything."

She would take him at his word, at least for now. Borrowing from her Irish legacy of masterful storytelling, she wove the "sad but true tale" of her family, punctuating it with a few well-placed tears and carefully leaving out several details. Eight years before, when her brother was only fifteen, he'd been beaten up by neighborhood bullies. Da had called him a coward for not standing up to the thugs, so Jimmy had left home and never come back. He'd written only one letter a year or so later, posting it from Del Norte, Colorado, and saying he was headed to Wagon Wheel Gap to do some silver prospecting. Now that their parents had died, the mention of which brought genuine tears to her eyes, at least for Mam, she knew she had to search for her only living relative before she settled down.

At this point she batted her eyes, sending a few tears down her cheeks, and then dabbed at them with a handkerchief and gave Rand a look that pleaded for understanding.

"I'm sorry to hear about your dad and brother not getting along." He shook his head and stared off with a thoughtful look. "Describe your brother to me."

Marybeth started. Could it be this simple? Was it possible that Rand knew him? "His name is Jimmy O'Brien." She couldn't keep the eagerness from her voice. "I haven't seen him since I was twelve years old. He was just a couple of inches taller than I was, so he may be about five feet, five inches now, if he takes after our father. He has red hair and hazel eyes." She searched her memory for other details, but none came to mind. She certainly would not mention Mam's silver locket, which she'd given him to keep Da from pawning it to buy liquor. Marybeth laughed softly. "And, as if you haven't already figured out, he's Irish."

Rand's frown of concentration intensified. "Does he speak with a brogue?"

"No." She shook her head. "We both worked hard to get rid of it so we could get better jobs." She had worked especially hard to speak without the brogue, hoping to find employment as a servant in an upper-class home, something a rich rancher couldn't possibly understand. "He did pretty well, and the ladies at my church were so impressed by my efforts that they sent me to Fairfield Young Ladies' Academy, where I met Rosamond." She bit her lip, hoping she didn't sound proud, wondering how much further to go. "I learned deportment, but I also learned typing and accounting skills." In her letters she'd mentioned the academy but not the training in office work.

"Typing." He scratched his head. "I've heard about those typewriting machines but haven't ever seen one. I did receive a letter written on one. Makes a real nice page, just like printing in a book."

She beamed a smile at him, encouraged that he didn't seem the least bit angry. "Yes. I'm hoping to find work, perhaps in a bank or for a lawyer."

"Work?" Now he frowned again, but still without anger. "But I'm responsible for your care. I've made arrangements with Mrs. Foster on the condition you would agree to live there until our wedding." His eyes narrowed. "Marybeth, please assure me that you didn't take advantage of my parents' kindness just so they would pay your train fare so you could find your brother."

"N-no, not at all." *Yes.* At least partly yes. "Please recall the part of our agreement stating that either of us has the right to cancel our wedding if we're not compatible."

"And in just forty-five minutes, you've decided we're not compatible?" The edge in his voice sent a shiver through her middle. "Seems you've already made up your mind." He raised his hand as if he wanted to hit something, and Marybeth prepared to duck. Instead he waved off the gesture and stared glumly out of the window.

To her surprise, instead of being angry he seemed wounded, even depressed, so much so that she felt sorry for him.

Could it be that he wasn't like Da at all? Could she trust him to help her find Jimmy? Despite being a gambler and gunfighter, maybe he had a core of decency she could learn to trust. But how could she really know for certain?

Rand wished he hadn't raised his hand that dismissive way, as he always did to show gunslingers that he wasn't planning to fight them, for the gesture appeared to have scared Marybeth. He turned to stare out the window to watch the traffic in the street. She hadn't even given him a chance. Maybe hadn't even intended to try. So much for his parents' and sister's harebrained idea of finding him a proper Christian lady to marry. He should have just married one of those nice girls who lived down in Bowen. There sure were enough of them to choose from. But Dad had wanted to bring fresh blood into Esperanza; ladies with fine manners like Mother's to help some of the wilder gals like Maisie improve their ways.

Thoughts of Mother always stopped him short. He

raised a familiar silent prayer that the doctors at the Boston hospital would be able to find out what caused her breathing problems. Dad had been so anxious about her health that he'd left Esperanza, the community he'd spent the past thirteen years building, the town that looked to him for guidance for every important decision they made. Yet Dad had willingly made the trip back East for Mother's sake. Rand longed for that same kind of marriage, where the most important thing was to take care of one another, no matter what the personal cost might be.

His folks had taken his sister, Rosamond, along to enroll her in the Boston finishing school Mother had attended as a young girl. There they'd met Marybeth, and Mother had decided she was the perfect young lady for Rand. Until today he hadn't cared much about those fine manners Dad insisted the local girls needed to learn. But after meeting Marybeth, he couldn't imagine marrying one of those cowgirls he'd grown up with. Still, he was beginning to wonder how his folks could have been so mistaken about Marybeth. Couldn't they see she'd had another plan all along?

Rand had made a few plans of his own. He'd envisioned someone who could grow a kitchen garden *and* a family and give him a little intellectual companionship on cold Colorado evenings. If he'd just married one of the gals who always smiled so sweetly at him in church, he wouldn't be sitting here feeling like a complete fool. But he also wouldn't have a bride who could talk about something other than the price of cattle or how the weather affected the crops.

Probably intent on listening to their conversation,

Lucy sidled up next to him and gave his shoulder a sisterly nudge with her elbow as she held out the coffeepot.

"You must be missing Seamus." He held his cup while she poured.

Lucy shrugged. "If you see him, tell him I do miss him." She sniffed. "Don't know why he has to be the one up in the hills with all them cattle all summer long. I don't have nothing to do on my days off."

Rand gave her a sympathetic smile. "He's the trail boss because he's the best man for the job. You can be proud of him for that."

"Humph. And what am I supposed to do while he's out there?" Lucy poured coffee for Marybeth and then took Rand's empty plate in her free hand. With a swish of her skirt that brushed fabric against his forearm, she headed back toward the kitchen.

Eyeing Lucy with a hint of disapproval, Marybeth put two lumps of sugar and a dash of cream in her cup, stirred and lifted the drink to her lips. Her graceful hands looked like white porcelain and her little fingers posed in refined arches as she held the cup. Beautiful, elegant hands, but not hands for a rancher's wife. What had his folks been thinking? This young lady was entirely too genteel.

Or maybe as she'd traveled farther west, she'd realized what she'd gotten herself into. Too bad he couldn't blame Maisie for this turn of events, but that wouldn't be fair. Even if she spilled the whole story, with her upbringing as a rancher's daughter, of course she'd be proud of his killing a horse thief.

Well, one thing was sure. With Marybeth making it clear they wouldn't be getting married anytime soon, if at all, he could postpone telling her about the fatal gunfight. He had no doubt Maisie had blabbed the story, so when they did get around to talking about it, he would have to reassure Marybeth that he wasn't proud of killing a man, no matter what other people thought. On the other hand, he was still responsible for her since she'd come all this way to meet him. Best get this all figured out.

"Now about that job you mentioned, how do you plan on getting it?" He couldn't keep the rancor out of his voice.

She lifted her chin and gazed down her pretty little nose at him. "As I said, I plan to work for a lawyer or in the bank." She blinked in a charming, innocent way. "You do have a bank, don't you? I thought I saw one on our way here."

"Yes, we have a bank. But everybody knows that's a man's job. Besides, what makes you think Mr. Means is going to hire you?" Rand felt justified being a little cross. Not only was Nolan Means young, wealthy and good-looking, he kept trying to finagle his way into community leadership, something the Northam family carefully controlled to keep out unsavory elements.

Marybeth's hazel eyes flashed at his challenge. "I will have you know I am very good with accounts. Not only that, but with my typewriting ability, I will be a great asset. If Mr.…Mr. Means, is it? If he doesn't need an accountant or secretary, I am certain some businessman in this growing town will be happy to employ someone with my skills."

Rand gazed at her, admiration mingled with annoyance. The girl had spirit, that was certain. But as he watched her, something else became evident in her bright hazel eyes—a look he'd seen in green gamblers who just realized they'd gotten themselves into a game with seasoned cardsharps. She had a secret, one that scared her. Why on earth did she think coming out West would solve her problems? But here she was, and despite her postponement—maybe even her cancellation—of the wedding, he had every intention of sticking to his plans to take care of her. A Christian man always kept his word, always saw to his responsibilities.

Bolstered with that thought, Rand scratched behind his ear and gave Marybeth one of his best "aw shucks" grins. "Well, Marybeth, I wish you all the best. And I will pray for your success."

Her eyes widened and she seemed to struggle a moment before answering. "Why, thank you, Rand. How very kind."

He shrugged. "I've been praying for you since last January when Mother first wrote to me about you."

"Oh." She looked down at her coffee cup. "Thank you."

He frowned. She seemed confused by his mention of prayer. Yet Mother had assured him she was a Christian. A real one, not someone who just went through the motions in church. Maybe she'd fooled them all. That meant he had more than one responsibility for this little gal. He had to take care of her *and* get her saved. He would take her to church every Sunday and let her hear some of Reverend Thomas's fine sermons. If he'd listened to those sermons when he should have, he'd never have killed a man, no matter how threatened he'd felt.

Another thing he could do for Marybeth was to write to the sheriff in Wagon Wheel Gap to see if he'd come across a man matching Jimmy O'Brien's description. Maybe if Rand found her brother, she'd forget working and decide to settle down with him. On the other hand, he needed to find out what she was hiding before he could marry her. That was quite a quandary, one the Lord would have to sort out.

"If you're done with your coffee, I'll take you over to Mrs. Foster's. She'll put you up until—" He shook his head. No longer could he think *until the wedding.* "Until you get things worked out."

He stood, pulled a half dollar out of his pocket and dropped it on the table to pay for their dinner, adding a nickel for Lucy's tip. When Marybeth continued to stare at him with some sort of unreadable expression, he sighed as he snagged his hat off of the peg.

"I guess I should ask if that's all right with you."

She gave him a tentative smile and her eyes seemed to glisten. "Yes, it's fine. Thank you. You're very kind, considering..."

Rand ducked his head to put on his hat *and* to hide a grin. Her eyes held that secretive look again, but this time with even more uncertainty. Maybe he had a chance with this pretty little lady, after all. And maybe his older brother could offer some tips on how to win a gal determined not to like him.

Chapter Two

"Shall we go?" Rand held out his arm and Marybeth set a hand on it.

Once again she could feel his muscles rippling through his fine cotton shirt. How nice it would be to depend upon such a strong man. But Da had also been strong before his final drink-induced illness, and his excellent physique had housed a deceitful soul. In fact, Marybeth had met few men, sturdy or weak, who kept their word. Was Jimmy any different, or had he become like Da? She'd prayed for years he hadn't fallen into such sinful ways, but she didn't hold out too much hope. After all, the American West was known for its lawlessness. Maybe Jimmy had chosen that path.

Even if he had, she was determined to find him and make him hand over the silver locket. Mam had told her it contained the key to a treasure that would take care of Marybeth all her life. Although Jimmy probably didn't know what lay hidden behind the tintype picture of their family, the locket still belonged to Marybeth. Of course she would share the fortune with him. Too bad Mam hadn't claimed the treasure herself and used it to escape Da and his abuse. Knowing him, he would have found her and forced her to turn over the money so he could gamble it away or use it in one of his get-rich schemes that always failed. The man had never known how to tell the truth or make a wise decision, other than marrying a good woman like Mam.

"It's not far, just six blocks." Rand glanced down at her high-top shoes, already covered with dust from the unpaved street. "But we can get a buggy if it's too far for you to walk."

His thoughtful gesture threatened to weaken her, so Marybeth forced her defenses back in place. "The wind has died down and it's a lovely day. Let's walk." She punctuated her cheerful tone with a bright smile. "Besides, Boston's a very hilly city and I walked everywhere there. This flat town is no challenge."

He chuckled—a pleasant, throaty sound. "If you're used to hills, I'll have to take you up in the mountains for a hike. That sure would challenge you." His teasing tone was accompanied by quick grin before a frown darted over his tanned face. "Of course we'd take a suitable chaperone." His hastily spoken addition showed once again his eagerness to please her.

Oh, how she longed to trust him. Yet how could she dare to when he hadn't even told her about that deadly gunfight Maisie was so proud of? When Marybeth spoke of delaying their marriage, his hurt feelings and disappointment had been obvious. Shouldn't he have bragged about the killing, assuming she'd regard him as a hero and change her mind? She'd been honest with him about her family, at least as close to honest as she'd dared to be, but he was hiding a very significant happening in his life.

"This is the street."

Rand steered her down a row of attractive two-story houses, several of which rivaled some of Boston's finer clapboard homes. One redbrick structure reminded her of Boston's older Federal-style mansions. Numerous houses were in varying stages of completion, adding to the picture of the growing community about which Colonel and Mrs. Northam had told Marybeth. Young cottonwood and elm trees lined the street, and several fenced-in yards boasted a variety of shrubbery and colorful flowers in the last blooms of summer.

"What a pretty town." Her words came out on a sigh.

"We like it." Rand smiled his appreciation of her compliment, and her heart lifted unexpectedly.

Peace hung in the air like a warm mantle, belying the town's Wild West location. Maybe Esperanza would be a good place to call home after she found Jimmy. It all depended upon the people and whether or not she fit into the community.

"Here's Mrs. Foster's house." Rand indicated a pretty brown house with a white picket fence, a stone foundation, a wide front porch whose roof was supported by slender columns, and gabled windows jutting out from the second floor.

A slender, gray-haired woman with a slightly bent posture bustled out of the front door. "Oh, here you are at last. Welcome, welcome." She descended the steps, holding the railing beside them, and pulled Marybeth into a warm embrace. "I'm so glad to meet you, Miss O'Brien. Welcome to Esperanza. Welcome to my home."

Tears flooded Marybeth's eyes. She hadn't been held in a maternal embrace in the four long years since Mam died, and oh, how she'd missed it. No formal introduction could have moved Marybeth as this lady's greeting did. She obviously possessed an open heart and generous spirit, just like some of the older ladies at her Boston church. "I'm so pleased to meet you, too, Mrs. Foster."

"Hello, Rand." The lady embraced him briefly and then looped an arm in Marybeth's and propelled her toward the stairs. "Come along, my dear. Tolley brought your trunk and carried it up to your room. If you need help unpacking, I'll be happy to assist you."

"Thank you." Marybeth glanced over her shoulder. Da never let Mam have friends, but Rand seemed pleased by Mrs. Foster's warm welcome.

Inside the cozy, well-furnished parlor, Mrs. Foster seated Marybeth on a comfortable green-brocade settee, waving Rand to the spot beside her. "You two sit right here, and I'll bring tea." She left the room humming.

"I sure am glad to see her so happy." Rand had removed his hat and placed it on a nearby chair. He brushed a hand through his dark brown hair and smoothed out the hat line. "She's been grieving for a long time. Probably will for the rest of her life." The hint of emotion in his voice revealed genuine compassion. "Having you stay here will be good for her."

Marybeth could not discern any ulterior motive in his words or demeanor. Once again she was confounded. Why would a gunslinger care about an old widow? "I'll be glad to help in any way I can." She eyed the piano. "That's a beautiful instrument. Do you suppose she would let me play it?" When Da wasn't around, Mam had taught Marybeth to play, using the piano in a neighborhood church. She'd gone to practice as often as she could, first to escape Da's anger, later for the sheer enjoyment of playing.

"I think she'd be pleased to hear you." Rand moved a hand closer to Marybeth's but pulled it back before he made contact, apparently rethinking the gesture. "I'd like to hear you play, too."

The intensity of his gaze stirred an unfamiliar sensation in her chest. Was it admiration? Oddly, traitorously, she hoped he did admire her. What girl didn't want to be appreciated?

"Well, I'd need to practice first. It's been a while since I played."

He seemed about to respond, but Mrs. Foster entered the room carrying a black-lacquered tray filled with all the necessities for a lovely tea. Rand stood, as any true gentleman would, until Mrs. Foster reclaimed her seat.

"Oh, my." He looked hungrily at the cake, the look every cook hoped for. "It's a good thing we didn't have any dessert at the café."

"The café!" Mrs. Foster blustered in an amiable way. "Why, I can outcook that Pam Williams any day." She raised her dark gray eyebrows and stared at Rand expectantly.

"Now, Mrs. Foster." He held up his hands in a gesture of surrender. "There's a reason I never volunteer to judge the Harvest Home baking contest or any other one. As a bachelor, I don't want to get in trouble with any of the many fine cooks we're so fortunate to have here in Esperanza. You don't know how much we depend on your good graces to have a decent meal from time to time."

He waggled his eyebrows at Marybeth and she bit back a laugh. It was their first moment of camaraderie, and it felt...*right.* Very much so. *Oh, Lord, hold on to my heart. Please don't let me fall in love with this man.*

"Humph." Mrs. Foster poured tea and passed it to her guests. If Rand weren't so used to Mother's Wedgwood china, he'd worry about breaking the delicate cup that was too small for his large hands.

Mrs. Foster served the cake and then focused on Rand. "Well, young man, you won't be a bachelor for much longer. Have you chosen your wedding date?"

He did his best not to choke on his tea. Mrs. Foster's question was understandable, but he hadn't had time to figure out how to tell folks the wedding was off. Besides, his family should hear it first and from him. The way gossip both good and bad traveled through the community, he'd get home and find out Nate and Susanna had heard all about the "postponed" wedding.

"I'm sure everyone knows how much planning a wedding requires." Marybeth sipped from her cup. "In fact, Maisie Henshaw tells me the church is planning to build an addition right after harvest, one that would accommodate large parties such as wedding receptions." She took a bite of cake. "Oh, my, this certainly is an award-winning recipe."

The smile she gave Mrs. Foster was utterly guileless, but Rand's chest tightened. Marybeth hadn't lied, but she hadn't told the whole truth, either. Of course, he still had some truth-telling to do, as well, so he mustn't judge her too harshly.

He noticed that Mrs. Foster's eyes narrowed briefly, as though maybe she hadn't been fooled by Marybeth's little diversion from answering the question. She didn't comment, however, just took a bite of cake. Food always provided a handy excuse for not saying something. Rand often used that ploy himself.

They passed several more minutes trading mundane information, as folks do when first meeting. Rand already knew everything Marybeth told Mrs. Foster, because she'd written it all in her letters. Too bad she hadn't felt inclined to warn him about her plans to postpone the wedding until she found her brother. Guilt smote him again. He should have written to her about the gunfight. Should have anticipated someone else bringing it up. He couldn't get over the idea that she already knew and that Maisie had told her. But what exactly did she know? What did she really think? These were things they needed to settle between the two of them, so he sure couldn't ask her those questions in front of Mrs. Foster. The dear old lady never hesitated to give her opinion on any topic under discussion.

Marybeth seemed weary from her travels, so Rand took his leave, promising to visit the next day.

As he walked toward town to see if Tolley was still around, a dull ache settled into his chest, replacing the growing joy he'd felt for weeks in anticipation of meeting and marrying Marybeth. This was no more than he deserved. What lady from back East would understand what he'd done? He didn't even understand it himself. Only his friends and neighbors proclaimed him a hero; only his younger brother wanted to copy his actions. He hated every memory of that fateful day and all he'd done that led up to it.

Shoving away those thoughts, he started his search for Tolley at Mrs. Winsted's general store. He remembered to pick up a packet of cumin and spool of white thread his sister-in-law, Susanna, had asked for, but didn't find his brother. Back out in the sunshine, he headed toward the livery and caught Tolley leading his saddled horse out of the stable.

"Say, shouldn't you be over at Mrs. Foster's wooing your pretty little bride-to-be?" Tolley's impish expression made Rand want to tweak his nose, as he used to when they were scrappy little boys.

"She's pretty tired from her travels." Rand tried to sound cheerful so Tolley wouldn't ask any more questions. "Did you order the rope from the hardware store?"

Tolley chortled. "Don't change the subject. Tell me—"

"Northam!" A well-dressed, black-clad man, gun strapped to his leg, stepped off the boardwalk and strode toward them. "Randall Northam."

Rand felt his dinner and Mrs. Foster's cake rise up in his gullet. Another gunslinger out to prove himself. Didn't he know better than to face two men? Tolley might be young and hotheaded, but he was a fast-drawing crack shot. *Lord, please don't let my brother get shot.*

He sighed. "I'm Randall Northam. What can I do for you, Mr.—?"

A sly smile crept across the man's face but his eyes remained as cold and deadly as a rattlesnake's. And surprisingly familiar. "Name's Hardison. Dathan Hardison. I believe you met my cousin Cole Lyndon about three years ago."

Rand went cold all over. Frozen cold in spite of the sunshine beaming down on his shoulders and the warm summer breeze fanning over him. If the man drew on him, he wouldn't be able to get his hand halfway to his holster. Somehow he managed to keep all emotion out of his face, a seasoned gambler's ploy. Except he wasn't a gambler. Not anymore. Nor was he a gunfighter, despite the gun at his side. But what could he say to the kin of the man he'd killed? *Lord, help me.*

"Yes, I 'met' Cole Lyndon. I'm sorry to say it was an unfortunate meeting." On the other hand, the no-good horse thief had robbed and beaten Susanna's father, leaving him for dead. The sheriff in Del Norte had said Cole had left a string of robberies and murders behind him. But no matter how often his friends called Rand a hero for outdrawing the wicked man, he'd never aspired to be an executioner. Never aspired to have every gunslinger from Montana to El Paso come gunning for him, risking his family and his town. So far he'd been able to talk himself out of another fight with humor or appeals to their better nature, even making a few friends of those who'd intended to face off with him. But revenge for injury to a man's family was entirely different. Trouble was, Rand knew he'd take it badly if anyone hurt Nate or Tolley. Especially Tolley, whose heavy breathing gave evidence of his rising temper.

"Unfortunate meeting. Is that what you call it?" Hardison's deadly cold tone hinted at imminent repayment for Rand's crime. The man glanced over his shoulder toward the Friday-afternoon crowds meandering along Main Street. He rolled his head and gave an unpleasant laugh. "Just wanted to let you know I'm in town." He slowly reached up to touch the brim of his hat in a mock salute, made as if to turn away and instead turned back. "Speaking of meeting, I almost had the pleasure of meeting a certain young lady from Boston on the train, but that sissified doctor and his cowgirl wife were playing nursemaid. I'll be looking for an opportunity to introduce myself to her."

Despite the horrifying pictures Hardison's words conjured, despite the sick feeling in Rand's gut, he sent up a prayer for grace. If this man hurt Marybeth… No, he wouldn't let Hardison rile him. "You'll find your sort of woman farther west, Hardison. Why don't you get back on the train tomorrow and head that way?"

He snorted and gave Rand a nasty grin. "Watch your back, Northam. We'll meet again."

"Yeah, well, you'd just better watch *your* back, mister." Tolley stepped slightly in front of Rand, his right hand poised to draw. "Why don't we settle this here and now?"

"Now, now, young'un." Hardison carelessly spat on the ground, but his right hand twitched. "Why don't you go home to Mama and let the men handle this?"

"Forget it, Tolley. Don't answer him." Rand half faced his brother but kept one eye on the gunslinger. "Don't say another word." He recognized the signs. Hardison had no plan to draw. At least not now. Part of his fun was stalking his prey to make them nervous.

"I'll be seeing you." Again Hardison touched the brim of his hat, turned his back on them and strode away.

"Why didn't you take him down?" Tolley pulled off his hat and slapped it against his leg, causing his horse to sidestep in alarm. "You're going to have to sooner or later."

"No." Rand gripped his brother's shoulder. "I made a deal with the Lord that I won't kill another man like I did Cole Lyndon." He'd do whatever was needed to protect his family and Marybeth, but never again would he kill someone to save his own life. Never again would he stare into the eyes of a man on his way to eternity, hopeless and without Jesus Christ because of him.

"Well, I didn't make that deal." Tolley glared after Hardison.

Rand swallowed hard as fear from his little brother gripped his belly. Why couldn't Tolley understand? He'd told him all about his guilt, about the horror he'd faced watching a man die by his hand. And now here was another consequence of his actions. Tolley just might get himself killed copying what Rand had done, maybe trying to protect him. No matter what it took, Rand had to keep his little brother—and Marybeth—out of trouble.

Chapter Three

Halting, discordant notes of piano music invaded Marybeth's senses and pulled her from a dreamless sleep. Mrs. Foster had said some of her students would have their lessons this afternoon, and this one clearly was a beginner.

Before Marybeth had lain down in the four-poster guest bed, her thoughtful hostess had brought a pitcher of hot water, but she'd been too tired to wash. Now, despite the tepid water, she freshened up from her travels, at least well enough to hold her until the promised Saturday-night bath. Her ablutions complete, she brushed the dust from her hair and wound it back into an upswept coiffure.

Still mellow from her nap, she studied her appearance in the dressing-table mirror, recalling with pleasure the way Rand had looked at her, how his gaze had lingered on her hair and then her eyes. His obvious admiration, gentlemanly in every way, would thrill any girl, as would his thoughtfulness.

Regret over her own behavior cut short her moment of joy. Perhaps she'd been hasty in her opinion of him.

Everyone she'd met or seen today regarded him highly. Perhaps she could open her heart to him, if only for friendship. He seemed interested in helping her find Jimmy, and even though he didn't approve of her working, surely he would understand her determination to support herself. When he came to take her to church on Sunday, she would ask for his help in finding a job.

She opened her trunk to lift out a fresh dress and then dug beneath the other garments for clean stockings. She caught a glimpse of white satin underneath it all and gulped back an unexpected sob. Mrs. Northam had insisted upon purchasing a wedding gown for her, and there it was packed in tissue. Shame brought an ache to her chest. She hadn't meant to lie to Rand's mother, at least not consciously. She'd merely grasped for an opportunity to search for Jimmy sooner than if she'd had to work for endless years to make enough money to come to Colorado. And now survival might force her to sell the beautiful satin gown. That would of course destroy her friendship with Mrs. Northam and Rosamond.

Marybeth shoved her emotions aside. Regrets and shame wouldn't do any good. Instead of waiting to see Rand on Sunday, she must get busy and solve her own problems. Today was Friday and most businesses would be closing soon. She must go back to the center of town and search for a job for which her skills suited her. At the least, she could locate the best places to apply on Monday. Once she changed out of her traveling ensemble and put on a black linen dress appropriate for office work, she grabbed her parasol and made her way toward the staircase.

As she descended, she smiled at the uneven three-four meter of the piano piece, which didn't quite obscure the melody of a Strauss waltz. Having had her own struggles to smooth out that same meter, she couldn't resist peeking into the parlor.

A dark-haired girl of perhaps twelve years sat ramrod-straight on the piano stool, her fingers arched over the keys. Mrs. Foster sat in a chair beside her, wearing a strained smile.

"My dear Anna, I don't believe you've been practicing enough this week."

"No, ma'am, I haven't." Anna sat back and crossed her arms in a rebellious pose. "I don't want to play piano. I want to learn to ride and shoot like Miss Maisie and her sisters."

"Laurie Eberly plays, Anna, and enjoys it very much."

"Humph. She's the only one."

While Mrs. Foster sighed, Marybeth ducked back out of sight and stifled a laugh. Oh, how she remembered the days of resisting Mam's lessons. Now she wouldn't trade her skill for the world. The memory of Rand's approval when she'd spoken of wanting to play caused a little hiccough in her heart. To reward all of his kindness, she would find out which songs he liked best and play them for him at the first opportunity.

"Well, my dear," Mrs. Foster said, "your brother insists that you learn, so let's try to get through this, shall we?"

After heaving out a loud sigh, Anna resumed her hesitant playing just as someone knocked on the front door.

Marybeth stepped into the parlor. "Let me answer that for you."

"Please do." The widow nodded her appreciation even as she frowned at Anna.

The front door boasted an oval window with an exquisite etching of wildflowers. Through the glass, Marybeth could see a well-dressed young gentleman, bowler hat in hand, gazing off toward town as he waited to be admitted. When she opened the door, he turned her way, stepped back and blinked in surprise. He quickly regained his composure.

"Ah. You must be Miss O'Brien." He gave her an elegant bow. "Welcome to our community. I am sure Randall Northam is happy at your safe arrival." He reminded her of the businessmen she'd seen at church back in Boston. Like some of them, he possessed plain patrician features that became more attractive when he smiled. "Please forgive my forwardness. I am Nolan Means, and I have come to escort my sister home."

It was Marybeth's turn to lose her composure. This was the banker Rand had mentioned. *Thank You, Lord!* Before she blurted out her amazement, along with a plea for a situation in his bank, her schooling in deportment took control. "How do you do, Mr. Means? Please come in. Anna is a charming child, and I believe her lesson is almost complete."

A sociable look lit his brown eyes as he entered the front hallway. "You have met her?" He chuckled. "How did she do today?"

Marybeth gave him a reserved smile. "I haven't met her yet, only observed her. I do look forward to making her acquaintance." How could she turn this conversation into a request to work at his bank? "She seems to be a delightful child who knows her own mind."

He chuckled again. "That is my sister, all right. And

you are gracious to say it that way. Her schoolteachers have never known quite what to do with her."

The waltz ended with a poorly done arpeggio, and Mr. Means grimaced. "Am I wasting my money and Mrs. Foster's time?" he whispered.

She shook her head and leaned toward him with a confidential air. "I resisted my lessons at first, but my mother's persistence paid off in the end. Now I love to play. Give her a little more time."

"Would you be so kind as to tell Anna that? Perhaps it would encourage her to continue." He regarded Marybeth with a friendly gaze. "Are you a music teacher, too?"

She swallowed a giddy laugh. The Lord had surely arranged this opening. "Why, yes, but only as my second occupation. I recently completed secretarial training and hope to find employment." His arched eyebrows foreshadowed the question she didn't want to answer. "Rand and I haven't set a wedding date, and I do want to keep busy."

"Ah. I see." His changing expression revealed myriad thoughts: surprise, speculation, perhaps even interest. Yet his brief intense look stirred no emotion within her as Rand's had. In fact, she was relieved when his face took on a businesslike aspect. "Secretarial training, you say? Perhaps our meeting is fortuitous, Miss O'Brien. I have need of a new employee at my bank. Did you also study accounting?"

Somehow Marybeth managed to control her smile. "I did, sir." She assumed the professional posture her teachers had taught her. "As well as typing."

"Typing?" He stroked his chin thoughtfully. "This is indeed a fortuitous meeting. I have obtained one of those Remington Sholes and Glidden typewriters for sending out business correspondence, but I have not found anyone to hire who can manage a letter without errors. Perhaps you can help."

She gave him a slight bow. "If you're speaking of the improved 1878 model, I learned on that very machine."

"Well, then, Miss O'Brien." He reached out to shake her hand and she responded in kind. "If you will come to the bank at nine o'clock on Monday morning, we can discuss your employment. That is, if you are interested."

"Nolly!" Anna dashed into the front hall and flung her arms around her brother's waist. "Oh, do say I don't have to take lessons anymore." The sob that accompanied her plea sounded a bit artificial to Marybeth.

Wringing her hands, Mrs. Foster appeared behind her student. In that moment Marybeth realized the dear lady needed the income from these lessons. Losing a student might create a serious problem for her. All the more reason for her to secure the job at the bank so she could pay for her room and board. She could not remain this dear lady's guest forever.

"Now, now, Anna." To his credit, Mr. Means seemed not to notice Mrs. Foster's anxiety. Nor did he appear embarrassed by his sister's behavior. "We will talk about it later." He questioned Marybeth with one arched eyebrow. "As well as what you and I discussed, Miss O'Brien?"

She returned a nod, assuming he meant both Anna's lessons and the situation at the bank. Even if he decided she wouldn't do for the job, she would be glad to encourage the child to continue. That would be a small repayment to Mrs. Foster for her hospitality.

They took their leave and Marybeth turned to her

hostess. "May I help you prepare supper?" She must keep busy until Monday to make the time pass quickly.

Mrs. Foster appeared to have recovered from her alarm, for she gave Marybeth a bemused look. "Nolan seems quite taken with you."

Marybeth coughed out a nervous laugh. She'd thought her demeanor was entirely proper. "Oh, I certainly hope not."

Mrs. Foster seemed satisfied with her answer. "Very well. Shall we get busy with supper? I thought chicken and dumplings would be nice." She beckoned to Marybeth then proceeded down the center hallway.

"That sounds wonderful." Grinning to herself, Marybeth complied. She couldn't wait to tell Rand about having the same supper dish Miss Pam had served them for dinner. The cooking rivalry between these two ladies clearly amused him, but following his example, she would praise her hostess's dish as nothing short of perfection.

Why had she so quickly thought of sharing such a thing with Rand? Perhaps because he'd been in her thoughts since last January and she'd often practiced what she would talk about with him. Even though she'd been uncertain about the marriage, she'd looked forward to making his acquaintance, perhaps even gaining his friendship. Now that she knew his true character, those goals seemed less appealing. What would he say when she told him she had found a job? What would he do?

Guilt and nervousness vied for control of Rand's thoughts as he drove toward town. Nate and Tolley had insisted they would take care of today's chores, but he still felt responsible for doing his share. It was all

Susanna's fault. She and Nate were staying in the big house while his parents and sister were back East, and his sweet little sister-in-law had wheedled the truth out of him about Marybeth's reticence to marry right away. She'd insisted he must get busy courting.

"If Lizzy were feeling better, I'd say bring Marybeth out here today," she'd told him over breakfast. Rand's two-year-old niece had come down with a cold and had clung to her mother while she ate. "First thing next week, you have to do that." She'd encouraged her fussy baby to take a bite of toast, but Lizzy had refused. "How about a picnic? Today isn't too soon. Nate and I went on a picnic my second day here. His courage in facing down those Indians made him a hero in my eyes and went a long way toward winning my heart."

Nate had beamed at his bride's praise as he'd nudged Rand's arm. "Go ahead, brother. Rita can pack a basket while you get old Sam hitched up to the buggy. You can drive into town and surprise Marybeth. Ladies like to be surprised, don't they, sweetheart?"

Susanna had batted her eyelashes at Nate as if they were still courting. Rand admitted to himself that he'd like to have Marybeth look at him that way. Seated across the table, Tolley had just groaned.

"*Sí*, Senor Rand." Rita, the family cook, had a little courting going on herself with one of the cowhands. "I'll have everything ready in fifteen minutes."

"Well," Rand had drawled, still uncertain. "I did promise Marybeth a hike in the mountains." He'd stirred a bite of griddlecake into a puddle of syrup on his plate. "I also promised we'd have a chaperone."

All eyes had turned toward Tolley, who'd shoved back from the table, shaking his head. "No, sir. Not me. I've got all those chores to do, yours and mine. Got cows to milk, stalls to muck out, mustangs to break, fences to check and a whole bunch of other stuff." He'd stood and started toward the door like a scared rabbit. "Helping with her trunk was one thing, but I refuse to play duenna while you two make eyes at each other. Find somebody else."

"But you'd look so purty in a lace mantilla," Nate had quipped.

Rita had giggled and Susanna had laughed. Tolley's response was to slam the back door on his way out.

Bouncing Lizzy on her lap, Susanna had said, "Why not stop by Maisie and John's and invite them along?"

So now Rand drove old Sam toward town with a large, well-packed picnic basket secured to the back of the buggy and a prayer in his heart that Doc and Maisie would be free today. If they weren't, maybe Mrs. Foster would go. Of course that would mean they couldn't go hiking because it would be too hard on the older lady, but they could go up to a meadow by the river. He couldn't decide which chaperone he preferred. Having either one hear his every word would only add to his nervousness as he tried to become better acquainted with Marybeth.

As if that wasn't enough indecision for a man to have, he also had to figure out what to tell her about Hardison. While Nate had advised him not to worry her with the gunslinger's threats, Tolley thought she ought to know what the man had said in regard to her. Rand usually took his cautious older brother's advice, and yet he couldn't entirely dismiss the idea that she should be on the lookout for danger. As peaceful as the Esperanza community was, as caring the folks were about one another, there was always a chance of getting bit by a sneaky snake in the grass.

At the Henshaws' two-story house several blocks from Mrs. Foster's, he found three waiting patients seated in the front hallway. He greeted them with concern over their health even as his heart took a dip. Obviously his friends wouldn't be able to get away for a picnic. Before he could leave, Doc came out of the surgery.

"You're just in time, Rand. You can give me a hand." Doc took him out the side door to a wagon, from which they unloaded a leather-topped oak examining table and carried it into the surgery.

With the new furniture in place, Doc eyed Rand up and down. "Now, what can I do for you? I should have asked you that before I put you to work."

"Say—" Maisie came in the room before Rand could answer "—shouldn't you be over at Mrs. Foster's house courting that pretty little bride of yours?" She punctuated her question with a wink, a rowdy laugh and a slap on his arm.

"Uh, yeah. That's where I'm headed." Why had he thought inviting them would be a good idea? Maisie had a good heart, and he loved her like a sister, but she also had a loose tongue. He wouldn't even waste time asking for sure if she'd told Marybeth about his past.

"But—" Doc said.

Not giving Doc a chance to finish, Rand made his escape, dashing back to the buggy and heading toward Mrs. Foster's house.

Pretty piano music came through the open front window and Rand paused to listen to the end of the song. If that was Marybeth, she wasn't bad, but not quite as good as Mrs. Foster. Of course she'd said she needed to practice, so he mustn't be too quick to judge.

When Mrs. Foster admitted him, however, he saw that Laurie Eberly was just finishing her piano lesson. At fourteen years of age, Maisie's next-to-youngest sister had a bit more musical talent than her four sisters, and she liked to sing. That was, when she wasn't batting her eyes at Tolley like all the other younger girls. No wonder his brother was skittish about courting with every young girl in the territory making eyes at him, and him not even ready to court. Rand had suffered through that same phase several years ago.

"Make yourself comfortable, Rand." Mrs. Foster waved him toward the settee as she started up the staircase. "I'll fetch Marybeth. I'm sure Laurie won't mind an audience, will you, dear?"

"No, ma'am. I'd love it." Laurie glanced over Rand's shoulder as if looking for somebody and then gave him a sisterly smile. "What's Tolley doing today? Busy at the ranch, I suppose."

"Oh, he's real busy." Rand had his own romance problems, so he sure didn't want to stir up anything that would annoy his younger brother. He sat, hat in hand, and realized his palms were sweaty. Who would have guessed courting could be so difficult?

"Maybe I'll ride out there after my lesson and visit Susanna." Laurie set her fingers on the keys and began to play a song Rand wasn't familiar with.

He couldn't figure out a way to discourage her from going out to the ranch and pestering Tolley, especially since Susanna probably would appreciate a visit. Like all of the Eberly sisters, Laurie would be a big help with the sick baby.

"Hello, Rand." Marybeth entered the parlor looking refreshed from her travels. Beautiful, in fact, with her pretty auburn hair piled high on her head and her eyes more blue than hazel today because of that blue dress. As he stood to greet her, his heart leaped into his throat. "I wasn't expecting you until tomorrow. Is everything all right?"

He had to clear his throat before he could talk. "Hello." Was that dismay or worry in her eyes?

"Now, Marybeth." Mrs. Foster stood by her with an arm around her waist. Their already comfortable relationship would encourage him if he weren't so nervous. "Can't a young man come calling unannounced?"

"Oh, yes. Of course." Marybeth seemed to force a smile. "How are you today, Rand?"

"I'm well, thank you." He felt the strain in his own smile. "And you?"

"Well, thank you."

They stared at each other for a moment until Marybeth looked down at her hands.

About now was the time when Maisie would slap his arm and tell him to speak up. Fortunately her little sister didn't seem so inclined. Laurie still sat at the piano, and even though she wasn't playing she didn't appear to be eavesdropping.

"I was wondering," he said, "if you would accompany me on a picnic—you and Mrs. Foster? We can go down by the river, enjoy the scenery and see what our housekeeper fixed for us. She's a great cook." He glanced at Mrs. Foster. "Of course, not as good as you, ma'am."

"Thank you, dear boy." Her beaming face showed how much she appreciated his words. How she must miss hearing her husband praise her cooking. "Rita is quite young, but she'll improve with a bit more experience." She looked between the two of them. "Thank you for inviting me to chaperone your outing. Unfortunately, on Saturdays, my teaching schedule and my organ practice for tomorrow's service keep me from accepting."

Was that relief he saw on Marybeth's face? Dismay wound through Rand's chest. Was she all that set against being with him? So much for Susanna's brilliant idea about courting.

Marybeth tried to hide her relief over Mrs. Foster's refusal. The last thing she wanted was to have the older lady present when she asked Rand how serious he was about helping her find Jimmy. Bless her kind heart, the lady was a gossip, as their late talk last night had revealed. She wasn't in the least malicious, but stated outright that folks had a right to know what was going on in their community. While Marybeth couldn't disagree, she didn't want her private business spread all over town and who knew where else. She must be the one who told Jimmy about Mam and Da being dead, an important piece of news she now wished she hadn't told Mrs. Foster. Yet how could she have kept it from her?

She scrambled around in her mind to think of a public place to go with Rand, a place where she'd feel safe or could walk away if need be. Perhaps that park she'd seen across from the church—

"If you need a chaperone, I'll go with you." Laurie lowered the fallboard over the piano keys and stood. "Before Maisie and Doc got married, I always tagged along to keep things proper." She gathered her music and put it in a leather satchel. "Since Tolley's busy and all, I can go fishing and see if the trout are biting." She gave Rand a look Marybeth couldn't quite discern. "Sort of planned to do that anyway."

Relief and amazement struck Marybeth at the same time. The Lord was still guiding her life in His mysterious way. While Laurie fished, she and Rand could talk privately.

"That's real nice, Laurie." Rand gave Marybeth a doubtful look. "Of course, if you had plans…"

"Not at all." She must have sounded too eager, because Rand's sad expression turned upside down. Gracious, he was handsome when he smiled. Handsome when he frowned, too, but of course smiles were much better. "Just let me change into something more suitable."

It didn't take her five minutes to slip out of her plain blue gingham and into her brown traveling skirt and white shirtwaist. Mrs. Foster offered her the use of a broad-brimmed straw hat to protect her complexion from the sun, and she carried her parasol for extra shade and a shawl in case a breeze came up. In a short time, they were on their way north toward the Rio Grande.

Marybeth sat next to Rand in his buggy, with Laurie riding her horse alongside them. Each time they went over a bump, Marybeth's shoulder jolted against his upper arm, and she could feel the solid muscles beneath the blue plaid sleeve. How pleasant that might have been if they were truly courting. Or if he weren't wearing that gun strapped to his right leg. Did he always wear it, even to church? She'd find out tomorrow.

The road smoothed out north of Esperanza and they picked up speed. Marybeth gazed east across the wide, flat valley toward the Sangre de Cristo Mountains. On the left, the San Juan range appeared nearer. Was Jimmy someplace up there? Or was she on a fool's errand?

"Thinking about your brother?" Rand offered that lopsided grin that made her silly heart skip. Or maybe it was his insightful question that moved her.

"Yes." She looked away from him toward the east again and brushed at sudden tears, hoping he hadn't seen them. "After all these years, I can't believe I'm this close. At least close to where his letter came from. Is Del Norte far? That's where he mailed it."

"Not far." For some reason he gave a little shudder at the mention of the next town over. "It's a long day's trip there and back."

"You go there often?"

His jaw tightened. "Haven't been there in three years."

Her question had bothered him, but why? Did it have something to do with his killing a man? Should she press the issue or let it go? With Laurie now riding twenty yards ahead, her long red hair swaying with the movement of her horse, she wouldn't hear their conversation. Perhaps the time had come for Marybeth to tell him what Maisie had said. His response would reveal a great deal about his character.

Rand knew God was pushing him to tell her about killing Cole Lyndon. He'd planned to do so today, but had hoped for a more comfortable setting, like after they both had full stomachs.

"Three years. That's a long time for such a close town." Marybeth spoke simply, with no apparent meaning behind her words. "Especially since Mrs. Foster tells me Del Norte has more places to shop than Esperanza."

Had Mrs. Foster told her anything else? He'd better hurry or everyone in the area would blurt out their own version of the story about the worst day of his life.

"I don't go over there because I used to gamble, and I don't want to be tempted." Those were the words of a coward sneaking in the back door.

Marybeth eyed him with surprise and maybe a bit of worry. "Gambling? You *used to* gamble?"

"Yes, ma'am." He gave a little shrug, bumping her slender shoulder without meaning to. It made his arm buzz pleasantly, but how did she feel about it? From her frown, he guessed she was thinking about the gambling and hadn't even noticed. "I had a real bad experience the last time I played poker and decided it wasn't the best way to spend my time."

"Tell me what happened."

Still frowning, she narrowed her eyes and now he could tell for certain she already knew the answer.

He pulled in a deep breath and exhaled long and slow. This was so hard. Should he explain that the man he'd killed had bragged about robbing and beating Susanna's father and leaving him for dead? That the gold lying on the table between them had come from selling the old man's horses? That the man and his partner had already cheated at that very card game? That Rand and his pal Seamus were about to quit anyway? Excuses, all of them. If he'd had a lick of sense, he'd have just walked away from the table that day and found the sheriff. A sick feeling rose up in his gullet.

"I killed a man."

She barely blinked, just looked away from him toward the river ahead. "I see."

"Maisie told you, didn't she?"

Marybeth nodded, still not looking his way. "She said you're a hero because the man was a horse thief who'd done his own share of killing."

He shrugged again, this time taking care not to touch her. "That still doesn't excuse it. Instead of losing my temper, I should have let the law handle him."

She looked his way, tears rimming her eyes. "So you regret it." Not a question, a statement. Maybe she understood.

"I do. Deeply."

She set her long, gloved fingers on his forearm. This time her touch imparted an odd sort of reassurance. "Have you asked God for forgiveness?"

A grim laugh escaped him. "Every day."

"Then you must believe He has forgiven you."

Marybeth enjoyed the sweet smile that blossomed across Rand's handsome face. This had been an important moment for them because so far they hadn't had a chance to discuss their faith. Yet nagging at the back of her mind was the memory of Mam always forgiving Da, but Da never changing. Had Rand truly changed, or did he still have the kind of quick temper that would make him draw a gun and kill a man…or who knew what else? She would wait and see.

"Thank you." Rand squeezed her hand.

"For what?"

"For reminding me of God's forgiveness." He tugged the reins to the left to direct the horse down the path Laurie had taken. "Mother wrote that you're a woman of faith, and it's good to hear you speak of it." His gaze lingered briefly on her lips. To her relief, he made no move to kiss her.

They arrived at a small meadow beside the slow-moving river, so Marybeth would have to postpone asking Rand questions about his faith. She didn't think she'd done much to help him, but her words had obviously encouraged him. At the very least, it was an opening she could refer to later.

He jumped down from the buggy and loosely secured the reins around a slender young pine tree so his horse could help himself to the abundance of grass at his feet. Laurie had already dismounted and found a branch to use for a fishing pole.

"Aren't you hungry?" Rand called out to her.

"Sure am." Laurie continued to work with her pole. "I just wanted to get a line out in the water to see what's swimming by today."

"Suit yourself." Rand gave Marybeth a hand in stepping down from the buggy.

"What a lovely place." She breathed in the fresh, cool air of the shady meadow. Closer to the river she spied some wildflowers but didn't recognize what kind they were. Peace settled over her and she made up her mind to enjoy the day.

"Yep. It's real nice here. 'Course we have fish in the streams near our ranch, but the best trout come from the Rio Grande. That's why I like it." He walked to the back of the rig, untied the picnic basket and pulled a blanket from beneath it. Then he searched for a good spot to lay it out.

Marybeth hurried to his side. "I'll help you."

"No, ma'am. You're my guest today." Finding a shady spot, he moved a few rocks and branches out of the way. "I'll take care of everything."

Nonetheless, Marybeth reached for the blanket and

helped him spread it out. She started to follow him back to fetch the basket, but he stopped and gently gripped her upper arms. "You don't mind very well, do you? Now go sit down and let me manage the rest."

Despite his crooked grin and teasing tone, a shiver went through her. *No.* She would not feel this way. He was just being nice, just taking care of her, as any gentleman would. She tried to return a playful grin, but it felt too wobbly to be convincing. Turning from him, she did as he said and made herself comfortable on the old woolen blanket. Or as comfortable as one could be on the rough ground. She reached beneath the blanket and pulled out a few more rocks.

He returned with the basket just as she threw aside a large sharp stone. Instead of the charming grin she expected, his expression twisted into something she couldn't even describe. Fear? Anger? Because she'd moved a rock instead of waiting for him?

He slowly set down the basket, slowly pulled his gun from his holster and slowly pointed it straight at her. "Don't move, Marybeth. Don't move an inch."

The rattler was just pulling itself up into a coil not three feet from Marybeth's hand. Yet the fear written across her pretty face wasn't from the danger she hadn't even noticed. She was afraid of *him.* In spite of his confession, she still didn't trust him. But this was no time to sort it all out. She had minded his order and sat like a statue on the blanket, her widened eyes squarely focused on his gun.

Dear God, don't let her move. Let me kill the rattler without hurting her.

Gunfire exploded several yards to his left. Snake

parts flew in all directions. Rand's knees threatened to buckle. He glanced at Laurie, whose rifle bore a telltale curl of smoke around its barrel.

Now he was just downright annoyed. Saving Marybeth's life would have made him a real hero in her eyes. Yet honesty demanded that he hand the honors to a fourteen-year-old girl.

"Good aim, Laurie." He needed to downplay the situation, make it sound like an everyday occurrence to calm Marybeth's fears.

"Looked to me like Marybeth was in your way." Laurie shrugged as she returned her rifle to the leather holster on her horse's saddle. "I had a better shot from over here."

Rand nodded his agreement. "Let's see now. Shall we move the blanket to a nicer spot closer to the river?" Someplace far away from the dead snake. "I don't know about you ladies, but I'm as hungry as a bear coming out of hibernation."

He grinned at Marybeth about one second before she fell over on the blanket in a heap.

Chapter Four

Marybeth had never fainted in her life. She'd always refused to surrender to the frailties of the silly society girls she'd known at the academy. But now she found herself looking at the world sideways and trying desperately to reclaim reality. The first thing to register in her mind was Mrs. Foster's scratchy straw hat, one side now crushed between her face and the hard ground. Her eyes couldn't quite focus on two round brown objects in front of her: Rand's bent knees? Laurie's voice reached her through a dull roar inside her head. Or was the roar from the nearby river?

"I dunno, Rand. You sure you want to marry a gal who can't handle a little incident with a snake?"

"Hush. Don't be rude." He tugged on the ribbons holding the hat in place and moved it back from her head. "Marybeth?" His work-roughened hands felt gentle on her cheek. "Are you all right?"

Air. She desperately needed air. Dragging in the life-giving oxygen so scarce at this high altitude, she whimpered with relief as her lungs expanded. Oh, mercy.

What a baby she was. This was far from the most frightening thing ever to happen to her.

"'M fine." She tried to infuse the words with confidence, but they came out on a strangled whisper. This really must stop. She pushed herself up on one elbow, with Rand's support under her arm providing the strength she lacked. After another gulp of air, she expelled an awkward laugh. "Gracious." No other words came to mind, so she just looked up at Rand and gave him a tremulous smile.

He shoved his hat back from his forehead and returned the same, his relief obvious in his eyes. "Would you like a sandwich?"

His playful smirk sent a giddy feeling shivering through her. In spite of Laurie's impertinent question concerning her apparent lack of fortitude, his gaze bore no censure.

"Yes. Thank you." No, not at all. Not with her stomach twisting inside her at the memory of the gory snake remains.

Dismissing the dreadful sight from her mind, she placed a hand in his offered one and they stood as one. Once again she had to draw from his strength, this time to gain her footing, and now she couldn't look away from him. For untold seconds they stared at each other as she tried to read his soul, as her minister used to say. Unlike Da's darting, half-penitent looks, Rand's gaze held no deception, nor did any manipulation or anger emanate from his eyes' green depths. Only kindness and concern and sweet gentleness. Cautious trust welled up inside her accompanied by a sincere liking for this cowboy, this good, decent man. Surely he would help her find Jimmy. And while she had a lot more to learn about him, she might just think more about their marriage bargain. She quickly shoved aside that hasty, dangerous thought, replacing it with another. At least now she understood why Rand carried a gun. She might even get one herself if snakes were a constant danger.

Through the fog of her musings, she became aware of Laurie's soft giggle.

"Guess I'll move the blanket." The girl grabbed an edge and tugged, forcing Marybeth and Rand to break their visual connection and hop off onto the grass.

While Laurie gave the blanket a shake and dragged it to a shady spot several yards closer to the river, Rand stepped away from Marybeth to pick up the basket and offered her an arm.

"Miss O'Brien, would you do me the honor of accompanying me on a picnic?" He winked and waggled his eyebrows, probably trying to cheer her.

With a giggle of her own, or maybe it was a laugh of relief, Marybeth set her hand on his arm. She would show young Miss Laurie Eberly *and* Rand just how brave she could be by making as little of the snake incident as possible. "Why, Mr. Northam, I would be delighted."

At Marybeth's sassy response, Rand almost fell over in relief. *Thank You, Lord.* She might have fainted, but she got right back on her feet. More than that, as they'd stared into each other's eyes for those brief seconds, he could see her determination to overcome the incident. Was he flattering himself to think he'd helped in some way? Not that it mattered. This little city gal had spunk, and it made him all the more resolute to keep on courting her. Even if they didn't end up getting married, he wanted to be her friend.

Yet as he held her hand to help her kneel back down on the blanket, he remembered her real purpose in coming to Colorado was to search for her brother. Had she deliberately lied to his parents so they would pay her traveling expenses? He mustn't let her pretty face and nice manners hide a lying heart, something he refused to bring into his family.

How odd that in the past few years he'd fended off a half dozen local gals who'd tried to capture his interest, honest Christian girls he just didn't happen to care for enough to court. Yet the bride his parents had chosen for him could end up being a disappointment to them. He already felt a little disappointed that she hadn't inquired about Susanna's health today.

On the other hand, he couldn't imagine how it would be to have only one family member still living and yet not know where he was. Rand loved his brothers and sister more than words could say. Even when they fought or just disagreed, they were always there for him. Dad and Mother, too. From what Marybeth had said about her father, her family hadn't been blessed in that same way. Maybe if Rand learned more about her and them, he could unravel the mystery of her character.

One thing was sure. After he took Marybeth back to Mrs. Foster's house, he would start his search for Jimmy O'Brien by writing to the sheriffs in Wagon Wheel Gap and Del Norte. In fact, if he had a little more confidence in his ability to avoid temptation, come Monday morning he would ride over to Del Norte and speak to Sheriff Hobart in person.

Laurie took charge of the picnic basket and dug out

a sandwich to hand to Marybeth. "You ever go fishing?" She handed one to Rand before taking a bite of a third one.

"Ahem." Rand gave her a scolding look. "Shall we pray before we eat?"

Laurie had the grace to bow her head without protest, while Marybeth, who hadn't taken a bite yet, gave him an approving smile. "Yes, please."

After a quick argument with himself over whether to mention the snake, he decided the Lord deserved their thanks for keeping Marybeth safe. He should have prayed right after Laurie shot the varmint. Dad said a Christian man needed to take spiritual leadership in any situation when a minster wasn't present. Rand and his older brother tried to follow Dad's example now that he was away from home.

"Father, we thank You that Laurie shot the snake before it could cause any harm." No need to belabor the point, so he hurried on. "We thank You for this food and the hands that prepared it. And thank You for making this beautiful day for us to enjoy. In Jesus' name. Amen."

He opened his eyes to see Laurie chowing down, while Marybeth was staring at him with teary eyes… and a smile. A feeling as warm and pleasant as the day spread through his chest.

"Let's eat." He bit into the sandwich, and flavor burst in his mouth and set it to watering. "Oh, man," he said after he'd chewed and swallowed. "I don't know what Rita puts into her mystery sauce, but nobody can beat her roast beef sandwiches."

"Not even Mrs. Foster?" Marybeth raised one eyebrow and gave him a teasing smile.

"Shh." He held a finger to his lips. "Don't tell her I said that."

She gave him another one of those cute smiles and he felt a slight tickle in his chest that he couldn't quite identify. "I can see that cooking is a source of great competition among the ladies." Turning to Laurie, she said, "How about you? Do you like to cook?"

"Not much." Laurie shrugged. "It's more of a chore than fun. I'd rather be fishing." She glanced over at her pole, still stuck in the riverbank with its line trailing downstream. "Or breaking horses." A glint in her eye warned Rand that mischief was coming. "Do you ride? 'Cause if you do, I have just the horse for you. Name's Malicia."

"How kind of you." Marybeth's expression was pure innocence, except for a slight twitch of her lips, revealing to Rand that she wasn't fooled by Laurie's offer. "Unfortunately, I've never had the pleasure of learning to ride."

"Too bad." Laurie finished her sandwich and excused herself to tend to her fishing pole. When she was out of earshot, Marybeth rolled her eyes.

"Malicia, eh?" She laughed softly. "Malice? I don't need to speak Spanish to figure that one out."

Rand chuckled. "The Eberly girls don't have any brothers, so they have to do all the work around their ranch, including breaking horses and mucking out barns. They don't think much of women who can't keep up with a man. They do everything from herding cattle to cooking mainly because they don't have the luxury of being pampered like city girls."

The instant the words left his mouth, he knew his

mistake. Marybeth's eyes dimmed briefly and her lips pinched together into a grim line. "Hmm."

Before he could correct his mistake, Laurie whooped.

"Got a big one on the line." She gave the pole a little jerk to set the hook, struggled briefly with her unwilling prey and then pulled the large trout up on the grassy bank. "Will you look at that?"

Marybeth got to her feet, snatching up a knife from the picnic basket and striding toward the scene. "That's a fine fish, Laurie. Must be at least two pounds. I'll be glad to clean it while you catch another one."

Laurie stared at her briefly, gave Rand a quick glance and held out her still hooked catch. "Sure. Here you go." Her tone of voice was friendly, but her eyes held a challenge. Rand wanted to tweak her nose for being so contrary with this city girl who'd already shown a healthy bit of grit by dismissing the snake episode.

Marybeth deftly unhooked the squirming silver trout and plunked it down on the grass. With the skill of a butcher, she gutted it in no time, tossed the innards into the river and scraped off the heavy scales that marked it as a fairly mature fish. "Did you bring a creel?"

Her eyes already wide with surprise, Laurie gave a brief nod. "On the back of my saddle." She tilted her head in the direction of her horse.

Marybeth hesitated only two seconds before approaching the large gelding. After putting the fish into the wicker creel, she untied the basket from the saddle and carried it to the river, dunking it into the water as though she knew exactly what she was doing.

Laurie once again glanced at Rand and nodded her approval.

Rand lay back and rested his elbows on the woolen

blanket, content to watch the girls, whose cooperative efforts suggested they were having fun catching and cleaning the fish. Marybeth had surprised and *impressed* him in a big way. In spite of her city upbringing, she didn't appear to be the least bit pampered, and if he knew what was good for him, he'd better not make any more remarks to suggest that she was.

Marybeth studiously avoided letting her face reveal the triumph she felt over showing she wasn't afraid of unpleasant tasks. Pampered, indeed. Maybe she couldn't ride a horse or even feel comfortable going near the large beasts beyond riding in a buggy. Yet before enrolling in the academy, she'd spent her entire life doing whatever honest work she could find to survive in a city not always kind to poor Irish immigrants. As to the cooking competition of the local ladies, she had a recipe or two she'd put up against the best of them. But again, she'd learned at Fairfield Young Ladies' Academy not to brag, a challenge to anyone of Irish descent. Her people had long been great storytellers and she'd learned the art at her parents' knees.

"Where'd you learn how to clean fish?" Rand asked later as they packed up to leave.

"In a Boston fishery when I was eight years old." With a cool look, she dared him to think less of her for her hardscrabble life.

Instead he nodded and grinned with seeming approval. "I was mucking out stalls when I was that age. Don't know which one's a harder job, but they're both pretty messy." After securing the picnic basket to the back of the buggy, he offered his hand to help her climb up.

"And smelly." She wrinkled her nose, which brought

the hoped-for laugh. "Boston Harbor usually stinks from all the fish and other seafood, and I wore the smell home with me every night. Not like this river. Everything here smells so fresh and clean. Even the fishy odor is mild and washed off my hands right away." She accepted Rand's help into the buggy and settled comfortably on the leather-covered bench. This moment of camaraderie encouraged her. He wasn't looking down his nose at her.

Maybe she should have trusted his parents enough to tell them everything about her childhood. They'd assumed she came from a middle-class home just because she attended a fine church and was a student at an academy for young ladies, but that was far from the truth. Yet Rand wasn't bothered by her working at a lowly job. Maybe he just didn't understand that only the poorest people took jobs cleaning fish at the fishery.

"I never thought about the smells of Boston." Rand settled beside her on the bench and grasped the reins. "I was born there, but we moved out here to Colorado when I was about ten, so I can't remember much about it. All I remember are the stories about the city's part in the American Revolution. My brothers and sister and I played Minutemen." His eyes took on a faraway look as if he were reliving those long-ago years. "Paul Revere's ride. Bunker Hill. Boston Tea Party."

"All the heroic events." She and Jimmy had also played those games with other children in their neighborhood. Better to reenact a war the Americans had won than the tragic Irish Rebellion her people had lost. Or the war that had been going on between the States during her childhood. Many a father hadn't come home from fighting for the Union, and her own da had suffered wounds that had plagued him until his death.

Rand nodded in response to her comment. "Heroics, yes. But being so young, I didn't appreciate the real history."

"Hey." Laurie had mounted her horse and swung him around toward the buggy. "You think Mrs. Foster would like these fish?" She held out the dripping creel.

"How thoughtful." Reaching out for the wicker container, Marybeth stifled the urge to dodge the river water flying about. She'd had much worse on her clothes working at the fishery. "I'm sure she'll enjoy them for supper."

"Well, if you two lovebirds can keep out of trouble, I'm going to ride on home." Laurie grinned at Marybeth and winked at Rand.

"Is that all right with you?" Rand asked Marybeth.

"Of course." If her teachers at the academy hadn't said ladies never winked, she'd have copied Laurie's impudent gesture. Winking at Rand might give him the wrong idea about her character, something she had guarded all her life.

"Go on." Rand waved his hand toward Laurie as if she were a pesky fly. "Git. And tell your pa I said hello."

"That's not all I'll tell him." The girl kicked her horse into a gallop, laughing as she rode away.

Marybeth wanted so badly to act shocked by the girl's cheeky behavior, to pretend that she herself was some fine lady who'd grown up with fine manners in a fine home. But she couldn't put the cat back in the bag, not after gutting fish and admitting she'd worked in the fishery. Yet neither did she have to revert back to the hoydenish behavior of her childhood in the slums, where both women and men had to be feisty and tough to survive.

The buggy rolled along in a syncopated pattern accompanied by the rhythmic squeak of the leather seats, the jangle of the harnesses and the clip-clop of the horse's hooves on the hard-packed ground. Reminded of an old Irish tune, Marybeth found herself humming along.

"Go ahead and sing." Rand shot her one of his charming grins before turning his eyes back to the road ahead. "I may even join in."

She eyed him, enjoying the cut of his strong jaw, high cheekbones and straight nose. If looks were all that counted, he'd be an easy man to love.

"Go on." He nudged her arm with his elbow and gave her another grin.

At least a month had passed since her last solo in front of her Sunday school class, so she took a moment to clear her throat and get back into the rhythm of the horse's gait.

"'While on the road to sweet Athy, hurroo, hurroo. While on the road to sweet Athy, hurroo, hurroo. While on the road to sweet Athy, a stick in me hand and a drop in me eye, a doleful damsel I heard cry, Johnny I hardly knew ye.'"

Caught up in the song and feeling a bit reckless, she infused her words with the Irish brogue she'd worked so hard to lose. To her delight, Rand whistled along in harmony. Before she realized what she was singing, she warbled, "'Where are your legs with which ye run when first you learned to carry a gun? Indeed your dancing days are done. Oh, Johnny, I hardly knew ye.'"

Rand quit whistling, and if she wasn't mistaken, released a quiet sigh. Regret filled her. Did the song about the Irish Rebellion remind him of his own gun battle, which clearly still bothered him, despite others considering him a hero? She stared out across a wheat field almost ripe for harvest. Why hadn't she chosen a different song? But once again, she couldn't put the cat back in the bag.

Rand wished he hadn't let the song get to him. After all, he'd insisted that she sing, and she did it very well. Yet when would he be able to put his gunfight behind him, to stop wishing he'd never "learned to carry a gun" and just enjoy life? In the back of his mind, he knew Dathan Hardison's appearance in Esperanza was part of the problem.

Lord, I need Your help. It's not fair to Marybeth for me to get all melancholy like this. He straightened his shoulders and inhaled deeply of the fragrant wheat field on their left. Soon it would be harvest time, a time that promised survival through the coming winter. Before the geese flew south or the passes were blocked by snow, he needed to survive this winter of his soul.

"I've been trying to think what's wrong with that song." He forced cheer into his voice.

"Oh?" She turned sad eyes in his direction.

"And I've figured it out. It's all about sorrow." He enjoyed the way she blinked in confusion.

"Of course it is. Poor Johnny comes home from war maimed and unable to care for his wife and child." She bit her lip as if sorry she'd said that.

"That's where you have it all wrong." He smirked. "This is the version we sang when our Boston boys—*and* my father—returned from fighting in the South."

He launched into a spirited song with the same melody. "'When Johnny comes marching home again, hurrah, hurrah. When Johnny comes marching home again, hurrah, hurrah. The men will cheer and the boys will shout; the ladies they will all turn out. And we'll all feel gay when Johnny comes marching home.'"

By the time he reached the hurrahs, she'd joined in singing with a gusto that matched his own. As the buggy rolled across Main Street toward Mrs. Foster's Pike Street home, they were both laughing together like old friends.

"If it's not too bold of me to say, we make beautiful music together, Miss O'Brien." He salted his words with a bit of the Irish brogue he'd learned from his friend Seamus.

"Aye, that we do, Mr. O'Northam." Her merry mood gave her face a pretty glow. "Do you play an instrument of any kind to accompany us?"

"No. I never had the time to learn." And regretted it now. Was it too late to take up the guitar or accordion, the instruments that had always attracted his interest?

"I'll just have to teach you. Then you can leave ranching behind and go on the road as an entertainer."

Now he let out a hearty guffaw. What a delightful young lady. He could spend the rest of his life getting to know her. If she would have him.

A glance down the street cut his joy short. Dathan Hardison leaned casually against a post in front of Winsted's General Store, his arms crossed and his hat tipped back from his face as he chatted with Mrs. Winsted. The widow's posture was nothing short of sociable, meaning Hardison was worming his way into her good graces. Maybe Rand and his brothers were wrong not to warn folks in the community about this man's reason for coming to town.

Forcing his attention to the road ahead, he also forced a smile he didn't feel. "I'll come by Mrs. Foster's at ten o'clock tomorrow to escort you to church." He could hear the strained, almost authoritarian note in his voice, so quickly added, "That is, if you'd like."

The flush of high-spiritedness faded from her face and she gazed off with a frown, as though the idea didn't particularly appeal to her. Once again, caution reined in his growing affection for her. If she balked at going to church, how could he commit his life, his love, to her?

Rand's mood had shifted so quickly that Marybeth stared down Main Street to see what had caused it. The pleasant scene betrayed nothing unusual, just an ordinary Saturday afternoon with people going about normal business. Perhaps he was just temperamental—not a good sign. Oh, she'd dispensed with the notion that he might be abusive like Da, but she wouldn't marry a man with a temper or even habitual cross moods. She refused to be like Mam, always hurrying to cheer Da when he came home in a bad humor just so it wouldn't get worse. How often she herself had tried to make things right in their home, to no avail.

Rand cleared his throat, recalling her from her musings. "You did plan to go to church tomorrow, didn't you?"

She detected a note of irritation in his voice and that habitual urge to make things right crept into her chest. She tamped it down and gave him a saucy grin. "I'll not be needing you to keep me on the straight and narrow, Mr. Northam. I'm well and good dedicated to it myself."

She tossed her head and sniffed. "In fact, Mrs. Foster tells me she goes over to the church early to make sure everything's in fine fettle for the services, so I'll be going along with her and setting out the hymn books."

Her impertinent tone must have pleased him, for he gave her one of his attractive smirks. "And maybe I'll just be showing up to help you set them out. What would you think of that?"

She tapped her chin thoughtfully with her forefinger. "Hmm. I might just be able to stand your company, providing you don't get all bossy and try to tell me how to go about it."

"Why, Miss O'Brien, I would na dream of it."

Their merry mood restored, she enjoyed the rest of the ride down Pike Street to Mrs. Foster's house.

"Won't you come in?" she said as he handed her down from the buggy.

"I'd like that very much, but Nate didn't give me the whole day off. I still have chores and Tolley won't take kindly to my leaving them all to him."

He held her hand a little longer than was proper, but for some reason she didn't mind. Gazing up into his green eyes, edged as they were with dark lashes, she thought once again how easy it would be to fall in love with this man, if looks were all that counted. If nothing else, today she'd learned he would keep her safe. That was worth a great deal.

"I should go in." She tugged her hand free and retrieved the creel from the floor of the buggy, where grassy water formed a small puddle. "Oh, dear. I hope that doesn't leave a stain."

"Aw, nothing to worry about. It won't take a minute to wash it out." He took the creel from her and offered his arm. "Let's take these fish around to the back door so they won't drip water through the house."

"As if I hadn't thought of that very thing." Seeing he really wasn't so eager to get to those ranch chores, she found herself in no hurry to lose his company.

"O'course ya did." His Irish brogue was entirely entertaining and she rewarded his remark with a laugh.

As they strolled along the flagstone walkway toward the backyard, Marybeth took in the scent of the roses planted in narrow beds against the two-story house. She hadn't had a chance to see the outside of the house and found it entirely charming. "How lovely to have roses growing right here. We never had—" She stopped short of saying "anything so grand at our house." Despite her admission that she'd worked in the fishery, she still didn't want to admit to him how poor her family had been, so she finished with "A knack for growing flowers." Or decent soil in which to grow them.

"Maybe Mrs. Foster can show you her gardening methods. If not, Susanna can. She's done a fine job of keeping up the flower garden at our house while Mother's back East."

"And when do you suppose I'll be introduced to this Susanna?" In truth, Marybeth wasn't certain she wanted to meet the young lady or at least not form a friendship with her. She'd had very few intimate friends in her life, and if she got too close to Rand's sister-in-law, she feared it would make it all the harder not to become a part of his family.

"She may come to church tomorrow if Lizzy feels better."

"Poor baby. I'll be praying for her." Marybeth adored children. In spite of her determination not to get close to his family, if she didn't have her appointment with Mr. Means on Monday morning, she might ask Rand to fetch her out to the ranch so she could help Susanna take care of the wee colleen.

Oh, dear! With Rand's teasing her in an Irish brogue, hers was returning like a rekindled fire, one she must stamp out right away. In Boston, the Irish garnered little respect, and she refused to invite such treatment out here. Not that anyone in the Northam family had disparaged her background. Brogue or not, with a name like O'Brien she could hardly fool Rand's parents, and they'd been more than kind to her. A twinge of guilt stirred within her. More than kind, indeed, if they wanted her for their son. It was nothing short of an honor to be regarded in that light. But was Rand as honorable as his parents?

Once at the back stoop, Rand handed her the creel and gazed at her, a half smile on his lips. He tipped his hat back, bent forward and placed a kiss on her cheek. "Until tomorrow."

He strode away, whistling, and disappeared around the corner of the house, leaving her standing there, fish in hand and a longing in her heart for Sunday morning to arrive very soon.

Chapter Five

"Thank you, Marybeth." Mrs. Foster ran a damp rag over the oilcloth that covered the kitchen table. "You've helped me so much. Bringing home those delicious trout for last night's supper and cooking them, and now washing breakfast dishes."

"You're very welcome." Marybeth put the last dish away and draped the damp tea towel over the rack at the end of the kitchen cabinet. "I believe everyone should help out, no matter what the work is." Just because Rand might be at the church didn't mean she was in a hurry to get there. Truly, it didn't. Never mind how much she'd enjoyed his company yesterday. Nineteen hours and a restless night of sleep had restored her senses.

Last night she'd dreamed about Jimmy, dreamed Rand had found him and brought him to her right here at Mrs. Foster's. Only, when she'd dashed out the door to greet him, he looked more like Da than her jolly brother. Older, bent with care, tortured eyes, darker hair shot through with gray. Surely that couldn't have happened to Jimmy. He was only twenty-three.

So she shook off the nightmare, mainly because she

didn't put too much stock in dreams. Still, she couldn't help but wonder what changes she would find in her brother.

"We'd best hurry over to the church." Mrs. Foster shoved a clean dust rag into the satchel containing her music and bustled out of the kitchen toward the front door, with Marybeth close behind her. "I always like to dust the pews and windowsills and sweep a bit before people begin to arrive. Our pastor is a single young man, and without a wife to help him, he has to do everything himself. So until he finds a suitable bride, we older ladies try to keep the dear man well fed and his clothes mended."

From her landlady's maternal tone, Marybeth imagined a pudgy, sweet-faced little man whose sermons kept his flock comfortable in their pews. On the other hand, if he was the bossy type, perhaps he would urge her to marry Rand right away. As she and Mrs. Foster walked up Pike Street toward the church on Main Street, her anxiety grew. The last thing she needed was a pushy preacher telling her how to live her life.

Contrary to the impression Mrs. Foster had given her, Reverend Thomas was a tall, rather handsome and well-built young man with kind eyes devoid of any high-handedness. If she didn't know better and he weren't wearing a fine black suit, she would have assumed he was a cowboy.

"Welcome, Miss O'Brien." The minister shook her gloved hand and gave her a slight bow. "I understand you and Rand will be setting a date soon. I hope you'll permit me the honor of joining you two in marriage." His warm smile, Southern inflections and the jolly glint in his eyes caused her to like him right away, even as his words made her heart sink.

"Oh. Hmm." She glanced at Mrs. Foster, who was already dusting the pews. "I understand you're building an addition to the church, so we'll probably wait until it's finished so we can have our reception there." Now she sounded as gabby as her landlady.

"Ah, very good." Reverend Thomas retrieved a broom from the cloakroom and began to sweep dust and leaves across the floor toward the front door. "I've always advised couples to get to know each other fairly well before marriage."

Relief filled Marybeth as she reached for the broom. "Please let me do that."

He released it without argument. "Thank you. I do want to go over my sermon notes one more time before the service." Without another word he strode up the center aisle and disappeared through a side door.

Marybeth had just finished sweeping the last of the dust down the front steps of the church when Rand arrived on horseback. His gaze landed on her and he reached up to touch the brim of his hat. "Howdy, Marybeth." There was a sweet, shy note in his voice that sent her heart into a spin. In fact, she was feeling a bit shy herself, as though they hadn't seen each other just yesterday. Oh, bother. Where was her resolve not to become attached to him?

"Hello, Rand."

Gracious, he looked handsome and capable as he dismounted and secured his horse to a railing under a nearby tree. His black suit, white shirt and black string tie added to his attractive appearance. When he turned and gave her that crooked smile of his, it was all she could manage to scurry back into the church before she gave her heart away on the spot.

No, no, no. She would not fall in love with his good looks. Hadn't the minister just said a couple should get acquainted before marriage? She'd been here only two days. Despite knowing Rand's parents for a brief time in Boston, she simply had too much to learn about their son before letting herself fall in love. Most important was whether or not he would keep his word about helping her find Jimmy. No matter how long it took, he must do that before she would even consider loving him enough to change her lifelong determination not to marry.

Entering the building, he removed his hat and ran a hand through his hair to get rid of the hat line. She'd already come to love and expect the gesture. "Howdy, Mrs. Foster. I'm here to help. Don't tell me you ladies have all the work done."

"You can help Marybeth set out the hymnals." Mrs. Foster nodded toward the cloakroom.

"Yes, ma'am." He turned to Marybeth, his grin still in place. "You first."

She scooted past him and into the narrow room where churchgoers could hang their hats and coats. Rand settled his wide-brimmed black felt hat on one of the four-inch pegs. It was a fine new chapeau, probably kept just for Sunday and special events. His light woolen suit also appeared to be of the finest quality. How many men could afford such a wardrobe? Rand's wife would probably never want for anything, except maybe the freedom of a single life. Mam had been imprisoned by her marriage, by Da's moodiness and temper.

At the end of the small cloakroom sat a three-shelf

bookcase covered with an old sheet to protect the hymnals from dust. She removed and folded the material while Rand scooped up a handful of the books. As his arm brushed hers, a pleasant feeling shot up her neck. From his quick intake of breath she guessed he hadn't minded the contact, either.

"Sorry to bump you that way. It's a little tight in here." He gave her an apologetic smile before making his way out to the sanctuary.

"It's all right," she whispered to his back, not trusting herself to speak out loud. What were these feelings he caused? Why did she wish he'd kiss her on the cheek again, as he had yesterday afternoon? She'd never felt this way toward any man.

Rand took several deep breaths as he headed toward the front pew. It might be Sunday, and he might be in church, but he'd had an almost overwhelming urge to plant a kiss on Marybeth's ivory cheek right there in the cloakroom.

The moment he'd ridden up to the church and seen her busy at work with that broom on the front steps, his chest had swelled with pride and appreciation not only for her beauty, but for her willingness to help, whether the work was sweeping a church or cleaning a fish. It was a bit too soon to say he was in love, but he had a feeling it wouldn't be long before he handed his heart to the lovely Miss O'Brien on a silver platter. It took some doing to remind himself that he still needed to discern her character and find out whether she'd lied to Mother and Dad.

She cut short his concerns when she brought a stack

of hymnals to the front and set them down. "How many should we put in each pew?"

He surveyed the wooden benches he'd helped to build nine years ago, ten on the right and ten on the left, each of which held six or more adults or an assortment of children. "Three ought to do it. Folks don't mind sharing, and we need to be sure everyone can see one. Reverend Thomas has a habit of choosing at least one song nobody knows just so we can learn more of them."

Chuckling in her feminine way, she disbursed the books down one side while he took care of the other. "Are all of the pews filled on a Sunday morning?"

"Pretty much." A mild sense of pride in his community brought a grin to his lips. Before he'd gotten right with the Lord, how often had he slept through Reverend Thomas's excellent sermons? Some cowboys still nodded off from exhaustion, but at least none from drunkenness. Dad had forbidden alcohol in the town he was building, and everyone who'd settled here agreed. There were plenty of saloons in the nearby towns to attract men who wanted to waste their money after the sun went down on payday.

Marybeth seemed right at home in the church. After she finished with the hymnals, she went down front to stand by Mrs. Foster and hold one of the books open as the older lady practiced at the pump organ. Sometimes Rand wondered how old Mrs. Foster could manage to pump with her feet and play at the same time, but she seemed to do it with ease. He recalled the husbandly pride beaming from Captain Foster's face on Sunday mornings over his wife's skillful playing. Rand couldn't wait to hear Marybeth take to the keyboard. No matter how well she played, he'd praise her efforts.

At the end of the hymn Marybeth gently closed the book. "Would you like me to help you during the service?"

"Thank you, my dear, but I've promised Laurie she could do it. She treasures the responsibility."

Promise. Rand had forgotten all about telling Marybeth how he'd kept his promise. As soon as she joined him in the center aisle, he offered his most charming grin.

"By the by, I almost forgot to tell you that I wrote letters about your brother to the sheriffs of Del Norte and Wagon Wheel Gap. Took them over to the general store and slipped them through the mail slot. Mrs. Winsted will see that they get out tomorrow afternoon."

Marybeth gripped his forearm with surprising strength and gazed up at him with the prettiest smile he'd ever seen. "Oh, Rand, thank you so much." Her eyes glistened with unshed tears. The strength of her emotions nearly undid him. "This means the world to me. You just can't imagine how much."

No, he couldn't. His family had always surrounded him, even at his worst. What must it be like to be alone in the world and searching for a long-lost brother? He placed a hand over hers and gently squeezed. "If Jimmy O'Brien is anywhere in the San Luis Valley, we'll find him."

She nodded but pursed her lips and didn't say anything more. He could tell she was having trouble reining in her emotions, and he had a little difficulty holding on to his own. But having a sister had taught him how to deal with women's tears. Sort of. Right now he longed to pull Marybeth into his arms to comfort her, just as he would Rosamond if she was all weepy.

Unfortunately the Archers and several other families were entering the church and beginning to fill the pews. For the past three years Rand had done all he could to maintain a spotless reputation, and he sure didn't want to damage Marybeth's before folks even met her, so he just patted her shoulder.

"Where would you like to sit?" He was glad to see her bright smile return.

"Where does your family sit?"

"Just about any place. We don't have special pews. The preacher put an end to that when a cranky older member chased a poorly dressed young couple out of a pew he'd claimed as his own. They were new to the community, and we never saw them here again. Later the preacher said they'd joined a church down in Waverly. These days we all try to welcome anybody who comes through those doors, no matter how they're dressed or what they look like."

"Oh, my." Marybeth's eyes had widened as he told the story and now she nodded thoughtfully. "That's what the second chapter of James teaches, isn't it? We're not to be a respecter of persons."

Rand eyed her with a new appreciation. If she knew the scriptures that well, it sure did say something good about her character.

They slid into the third row on the left just as Tolley and Nate entered the church. Rand waved them over, pride surging through his chest at the idea of introducing Marybeth to his older brother.

Marybeth's pulse began to race at the prospect of meeting more of Rand's family. There was no mistaking the resemblance between Rand, Tolley and the tall man with him. She could find no fault in any of their similar features, yet somehow Rand's face appealed to her, whereas his brothers' did not. Maybe it was that crooked boyish grin.

"Marybeth, you've met Tolley. Here's our older brother—"

"And warden," Tolley quipped.

Rand shot a scolding look at him. "Our older brother, Nate," he finished.

"Hello, Tolley. How do you do, Nate?" Marybeth reached out to shake his hand. "I'm so happy to meet you. Did Susanna have to stay home with baby Lizzy?"

Her simple question seemed to please Nate. Behind his regretful smile, pride in his wife and baby girl glinted in his eyes as he shook her hand. "I'm mighty glad to meet you, too, Marybeth. And thanks for asking about my girls. Yes, they'll have to stay home for just a few more days. Lizzy's getting better, and Susanna's eager to meet you, so they'll be coming to town by Wednesday or Thursday, I'm sure."

The friendly warmth in his gaze made Marybeth regret her earlier doubts about meeting Susanna. What a dear, good family they all were. What would it be like to be accepted as a part of it? Would she even know how to act? Or how to feel accepted?

Mrs. Foster started to play quietly on the organ and people began to settle into their places. Rand moved down to the end of the pew, and she followed him, while the brothers filed in after her. Seated between Rand and Nate, Marybeth felt the power of their well-built physiques. Though a bit intimidated, she also had never felt so safe and protected.

Reverend Thomas welcomed everyone to the service and then announced the hymn. Rand held out the hymnal for her as they joined in a rousing "Onward, Christian Soldiers." Standing between the two brothers, Marybeth could hardly suppress a laugh. While Rand's pleasant baritone provided an admirable bass harmony just as it had yesterday, Nate's enthusiastic efforts weren't even in the same key. Or any key, for that matter. If she did decide to marry into this family, she was glad her husband would be the one who could carry a tune.

Marry? Husband? The words stopped her. She'd always vowed never to have a husband, and here she was thinking of marrying Rand. But how could she not look favorably on him when he'd kept his promise about writing those letters? When he'd stood here not ten minutes ago and promised to find Jimmy, if he was to be found anywhere in this great valley?

Lord, what am I going to do? Maybe the minister's sermon would have an answer for her. After all, when she'd prayed about accepting Colonel and Mrs. Northam's offer to pay her train fare to come west, hadn't the minister in their church preached that very Sunday about Abraham being called out of his homeland to a new land of his own? She'd taken that as a sign she was to begin her quest to find Jimmy. But it didn't mean she had to marry Rand. Did it?

As the hymn ended and the congregation took their seats, Rand sensed that same unease in Marybeth he'd noticed from the first. Although she seemed happy to be in church and certainly enjoyed the singing, if her smile was any indication, her mood had grown sober at some point during the hymn. He doubted it was Nate's poor excuse for singing that caused her sudden change, but he couldn't imagine what had brought on that furrowed brow.

Reverend Thomas announced a meeting of the deacons after the service, so that meant Rand would be staying. He was sitting on the church board while Dad was out of town. The preacher also mentioned the ladies' fund-raising quilting bee on Thursday. Rand hoped Marybeth would consider attending the bee so she could become friends with the other ladies at church. If she could see what a fine community Esperanza was and how genuine the people were, maybe she'd decide marriage to him wouldn't be so bad. He hoped and prayed that would happen, even as his concerns about her truthfulness whispered a word of caution to his mind.

After a few other announcements and another hymn, during which the offering was taken, the pastor moved to his place behind the pulpit just as the church door banged open. Although Rand's parents had taught him to keep his attention on the preacher no matter what happened at the back of the church, he couldn't help turning around to see who the noisy latecomer was.

Hardison!

Rand's first instinct was to reach for his gun. But this being Sunday morning, he'd left it in his saddlebag in deference to the preacher's wishes about no guns being brought into the church building. Everyone honored that wish, except maybe Maisie and her sisters, who probably carried derringers in their reticules. Right now Rand wished he'd stuck his sister's small firearm in his pocket. Then again, he never imagined Hardison would dare to complete his threats right here in God's house.

Tolley shot him a look and a nod, but Rand frowned

and shook his head. They wouldn't chase the man out, not after his speech to Marybeth about this church welcoming everyone to its services. He prayed he wouldn't have to eat those words.

Before he could figure out what to do, Hardison whipped off his hat and gave the preacher a nod. "Sorry," he whispered, sounding as though he meant it.

"Welcome, friend," the preacher said. "We're glad you're here."

Hardison walked around to the window end of a back pew and slid in next to Susanna's father and stepmother. He gave them a friendly smile, one so sincere that Rand almost believed it. Apparently, Edward MacAndrews did believe it because he shook hands with Hardison, while his wife, Angela, returned a maternal smile.

Rand's insides twisted at the deception. What was this man doing here? After threatening Rand and his family and Marybeth, why would he intrude on this holy time?

On the other hand, Reverend Thomas seemed pleased at the intrusion, perhaps even a little bit more invigorated than usual. He read the scripture passage from Psalm 119. "'Wherewithal shall a young man cleanse his way? By taking heed thereto according to Thy word.'"

Ordinarily, Rand would sit up and take notice. Since killing Hardison's cousin, he'd tried diligently not only to listen carefully to each sermon but also to cleanse his way of every possible sin. But it was no sin to protect those he loved, those he was responsible for, was it? He'd been assured by friends and family that it had been a righteous execution of a killer, yet he still couldn't reconcile himself to being the executioner.

The preacher went on. "'With my whole heart have I

sought Thee. O let me not wander from Thy commandments. Thy word have I hid in my heart that I might not sin against Thee.'"

Only by force of his will could Rand take in the lesson from the sermon. Had he truly been seeking God with his whole heart these past three years? When was the last time he'd worked on memorizing passages that spoke to him? Despite knowing it was wrong to judge people according to their wealth or position or clothing, he hadn't known that verse about not being a respecter of persons was in the book of James. He would have to look it up when he got home. This morning he'd been so eager to get to town that he'd forgotten his Bible, another lapse.

As Reverend Thomas always did, especially when a stranger attended services, he ended his message with the gospel. He explained how Jesus' death on the cross paid for everyone's sins, no matter how bad a person was. All a man had to do was to reach out and accept the gift, just like a birthday present. He spoke of Christ's resurrection as the promise to all believers that they would one day be in Heaven with Him.

Usually, Rand loved to hear the simple gospel that had turned his life around three years ago, especially the way Reverend Thomas delivered it. The preacher didn't pound the pulpit, nor did he holler or pour shame and condemnation on his congregants, like some preachers Rand had heard as a boy. Like Jesus, Reverend Thomas led them like a flock.

If he weren't so concerned about Hardison, he would let the message settle over him like a warm blanket to chase away the chill of guilt that often plagued him. Instead he prayed for God's protection on everyone in the congregation because he had no doubt the gunslinger would do something to disturb the peace in this holy room.

Sure enough, just as the preacher finished his invitation to anyone who wanted to accept Christ's free gift of salvation, Hardison stood and walked to the front, brushing invisible tears from his cheeks as he walked.

While others whispered "Praise the Lord" or "God bless him," Rand ground his teeth. Even Tolley seemed more puzzled than disbelieving. But Rand would believe the gunman had been converted when Mount Blanca crumbled into sand and spread across the Valley floor.

Marybeth blinked in wonder as a man strode up the aisle toward the preacher. Her Boston church didn't have altar calls, but Rosamond had told her about them. How wonderful that during her first visit to this place of worship a man became convicted of his need for Christ and was willing to make his new faith public.

The pastor invited him to kneel and then knelt beside him and put an arm around his shoulders while they prayed. As she watched them stand and the pastor introduce Dathan Hardison to the congregation, she realized he was the man who had stared at her so boldly on the train. At the time she'd felt very uncomfortable under his leering perusal and more than a little grateful for the companionship of Dr. and Mrs. Henshaw. Perhaps now that he'd become a Christian, this man would behave in a more seemly fashion toward ladies. At least his expression bore signs of repentance, for which she could only rejoice.

She glanced up at Rand to share this joyous moment, only to see a scowl on his face. A quick glance at Nate revealed less hostility, but still a decided lack of approval. Impatience and annoyance swept through her. A man had just come to the Lord. Why would they not be pleased? This was the first real flaw she'd seen in the entire Northam family's character. What other disappointments would they hand her in the coming days?

On the other hand, Nolan Means, seated across the aisle with his sister, Anna, wore a pleased, even interested, smile. That spoke well of the banker. Maybe he would befriend Mr. Hardison. She had an idea Rand and Nate weren't planning to.

After church, Rand excused himself from walking Marybeth back to Mrs. Foster's, telling her he had a deacons' meeting to attend. "I'll leave you in Mrs. Foster's capable hands." He gave her that cute smile of his, but the troubled look in his eyes conveyed another feeling altogether. "She'll get you safely home."

As if she couldn't get herself safely back to the house. But she wouldn't challenge him about that. "Is everything all right?" Maybe she could get him to explain his disapproval of Mr. Hardison.

He gently squeezed her forearm. "Nothing for you to worry about. Just church business." His attention now on Nate, he seemed in a hurry to get away from her for the first time since they'd met.

Fine. If he wouldn't share his concerns with her after she'd told him so many of hers, then so be it.

"Well, I'll bid you good day." She edged past the brothers and joined her landlady down front by the organ. "Your music was lovely, Mrs. Foster. It certainly put me in the mood for worship." And Rand just ruined it all.

As she shook hands with the minister on her way out

into the summer sunshine, she decided to let her negative feelings go, as Mam had always urged her to do. That had been Mam's way to survive her miseries, but Marybeth had never quite mastered it.

Mrs. Foster introduced her to several people, including Susanna's father and stepmother, Mr. and Mrs. MacAndrews, who welcomed her as if she were already part of their extended family. Maisie and Doc made sure she met the rest of the Eberly family: the parents, of course, and sisters Beryl, Georgia and Grace, who at twenty years old was half a head taller than her own father. Laurie gave Marybeth a wave and now was busy with the other girls her age, probably waiting for Tolley to emerge from the church.

All in all, Marybeth felt the warmth of Christian love around her. Several men surrounded Mr. Hardison and chatted with the new convert as if he were an old friend. When he glanced her way, he smiled and tipped his hat but made no move to approach her. That spoke well of him. No doubt he would wait for a proper introduction, as a gentleman should. She would forgive and forget his inappropriate stares on the train.

Mr. Means spoke to Marybeth briefly and reminded her of their appointment tomorrow morning. As if she could forget it. A job at the bank was exactly what she needed to support herself and to keep her from being forced to marry Mr. Randall Northam, with all of his changing moods.

After Marybeth and Mrs. Foster left, Rand stayed in the pew to talk with his brothers about Hardison before the deacons' meeting.

"Everybody believed his act," Tolley said in an urgent whisper. "We need to expose him for what he is."

"Hang on, brother." Nate blew out a long breath. "I'd be one of those who believed him if Rand hadn't told me his name and described the encounter you two had with him." He looked toward the door, where the last few church members lined up to shake hands with the preacher on their way out. "Besides, who's to say he wasn't convicted of his need for the Lord during the preacher's message? It was one of his best sermons, and that's saying something."

The familiar nudge of conviction for his own sins stopped Rand's protest before he could give voice to it. He wished he'd listened more intently to the preacher's words when he was younger.

"Another thing." Nate went on. "We don't want to alarm the townfolks or take a chance on turning them against a new Christian. That is, if he's sincerely converted."

"You weren't there when he threatened Rand." Tolley scowled at his oldest brother. "Tell him, Rand."

"No sense repeating what I told him Friday night." Rand saw Reverend Thomas and the other deacons returning to the sanctuary. "Nate, can you stick around until after the meeting? Maybe we can ask the preacher what he thinks."

"Sure." Nate set a hand on Tolley's shoulder. "Would you mind riding back to the ranch and making sure Susanna and Lizzy are all right? And say I'll be a little late for dinner?"

Tolley shrugged off his hand. "'Course not. Won't mind at all. No, sir. Not me. I'm old enough to be your errand boy but not old enough to sit in on a meeting with the men." He marched up the aisle, snatching his hat from the cloakroom and clapping it on his head as he exited the church.

Rand cast a rueful look at Nate. "We've got to let the boy grow up someday."

"Maybe." Nate shrugged. "When he cools that temper down a bit."

Rand nodded. Nate had fought his own battle with a strong temper and with God's help had won. Now he had a cool head and steady hand, which was reason enough for Dad to leave him in charge of the ranch. Rand was glad to leave the authority to him, something he couldn't have said three years ago when he'd chafed under his older brother's authoritarian ways.

Which was why Rand had been more than a little surprised when Dad had left him, not Nate, in charge of the family's church responsibilities. Especially considering that the deacon board was, in effect, the town council, until Dad returned and organized the setting up of an official city government. So far Esperanza and the surrounding community had grown peaceably on their own, with good people moving in every week, folks taking responsibility where they saw a need, and no one stirring up trouble. Until Hardison.

"All right, men." Reverend Thomas waved the seven deacons and Nate to their seats in the two front pews. "Let's make this short and sweet. Mrs. Foster's invited me to dinner, and I don't want the fried chicken to get cold."

While the other men laughed, a jealous itch crept into Rand's chest. He refused to let it bite him. The preacher would never intrude on another man's territory. Still, he wished he were the one having dinner with Marybeth and her landlady. To ease his own mind, he'd need to stop by the house on his way home to see whether Mrs. Foster had opened her home to Hardison. She or someone else usually fed newcomers…and strays.

After a prayer for the group to make wise decisions, Reverend Thomas beckoned Rand to the front. "What's on the docket today?"

Rand had overcome his nervousness at leading older men several months ago. They all had come to respect him, and of course they all respected the Northam name. Today, however, the specter of Dathan Hardison and his dead cousin hung over him as he dug notes out of his shirt pocket. Only willpower helped him get through the bits of business.

In the end, the men decided that enough children now attended the church to warrant the establishment of a formal Sunday school, so once the addition was built, they would have to line up some teachers with Bible knowledge. The ladies' fund-raiser was a priority for their support, so Rand urged the men to let their wives participate. Finally, citing the scripture about caring for aged widows, Rand encouraged the board to offer Mrs. Foster some payment for her faithful organ playing, her being a widow lady with no family nearby to take care of her and only piano lessons and her husband's pension from the war to live on. All measures were passed unanimously.

"Well, if there's nothing else, we can dismiss the preacher to his fried chicken." Rand made a final note on his scrap of paper about Mrs. Foster and stuck it back in his pocket.

"Actually, I do have something else." Nolan Means

stood in the second pew and leveled a benign look at Rand. "If I may?"

Rand gave him a short nod. "Sure. You want to come up here?" Dad had warned him that bankers often liked to take over the leadership of a town simply because they had money. Despite their own wealth, Dad insisted the Northams would not rule the town, just try to lead it with the Lord's help. Rand didn't know Means well at all, but he'd keep an eye on him.

"No, thanks. I can speak from here." The banker, around twenty-four years old and impeccably dressed in his black suit and white linen shirt, glanced around the group. "As you all may know, the new bank is my first to manage under my uncle's backing."

Rand found it interesting that the man seemed surprised by his own statement, much as he himself had been surprised by Dad's faith in him.

"Of course, I want to make it a success," Means went on. "Which keeps me on my knees." He chuckled and the other men joined in. "I know Esperanza is a fine town, but I'm concerned about outsiders, especially those riding through on their way to the silver fields. Not that I expect a robbery, but it's always a possibility."

When several men murmured their surprise, he hurried on. "I believe it's time our town hired a sheriff, someone full-time to watch out for our interests."

"Not a bad idea," Edgar Jones, the barber, said. "Mrs. Winsted next door to me tells me she's been missing small things from the general store. Mostly candy, so it's probably mischievous boys, but other items, too, that can slip easily into a pocket. The presence of a lawman in town would discourage such shenanigans."

Again the other men murmured their concerns.

"I think Mr. Hardison might be a possible candidate," Means continued. "I spoke to him after church, and he told me he has had a long history with the law."

Rand almost choked over Hardison's wily words. Until this moment he'd been willing to listen to Means, but this was going too far. He opened his mouth to tell these fine men exactly what Dathan Hardison was up to. Even cool, calm Nate frowned and moved forward on the pew as if he were about to stand in protest.

"Hold on." Reverend Thomas stood beside Rand. "Let's not load so much on a new convert. Let me disciple him for a while." The look in his eyes told Rand he had a deeper meaning behind his words.

Means started to voice his protest when old Charlie Williams stood next to him, his mountain-man hackles raised like a grizzly bear's.

"The Colonel said he'll hire a sheriff when he comes back. We'll wait for him on this." While the other men talked all at once, Charlie gave Rand a curt nod, as if to say, "Don't lose control, boy."

Suppressing a grin, Rand raised his hands over the hubbub. "All right, all right." When he had their attention, he said, "Charlie's right. We'll wait for the Colonel, but in the meantime, I'll write to him about our concerns. Will that be enough for you all?"

That promise seemed to settle everyone down. "All right. If there's nothing else, this meeting is adjourned."

Nolan Means didn't exactly look pleased, but his expression held no anger. If he really had concerns about a bank robbery, they most certainly would have to address the matter.

After the other men left the church, the preacher released a long sigh. "We dodged that bullet, didn't we?"

"What?" Rand and Nate chorused together.

The preacher chuckled. "Friends, I don't consider myself as wise as Solomon, but I do know a real conversion when I see one. Unfortunately, Hardison will have to go a long way to prove he's redeemed before I believe him." His eyes exuded a pastoral sadness that spoke well of his character.

Rand and Nate exchanged a look.

"Is it time to tell him the whole story?" Rand asked his brother.

"Be my guest," said Nate.

As Rand unfolded the tale of Hardison's threats to Reverend Thomas, the weight of fear he'd felt on his chest for the past three days seemed to lift a few notches. But he couldn't help thinking Hardison had a hidden agenda that included more than just revenge for his cousin's death. Why didn't he just confront Rand for a shoot-out? Why was he trying to inveigle his way into the close-knit community of Esperanza?

Chapter Six

"I'll answer the door." Marybeth removed her apron and laid it over the back of a kitchen chair.

"Thank you, dear." Fork in hand, Mrs. Foster turned a chicken leg in the frying pan and brushed a sleeve over her damp forehead. "This will be done in just a few minutes, so have the preacher take a seat in the parlor."

Anticipating a pleasant dinner with Reverend Thomas, Marybeth made a quick trip through the dining room to be sure the table was still properly set. Last evening she and Mrs. Foster had polished the silver and set it out with the gleaming rose-patterned china. Crystal goblets awaited tea now stored in the icebox—iced tea for a Southern gentleman—and white linen napkins lay beside the plates on the white damask tablecloth.

Pleased to see her landlady's cat had not gotten on the table and disturbed the settings, Marybeth hastened to the front door. Through the oval etched-glass window, she saw the preacher was not alone. Rand! Her heart skipped and her hand trembled as she opened the door.

"Good afternoon, gentlemen. Please come in." She

stood aside to let them in. *Oh, bother.* Her voice was shaking, but due to which of these men? Until this moment she'd been too busy helping Mrs. Foster to be nervous. Of course she'd felt a little concerned about the preacher because he might ask too many questions about her wedding plans…or lack thereof. But Rand's appearance also made her a bit nervous. Why had he come?

Both gentlemen greeted her as they removed their hats and stepped over the threshold. The preacher hung his hat on the walnut hall tree beside the door, but Rand stood just inside.

"I can't stay," he said in answer to her questioning look. "I just wanted to be sure you and Mrs. Foster got home all right." She could see the relief in his eyes, but for what?

"Of course we did." She glanced at the preacher. "It's just a short walk. What could happen in three blocks in this lovely, peaceful town?"

The men traded a look, which both irritated her and made her feel good. She dismissed the irritation born of her desire, her *need* for independence. Rand's obvious relief over her safety touched her. Once again, she could see he wanted to take care of her, an admirable quality she could not disregard. Even as she thought it, she also remembered all those cozy feelings could be a trap from which she would never escape.

"Probably not much would happen on a Sunday." Rand turned his hat in his hand. "I guess I just wanted to see you again. I won't be able to visit you until late tomorrow morning. Ranch chores, you know." He gazed down at her with those gentle green eyes, and her pulse stuttered.

"Oh." She glanced at Reverend Thomas, whose benign expression showed interest without being intrusive. It also convicted her. Should she tell Rand about her appointment at the bank? Her mouth took over before her mind decided. "I may not be here."

He blinked. And frowned. "Where will you be?" The crossness in his voice reminded her that his moods changed quickly. Too quickly, and for no apparent reason.

"Why, I… I—" She shouldn't lie. *Must* not lie. "I have an appointment with Mr. Means at the bank. A job interview." She ended breathlessly so he wouldn't bark out another question.

But now his expression changed from cross to worried. He traded another look with the preacher before gazing at her again. "What time is your appointment?"

"Nine o'clock."

"Maybe I'll ride into town about then and walk you over to the bank."

"I could walk her over for you, Rand," Reverend Thomas said. "That way you could complete your chores without worry."

Marybeth felt the urge to stamp her feet like one of her spoiled classmates often did back at the academy. Growing up, she'd never had the luxury of expressing her feelings so strongly. "What's the matter with you two? I can walk to the bank by myself."

Maddeningly, they traded another one of those paternalistic looks. Finally the preacher said, "She'll be fine. I'll make sure."

"All right. If you insist." Rand placed his hat on his head. "I'll come by the bank and walk you home." He turned toward the door and then back to her. "I should say 'may I come by to walk you home?'"

The annoyance in his tone and expression struck Marybeth's funny bone, and she couldn't stifle a laugh. "You won't know what time."

He raised his fists to his waist. "Then I'll just sit outside the bank until you come out."

The preacher laughed. "I think he has you there, Marybeth. Why not let him escort you home?"

She cast him a saucy grin she hoped didn't seem irreverent. "Oh, very well. I suppose I'll be finished with the interview by ten o'clock. Or ten minutes after nine, if it doesn't go well." *Lord, please let it go well.*

"Good. I'll be waiting outside the bank at ten minutes after nine." Rand frowned. "I don't mean to say I hope it doesn't go well. Actually, I do hope it doesn't—"

"Quit while you're ahead, Rand." The preacher chuckled.

"Good idea." Rand gazed at Marybeth for another long moment. Then he spun on his heel and marched out the door and down the steps.

Good manners demanded that she turn her attention to Reverend Thomas, but she would much rather watch Rand ride away. Gracious, he was a good-looking man. A determined, capable man. She had no doubt whatsoever that he could accomplish anything he set his mind to.

Which stirred up no little concern inside her. While those were good qualities when it came to his finding Jimmy, she wasn't so sure she wanted them turned her way if he decided he was going to marry her.

"I could not be more pleased with your skill, Miss O'Brien." Mr. Means stood beside Marybeth's chair and bent over her shoulder watching her progress as she copied a handwritten letter using the Remington Sholes and Glidden typewriting machine. "I cannot see a single error in your transcription."

"Thank you, sir." She smothered a wide smile that might reveal how violently her heart had skipped at his compliment. She felt not the slightest attraction to the man, but his easy manner suggested he would be a pleasant employer for whom to work. "Would you like to try dictation?" Her fingers itched for the challenge.

"Hmm." He stared off as though considering the matter. "No, better not. You see on this page—" he held up the handwritten letter she'd just copied "—how many times I scratched out my words when better ones came to mind. No need to waste paper." He reached out as though to pat her shoulder but then seemed to think better of it. "I will be delighted to sign and send this letter to my uncle in New York. He went to a great deal of trouble to acquire and send this machine for the bank, so it will give him great satisfaction to finally receive a letter written on it."

"Very good, sir." Marybeth rolled the bar to release the sheet and handed the letter to him.

"Will you be able to start work right away?" He studied the typed page with interest as he spoke.

"Today?" She could hear the giddy squeak in her voice, but he had the good manners not to laugh.

"If you can. I have several letters I would like to send out with today's three o'clock post."

Once again her heart skipped. Rand's letters asking the two sheriffs about Jimmy would go out this afternoon, too. How long would it take them to reach their destinations and answers be returned? If she didn't keep busy, she'd find herself fretting over the situation.

"I'd be happy to start today." She ran her hand over the corner of the polished oak desk where she would be assuming her duties. Nearby stood a dark walnut hat rack that held her hat, gloves and reticule. It also could serve as an umbrella stand, but Mrs. Foster told her the San Luis Valley had very little rainfall. Coming from Boston, Marybeth found that quite remarkable.

"Good. I'll write those letters and bring them to you. In the meantime, would you go over to the café and fetch me a pot of coffee?"

He was still looking down at the letter, so could not have seen her shock. She quickly schooled her face back to a pleasant, professional smile.

So it was true, what she'd learned in her secretarial training. Ladies who worked as secretaries must also serve coffee and tea and whatever other refreshments their bosses required. Never mind their advanced training, they were still just maids with extra skills.

"Of course, Mr. Means. Would you care for cream and sugar?"

He glanced up at her, not seeming really to see her. "Yes, please. And perhaps one of Miss Pam's pastries. She knows the ones I like."

"Very good, sir." Marybeth put on her hat and gloves before proceeding out the front door of the stone bank. She carried her reticule, although it held no money. Surely, Mr. Means didn't expect her to pay for the coffee and pastries. She would tell Miss Pam to put the cost on the banker's account.

"It's about time." Rand leaned against the bank's hitching post, arms crossed and hat low over his eyes.

"It's almost eleven o'clock. What were you doing in there?"

"Rand." She gasped softly. She'd forgotten all about his offer to walk her home. But his cross tone of voice cut short her regret. "Well, if you must know, Mr. Northam, I've just been hired to work at the bank. I start today."

"Is that so?" He pushed his hat back to reveal those appealing green eyes filled with disappointment and a dash of annoyance. Marybeth steadied her swaying emotions. She would not let him change her course.

"Yes, it is." She tugged at her gloves and stepped off of the boardwalk into the dusty street. Which only served to remind her of how tall and well formed he was. She huffed out a cross breath over her own ambivalence. "Now, if you'll excuse me, I have an errand to run."

He gave her a mischievous grin. "Ah, I see. You're the new errand boy. What happened to the typewriting job?"

She could feel her temper rising, but she wouldn't give him the satisfaction of seeing it. "Why, you're entirely mistaken. Mr. Means is delighted with my typewriting skills. While he writes some letters for me to transcribe, I'm fetching us a pot of coffee and some pastries."

As she walked away from him, guilt smote her. Mr. Means hadn't said anything about coffee for *her*. She'd often told half-truths to Da to keep from getting hit, yet Rand hadn't done anything to deserve such treatment. Nor did she think the Lord approved of such deceptions. Before she could turn around and tell Rand the truth, he fell into step beside her.

"I might just have one of those pastries myself." To her chagrin, he offered her his arm. "Nobody makes them like Miss Pam, but don't tell Mrs. Foster I said that."

She couldn't very well let him walk along beside her with one arm bent and sticking out, so she set her hand on it. Mercy, he had powerful muscles. "You know, Mr. Northam, I've looked up and down this street and I can't see any reason why I need your protection as I walk around town."

"Maybe not." He gave her that devastating smile. "But I just want to make certain everybody knows you're taken."

She stopped in the middle of the street and glared up at him. "I most certainly am not *taken*." Staring up that way, she felt her hat slipping off the back of her head and reached up to catch it, bringing a low chuckle from Rand. "Now, if you'll excuse me, I need to complete my errand and get back to work." She started to march off in a huff when he gently gripped her upper arm and turned her back.

"Do you mind?" She wanted to struggle against his hold, but that would make a scene to shame them both.

"Now that you mention it, I do mind." He tipped his hat back again. "Marybeth, you don't need to do this. You don't need to work at a job while we're searching for your brother."

The pain in his eyes cut into her, yet not so deeply as to change her mind. "But I want to, Rand. I want to earn my own livelihood, not be supported by you. How would that look if we end up not getting married?"

He winced visibly, stared off and then slowly returned a sad gaze to her. "All right. But I'm going to walk you home every day. And the preacher is going to be watching out for you when you walk to work in the morning."

Something in his voice held a warning she could not easily dismiss. "Why? What are you not telling me?"

Again he stared off, but this time he seemed to study the numerous people going about their business on the street. "I don't want to worry you, but you have a right to know. There are always unsavory elements passing through Esperanza on their way to the silver mines. Not all prospectors are dangerous, but some like to prey on the unsuspecting. Some transients get their prospecting stake by robbing good people as they travel west. They cause havoc and then disappear before anyone can call them to account for it or even know who they are."

"Oh." Marybeth knew well which parts of Boston held that same danger. She'd lived in a poor, rough neighborhood but had known of rougher areas closer to the waterfront. "Very well. I accept your offer to escort me home each day." She started to turn away but instead set a hand on his arm. "Thank you, Rand."

Relief blossomed across his tanned face and that charming smile appeared again like sunshine. "Now, let's get Mr. Means his coffee before he fires you."

His teasing tone lightened her mood considerably. "Humph. You didn't see how pleased he was with my typewriting. Why, I'm going to be indispensable to him. You just wait and see, Mr. Rand Northam."

His chuckle held a hint of ruefulness. "I don't doubt that for one second, Miss O'Brien, and that's what worries me."

Rand might have continued to argue with Marybeth about her job if he hadn't noticed the pride and self-respect just being hired had already given her. He didn't understand why any lady would want to earn her own living when she could get married and have a husband to provide for her. Yet something in Marybeth's past must have left a hole in her heart that needed to be filled up. She'd made it clear he wouldn't be able to do that, which stung a little. A lot, actually.

Still, if she needed this job to bolster her spirits, he couldn't object. Maybe she was like Tolley, who still felt the need to prove himself. In fact, Rand knew that feeling himself, and all too well. Further, Marybeth was right that folks wouldn't think too highly of either of them if he supported her and they ended up not getting married. She didn't need to know he was paying her rent. Mrs. Foster had promised not to give away their little secret. The old dear might talk about many of the happenings in town, but she also could keep a secret if asked to.

So he'd learned a few things about Marybeth today that might help him if their relationship continued to move forward. She had something in her past still affecting her, and because of that, she needed to prove herself. Also, she wasn't hard to persuade about a matter if he gave her good enough reasons. He hadn't lied about dangerous transients passing through, but saw no reason to warn her specifically about Hardison.

Best of all, she looked awful cute when she got riled. He'd have to play that to his advantage. In the most innocent way, of course.

Her workday ended at four o'clock and Rand made sure he was waiting outside the bank door, leaning against the hitching rail as he had that morning. He hadn't seen Hardison during either trip to town, and the preacher said he hadn't, either. For a man who'd been so broken up about his own sin the day before, the gunslinger didn't seem to be in any hurry to learn about how to live the Christian life.

When Marybeth emerged from the bank, Rand straightened, swept off his hat and gave her a deep bow. "My, my, Miss O'Brien, you sure must have an easy job 'cause you look fresh as a daisy, just like you did this morning." Earlier he'd forgotten to compliment her, which Nate had told him was an important part of courting.

"Humph." She stuck her pretty little nose in the air. "Don't think you can sugarcoat your obvious disdain for my job, Mr. Northam. I'll have you know I've been busy all day—"

"Fetching coffee all day? Are your feet tired? I can hire a rig to drive you home."

"Oh, you." She smacked his arm and strode off down the boardwalk.

With a laugh he caught up and fell into step with her, having to shorten his long stride considerably to do so. "How was your day, Marybeth?"

She shot him a sweet smile. "Very exhilarating, thank you very much. I love typewriting almost as much as I love playing the piano."

"Mmm. Glad to hear it." Glad to see the sparkle in her eyes even though he hadn't put it there.

"Why, thank you." She rewarded him with another of those smiles.

Oh, mercy, how he wanted to plant a kiss on her pretty ivory cheek. When he'd done it before, she hadn't objected. Maybe he would when they reached Mrs. Foster's front porch. Or maybe he'd at least ask her permission. Yes, that was the idea. Make sure she didn't mind before he started acting like he could kiss her anytime he wanted to. In the meantime he wanted to stay on her good side, and he knew just how to do it.

"I checked with Mrs. Winsted over at the general store," he said. "She made sure my letters got on the train headed over to Del Norte. Sheriff Hobart will have his in the morning. The other letter will take another day or so to get to Wagon Wheel Gap by stagecoach, depending on roads and bridges." He inhaled deeply after that long speech and enjoyed the delight on Marybeth's face.

"Oh, Rand, thank you again. I won't be able to sleep tonight wondering what the sheriffs will have to say. This is so exciting." She executed a happy little skip and then put a dainty gloved hand to her lips and resumed her more sedate pace. "Goodness. What will people think if they see me hopping down the street?"

Rand chuckled. "I would hope they'd think you were happy to be with me." *As happy as I am to be with you.*

She looped her arm in his as they turned down Pike Street. "I am, Rand. Just be patient with me, will you?"

From the bright look in her eyes, he believed her, and he'd do all he could to be patient, to give her all the time she needed to decide she liked him enough to consider marrying him.

They reached Mrs. Foster's front porch where he walked her up to the door. When she paused before going inside, Rand removed his hat and cleared his throat.

"Marybeth, I don't want to presume anything, so I'm asking your permission to...well, I'd really like to give you a peck on the cheek."

"Why, Mr. Northam, I don't recall you asking permission the last two times you kissed me. Why so shy all of a sudden?" Merriment danced in her eyes. Was her happiness due to being with him or his writing letters about her brother or her good day at work?

"Well..." He drawled the word out slowly. "Nate got after me for kissing you without asking, so I thought I should ask this time."

Suddenly serious, she blinked, and her eyes reddened just a little. "That's very sweet of both of you. It makes me feel...very special."

"You are." Now he knew one more thing about her: she didn't know what a fine lady she was. Maybe over time he could remedy that. "Well?"

She laughed. "Oh, all right. Just a quick kiss."

He did make it a quick one. Then he let out a whoop, jumped down the front steps and barely felt his feet touch the ground all the way back to the livery stable to pick up his horse.

"Do not be nervous, Miss O'Brien." Mr. Means stood off to the side as Marybeth took her place in the teller's cage. "You have watched Mr. Brandt for two days now, so you know what to do."

She gave him a shaky nod just as the bank's front door opened, jangling the bell that hung above it. She turned a smile toward the customer but had to force herself to keep it in place. The leering man from the train. She hastened to remind herself he was also the one who'd prayed with Reverend Thomas in front of the whole church last Sunday.

Removing his hat, he approached the cage wearing a smile of his own. "Good afternoon, ma'am." He glanced around the area and seemed to notice Mr. Means in the background. "Good afternoon, sir." Now he settled a pleasant gaze on Marybeth, one devoid of any impropriety. Without the leer, he wasn't bad-looking, though in no way could he compare to Rand.

Rand, who would be coming soon to escort her home from work. She'd enjoyed their walks back to Mrs. Foster's these past few days. It always made her days even more pleasant. First, though, she had work to do.

"Good afternoon, sir." She swallowed hard. Her first time to help a bank customer! "How may I help you?"

"I'd like to open an account, if I may." He reached into his nicely pressed black frock coat and pulled out a leather wallet that looked new.

"Of course, sir." Marybeth reached into a drawer for a ledger, a small booklet in which she would record the deposit. She turned to the front page and dipped her pen into the inkwell. "What name, please?"

"Dathan Hardison." He bent forward to watch her write, but the bars of the cage kept him from coming too close. Still, she caught the pleasant scent of his shaving cologne. He spelled out his name as she carefully printed it on the page.

When the ink dried, she turned to the first lined page. "And how much will today's deposit be?"

He pulled some large bills from the wallet, along with a handful of five-dollar gold coins from his trousers' pocket, and shoved it all through the small opening below the bars. "Three hundred and eighty-five dollars."

Marybeth did her best not to gasp. That was a small fortune. Maybe there was more to Mr. Hardison than she'd thought. Maybe he'd come to Esperanza to open a business. "Very good, sir," she said in a monotone voice that mimicked Mr. Brandt's.

She counted the money, put it in the drawer and recorded the amount in his ledger, adding her initials beside the figures. Before handing the booklet to him, she also wrote the amount in her teller's ledger. "This booklet will serve as your receipt, Mr. Hardison. Whenever you wish to make a deposit or withdrawal, be sure you bring it with you."

"Yes, ma'am." He gave her a friendly smile that included Mr. Means. "Begging your pardon, ma'am, but would it be too forward of me to ask your name?"

To her relief, Mr. Means stepped forward. "Good afternoon, Mr. Hardison. Permit me to introduce you to my new assistant, Miss O'Brien. Miss O'Brien, this is the gentleman who joined the church on Sunday."

"Oh, yes, of course." Marybeth thought her response sounded better than saying right out that she recognized him. "How do you do, Mr. Hardison?"

"Miss O'Brien." He gave her a gentlemanly bow before turning his attention to Mr. Means. "If I may, I'd like to make an appointment with you regarding some business matters."

"I happen to be free right now." Mr. Means stepped over to the locked door leading out of the teller's cage. "Miss O'Brien, you may close up here now." He gave her a meaningful look and she returned a nod. "I shall see you tomorrow morning."

"Yes, sir."

While her boss exited the tiny chamber and relocked it from the other side, she gathered the deposits of the day, counted them and made sure they matched the numbers in the ledger. After initialing the entries, she carried everything to the unlocked safe in the darkened back corner of the room. Mr. Means hadn't given her the combination to the safe, which was fine with her. He'd left it open, however, so she put everything inside, closed the heavy door and spun the dial to secure the money.

Satisfied that she'd done everything properly, she took the key hanging at her waist and unlocked the teller's cage, exited and relocked the door. Finally she untied the leather strap from her belt and dropped the key in the lockbox outside Mr. Means's office. After a last look around the wide bank lobby, she went to her desk to retrieve her hat and gloves.

How proud she felt of her first four days of work. In addition to typewriting the letters Mr. Means had written, she'd learned the duties of a teller so she could take Mr. Brandt's place when he went to dinner or perhaps became ill. Marybeth had learned his wife was expecting a happy event, so he would need some time off for that. She would be more than pleased to fill in for him any time Mr. Means asked her.

Wouldn't Da be amazed that a daughter of his could handle money so impartially, never once thinking of stealing it for her own use? Marybeth lifted a silent prayer that Jimmy had taken after Mam, not Da, in regard to money. As for Marybeth, she had decided the best way to avoid temptation was to regard the bills as pieces of paper and the coins as bits of metal. The only money she wanted was what she earned and what Mam had left to her. If Jimmy still had that locket, the two of them would be set for life and never have to depend on anyone else.

Outside in the afternoon sunshine, Rand waited in

his usual spot. When he straightened and gave her that wonderful smile, she felt a twinge of guilt over her recent thoughts, and even more so when he stepped over and bowed, one hand behind his back.

"Marybeth, I don't know how you do it. A long day at work, and you still look as fresh and pretty as one of my mother's roses." To emphasize his words, he pulled a bouquet of red and white roses from behind his back. "For you."

"Oh, Rand, what a lovely surprise." She took the flowers and breathed deeply of their sweet, heady scent. "Thank you."

She took his offered arm and they ambled down the boardwalk under a sunny sky. Happiness bubbled up inside her such as she'd never known. Yet she couldn't decide whether it was being with Rand or having a successful day at work.

"That's not my only surprise for you today." He gave her a smug grin that threatened to undo her giddy heart.

"Indeed? Well, then, surprise me again."

"First of all, Susanna's waiting at Mrs. Foster's to meet you."

"How nice." Marybeth's pulse quickened. Would his sister-in-law like her? Would they become friends? "Is the baby well? Did she come, too?"

The questions appeared to please Rand, because his grin broadened. "She did. Say, do you like children?"

"Yes, I do. Very much." Of course she would have to marry to have children of her own. Maybe she'd have to settle for enjoying other people's children. "I'm looking forward to meeting Lizzy."

"She's a sweetheart."

As they turned down Pike Street, Marybeth started

to ask Rand what her next surprise was. Before she could speak, a rider came along beside them.

"Good afternoon, folks."

Marybeth shaded her eyes and looked up into Mr. Hardison's smiling face. At least it seemed like a smile. With the sun behind him, it was a little difficult to tell. When she started to greet him, Rand stopped beside her, his posture suddenly stiff and his shoulders hunched up.

She shuddered. There he went again with those changing moods of his. When Da's shoulders used to hunch up like that, there was sure to be a brawl. What was it about Mr. Hardison that set Rand off this way? If they fought, she would walk away and refuse to speak to either of them ever again.

Chapter Seven

Rand ground his teeth and moved between Marybeth and Hardison. What a cheap trick to pull, coming up on them on horseback to give himself an advantage. If he wanted to kill Rand, why not just bushwhack him and then run off to Texas or someplace? He swallowed hard, knowing he had to answer the man.

"Afternoon, Hardison." His hand under Marybeth's elbow, Rand resumed his walk and continued to guide her down the street.

"Mind if I tag along with you folks?" He reined his horse a little closer to Rand's right side, making it impossible for him to draw his gun if he needed to protect Marybeth.

"If you hadn't noticed, we're busy having a private conversation, so, yes, I do mind." Rand kept his eyes straight ahead.

"Ah. Then I won't interrupt you." He gave a throaty chuckle that seemed to hold a hint of a threat. "I'll leave you to it. Good day, Miss O'Brien."

The jangle of reins and clip-clop of hooves gave evidence that he'd turned back, but the oily, familiar way he addressed Marybeth sent an icy shiver down Rand's back.

"Where did you meet that—" Rand glanced down to see her disapproving frown. He met it with one of his own. Instead of saying "polecat," as he felt inclined to, he finished his question with, "man?"

"He came into the bank today. Mr. Means introduced us." Her defensive tone did nothing to calm Rand. Had he merely been a customer or was Hardison seeking her out? Worse, was she somehow attracted to the well-dressed gunslinger? He didn't ask her any of those questions because he didn't want her upset when she met Susanna.

"Well, I suppose if you had a proper introduction, it's all right." Far from it, but Rand wouldn't tell her. He'd stick with the plan he, Nate and the preacher had come up with and just watch the man. Only trouble was that Hardison wasn't doing what they expected, which was calling Rand out at some inconvenient moment when a lot of people he cared about could get hurt. The gunslinger was weaseling himself into the good graces of those people. Even Miss Pam had remarked out of the blue that the "new Christian" ate at her café three times a day. Rand knew she was glad for the business, and he supposed even polecats needed to eat. He also had no idea of how to figure out what Hardison's next move would be.

They were about to arrive at Mrs. Foster's house, so he decided to warm the coolness between him and Marybeth. Only one thing was sure to work. "I hope Lizzy's not down for a nap so you can see her at her best. When she first gets up, she can be a little cranky."

His ploy worked because Marybeth looked up at him and her eyes brightened. "I wish we'd stopped by the general store and bought some candy. That's a sure cure for crankiness."

He gave her a smug, teasing grin. "All taken care of." He retrieved a small brown paper sack from his trouser pocket and handed it to her. "You can give her one of these lemon sticks, and she'll be your best friend."

"Aren't you clever?" Marybeth peeked inside the bag and then tucked it into her reticule. Her smile of appreciation eased Rand's concerns considerably.

He still couldn't imagine why she seemed friendly to Hardison. The man was years older, probably in his midthirties. While he was well-dressed and could put on proper manners, he didn't seem to have anything to recommend him to a young girl. Or maybe Rand was misreading her reactions. Other than his mother and sister and the Eberly girls, he didn't have much experience with women, and he didn't understand a single one of them.

How would Marybeth react if he just plain out told her Hardison was out for revenge and they all needed to be careful around the man? Of course he wouldn't without first talking to Nate and Reverend Thomas. But he sure would like to gain her trust. Maybe the letter in his pocket would help him do that. He hadn't opened Sheriff Hobart's reply yet because it was his third surprise for her. He thought she'd be pleased if they opened it together. A prickle of excitement spiked inside his chest. Yes, reading the letter together would be just the thing to gain Marybeth's trust and maybe make her real happy in the bargain.

"Here we are." Rand kept his hand cupped under Marybeth's elbow as they climbed the steps and approached the front door.

She could hear ladies' voices coming through the

open front window, and her nervousness returned. Not that it had completely disappeared or been helped by the encounter with Mr. Hardison. She couldn't understand why Rand disliked the man.

Now, as he smiled down at her, his hand still under her elbow, an odd and slightly thrilling thought popped into her mind. Was Rand jealous? Was he concerned that because she'd put off their marriage, she might find some other man to care about, to marry? Indeed, that must be it. Her heart gave a little twist at the thought. As kind as he'd been to her, he deserved to know she would do no such thing. Maybe if she revealed her nervousness over meeting his sister-in-law, he would forget all about their encounter with Mr. Hardison.

"Stay close to me." She leaned toward him and spoke in a whisper. "I do so want Susanna to like me."

"How could she not like you?" The way his face brightened and the gentle squeeze on her arm assured her she'd said just what he needed to hear. But unlike the manipulations she'd used on Da to avoid his tempers and beatings, this was a good thing. Now a pleasant warmth flooded her chest, and somehow she liked Rand all the more for it.

He opened the door and nudged her over the threshold and into the parlor. "Good afternoon, ladies."

Mrs. Foster and her guest set down their teacups and rose to greet them.

"Wan!" A darling little blonde girl in a pink calico dress toddled toward Rand, her hands reaching out. "Up, up."

"Hello, little dumpling." Rand lifted her to the ceiling and the child rewarded him with squeals and giggles.

Then he lowered her and nuzzled her neck, bringing more squeals.

Marybeth thought her heart would melt on the spot. This big, strapping cowboy playing with a baby and obviously adoring her. She'd never seen a man so taken with a child.

Rand settled the baby on his left hip and beckoned Marybeth forward. "Good afternoon, Mrs. Foster. Susanna, this is Marybeth, my…" His pause caused the room to go silent…and yet another thread of guilt to wind through Marybeth. He'd almost introduced her as his bride-to-be, yet he had the good manners to respect her wishes in that regard.

"You don't have to tell me who this is." Susanna rushed over and grasped Marybeth's hands. "This is Marybeth O'Brien. I would know you anywhere from Rosamond's description. She's written all about you." Shorter by several inches, she stood on tiptoes and kissed Marybeth's cheek. With blond hair a little darker than her daughter's, Susanna was a true beauty, even more so because she was expecting and had that maternal glow many women took on when a baby was on the way. Her soft Southern accent only added to her charm. "Welcome to Esperanza. We all hope and pray you'll love it here."

The warmth of her greeting soothed away Marybeth's concerns and brought tears to her eyes. "Thank you. How could I not love this town? Everyone's been so kind."

Susanna tugged Marybeth over to the settee. "You sit down. I'll make a fresh pot of tea."

"No such thing." Mrs. Foster picked up the silver tea

tray. "You two girls sit down and get acquainted, and I'll fetch more tea." She looked at Rand. "Coffee for you?"

"Tea's fine. Thank you, ma'am." He sat in the chair nearest Marybeth, the baby still content in his arms. "If you haven't figured it out yet, this is Lizzy."

"How do you do, Lizzy?" Marybeth reached out her hand.

Lizzy turned away and burrowed her face in Rand's shoulder. He gave Marybeth a significant look, glancing down at her reticule, where she'd hidden the candy. She leaned over toward Susanna and asked in a whisper, "May I give her a lemon stick?"

Susanna's enthusiastic nod caused her blond ringlets to bounce, adding to her charm.

Marybeth caught Lizzy's eye. Then, with lavish gestures, she opened her reticule and pulled out a lemon stick. She made as if to put it in her mouth just as Lizzy's hand shot out.

"Me."

"Oh, do you want this?"

She nodded solemnly.

"Mama, may she have it?"

"Why, yes, she may."

"Here you are, Lizzy." With great ceremony, Marybeth presented the candy.

Lizzy's eyes sparkled as she grasped it and stuck it in her mouth.

While Susanna instructed her baby in how to say "thank you," Marybeth glanced up at Rand. The sweet, intense look in his eyes almost took her breath away. Approval? No, more than that. But surely not love, either, after knowing her less than a week. Yet she basked in the glow of that look through her entire visit with Susanna and late into the evening.

Only after she went to bed did she remember he'd hinted that he had more surprises. Apparently he'd forgotten all about it, too. Or maybe it was the candy. Surely it was too soon to have letters back from the sheriffs about Jimmy. Either way, she'd enjoyed being with Rand and meeting Susanna and Lizzy. It wouldn't be too hard to feel at home with this family. Except that she desperately longed to find her brother, the only family she had left in the world. Until she learned the truth about Jimmy's whereabouts, even if he'd gone to Mexico or California or who knew where, she would never have peace.

Rand had driven Susanna halfway home in the buggy before he remembered the letter. She needed to get home to put Lizzy down for her nap and start supper, so he couldn't very well turn around and go back to town. Maybe it was best this way. If Sheriff Hobart had bad news, he could find a way to tell Marybeth without her going into shock.

After supper and evening chores, he went to his room to read the letter. Sure enough, it was a disappointment. The sheriff hadn't seen any short, wiry, red-haired Irishmen in the area over the past seven or eight years. The lawman was well-known for his memory of faces, names and happenings, so Rand took his word without hesitation. Somehow he'd have to tell Marybeth, and the sooner the better.

Cautioned by the way things had turned out on Thursday, Rand opened his mail right away on Friday. The letter from the sheriff of Wagon Wheel Gap said he couldn't recall anyone of Jimmy's description. Irishmen, yes, but none with such bright hair, short stature and no brogue. He added that he'd been there less than a year and so would ask the old-timers if they knew anything about a Jimmy O'Brien.

Rand's heart ached for the disappointment Marybeth would experience when he gave her the news. But it wouldn't be fair to her if he put it off.

At four o'clock he met her at the bank and invited her to an early supper at Williams's Café. "I went by Mrs. Foster's and told her I planned to ask you out. She said it was all right with her as long as I brought you home before dark." He gave her a smile he didn't really feel, but it seemed to work.

"Thank you, Rand. I understand Miss Pam fixes roast beef on Friday nights, so this will be a fitting end to a wonderful week."

They walked the block and a half to Williams's Café, speaking to several people as they traveled. Marybeth had met some of them at church and some at the bank, so introductions were few. In a way, Rand felt a little jealous that he hadn't been the one to introduce her, but in another way, he was proud that everyone seemed to like her…and especially that she seemed to like everyone. Maybe that was why she had been pleasant to Hardison. She'd never made an enemy.

Seated across the table from him in the café, she looked as pretty as a picture. Before he could give her the bad news about the letters, she spoke.

"Rand, I've noticed this town doesn't have a saloon. In all of the stories we've heard back East about the Wild West, it seems there's always a saloon where the

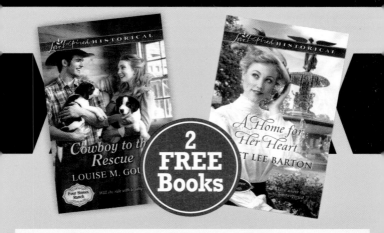

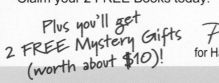

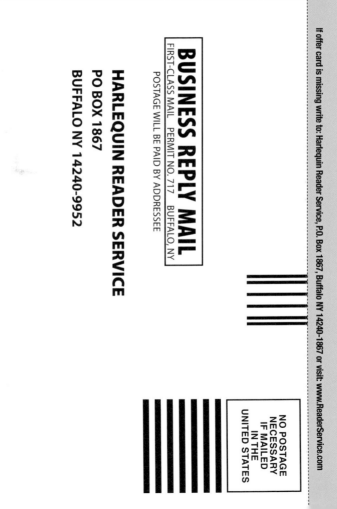

troubles begin." Her innocent, trusting gaze bored just a bit deeper into his heart.

"That's because my dad and the other founders of the community voted to keep spirits out." He tried not to sound too proud, as though he'd been responsible for the decision. After all, he'd ridden over to the saloon in Del Norte plenty of times to play poker, and look where it had gotten him. He'd killed a cardsharp whose cousin now wanted revenge. "We want people to feel safe and be safe here in Esperanza." And if they weren't safe, it was his fault.

"No liquor." The wonder in Marybeth's voice and eyes was something to behold and resembled her expression just after she'd been rescued from the rattlesnake, as though she couldn't quite believe it. "That's remarkable."

"I suppose." Rand shrugged. "If more towns adopted that law, there'd be a lot less wildness to the Wild West."

She laughed, and he detected a note of relief in it. He wanted to ask what that was all about, but Lucy approached the table to take their order. They'd have to talk about it later because he had an idea it meant something significant to Marybeth.

"You're looking mighty fine this afternoon, Rand." Lucy stood close to him, her skirt brushing against his shoulder. "What can I get for you, sweetie?" He wished she wouldn't be so familiar with him, but the poor girl was still missing Seamus, so he'd tolerate it for now.

"Two roast beef dinners." He looked at Marybeth. "That is, if you'd like the same?"

She didn't so much as glance at Lucy. "Yes, thank you." The chill in her voice rivaled a winter wind off of the San Juan Mountains.

As the waitress moved away from the table, Marybeth finally slid a look at her departing form through narrowed eyes and her pretty lips formed a disapproving pucker. To her credit, she didn't say anything, but Rand had an idea she wanted to. He'd best move the conversation on to the letters, no matter how hard it would be to disappoint her.

Reaching across the table to give her hand a squeeze, he cleared his throat. "I heard back from the sheriffs."

Hope lit up her face like sunshine, but she must have noticed his frown, because that hope quickly vanished, replaced by reddened eyes. "They haven't seen him." Her voice broke.

He shook his head, emotion blocking any words of sympathy he might try to speak.

"Oh, Jimmy, where did you go?"

Her forlorn tone broke his heart and he didn't have much at hand to cheer her. Just one thing came to mind.

"Is it possible your brother changed over the years?"

"I don't think so." Her frown deepened. "He was always a younger version of our father, except he had Mam's red hair. I wish I still had the letter he wrote from Del Norte. Maybe the postmaster over there would remember him." She stared toward the café door as if she wanted to go right now and find out.

"Say, that's a good idea." He liked anything that might encourage her, and he hadn't even thought of the postmaster. Or, in this case, the postmistress of many years. She would have been the one to handle the letter, and maybe Marybeth's brother just never crossed paths with Sheriff Hobart. The only other possibility, one he'd refused to give much thought, was that maybe Marybeth had made up the whole story. Maybe she didn't even have a brother. But that didn't make any sense. Why would she have agreed to come out to Colorado, not even wanting to get married, if there was no Jimmy O'Brien?

He tried to dismiss the notion, yet he couldn't resist testing her. "Tell you what. How about we ride over there tomorrow and find out?" As much as he hated to return to the town where he'd killed a man, he had to find out the truth about this matter. He'd always known he'd have to go back if he had a good enough reason. This seemed to be it.

Again, her face lit up like sunshine. "Could we? You said the other day it's a full day of travel to go both ways. If we left early, would we be back before dark?"

Her eagerness dispelled his suspicions. It also reminded him that she didn't ride. They'd have to take the buggy, which would make the trip slower.

More time in her company. More time to prove to her that he might make a pretty good husband, after all. Of course they'd have to take a chaperone. He'd ride over to the Eberly place to see if any of the sisters was free to go along.

Saturday brought sunshine and warmth with just enough of a breeze to make the trip to Del Norte pleasant. Their picnic basket once again tied to the back of the buggy, Marybeth sat beside Rand, with Beryl Eberly perched on a makeshift seat behind them. The hilly scenery and an occasional fluffy cloud floating over the distant San Juan Mountains only added to the enjoyment of the ride. Hope and excitement filled Marybeth's heart. Perhaps today they would learn where Jimmy had gone. But even if they didn't, she would be grateful to Rand for trying to find her brother.

She could hardly believe his generosity and that of his neighbors in helping her search. Truly this community was a warm, wonderful place to live. Not like Boston, where the Irish were still fighting for respect. Here no one blinked or frowned upon hearing her last name. In fact, she'd met several folks with Irish names, though none of them from Ireland itself, just second- or third-generation Americans. While she and Jimmy had been born in the old country, they'd come to America when she was a baby and he was not quite five years old. Da had come for the opportunity to better himself, or so he'd always said. But Mam, in one of her weaker moments when his cruelty had beaten her down, had revealed Da had left behind many debts.

Shoving aside bitter memories, Marybeth leaned back in the buggy to enjoy the ride. They traveled a fairly wide and well-worn road, which Rand told her had been an Indian trail, a path for prospectors and finally a stagecoach route extending all the way to Wagon Wheel Gap. Each time she heard the name of the mining town far up in the mountains, her heart skipped. On another day, would Rand take her that far if they learned Jimmy had gone there? Or would she have to purchase a stagecoach ticket and go on her own? It would be some time before she could afford to do that.

For today, she would use the fourteen-mile trip each way to become better acquainted with another Eberly sister. Beryl was the middle sister and somewhat quieter than Maisie and even Laurie. Still, with a little coaxing, Marybeth was able to persuade her to describe the various plants and trees they passed.

"Up in those hills—" she pointed south of the road "—those are aspen. They turn yellow in the fall and look real pretty fluttering in the wind. Farther down you can see the piñon trees." She indicated a grove of tall, bushy trees that appeared to be evergreen. "They bear nuts that are right tasty. We gather them in the fall and use them for baking."

"Don't tell anybody I said this—" Rand waved a hand toward the picnic basket "—but Beryl's the best cook in the whole Eberly clan."

While Beryl snorted, grinned and gave his arm a shove, Marybeth bit back a laugh. Rand needed to be careful with all of his compliments about the cooking of his various female friends. If those women ever got together and compared his praise, probably none of them would invite him to a meal again. And if they were all such fine cooks, what would he say about her skills if they got married?

Oh, dear. That thought was occurring entirely too often these days, and she'd only known him a week, not counting the six months they'd been writing back and forth. If she didn't watch out, she'd find herself more than liking him. She'd fall mindlessly in love with him, and then where would her search for Jimmy be?

They reached the outskirts of Del Norte in good time due to dry roads and no headwinds. Rand drove the horses off the trail to a shady spot under the tall cottonwoods that grew along the Rio Grande. If Marybeth was going to get more bad news, better to hear it on a full stomach. Beryl had kindly offered to prepare the picnic, and she'd packed a fine basketful, with chicken sandwiches, potato salad, pickles, apple crumb cake and cold coffee.

Not for the first time, Rand wondered whether Marybeth liked to cook. She hadn't been bothered by his compliments to other ladies' cooking, which could mean either she had confidence in her own skills or she'd never learned and didn't care to. He wasn't sure how that would work out if they married. All the women he knew, especially ranch gals, were pretty jealous about their cooking, so he was always quick to praise their efforts.

Odd the random thoughts he had about Marybeth. What kind of music did she like, other than hymns and Irish folksongs? Did she like Christmas as much as he did? Would she feel trapped being a ranch wife like a few local women he knew? Or would she be like Susanna and find her calling in having her own home and children to care for? At least now he knew she loved children. Lizzy had been won over by a lemon stick, but Marybeth had been won over by his niece's sweet baby ways. Did she want to have a few children of her own? Not a question he could ask until he'd won her heart.

As he lifted her down from the buggy, he couldn't help but notice her nervous glances around the site, so he gave her hand a squeeze.

"Looking for snakes?" Beryl quipped with a grin.

Rand wanted to throttle her, but Marybeth laughed. A shaky sound, but still a laugh, which showed her spunk. He liked that.

"Yes, indeed. I suppose Laurie told you all about our encounter last Saturday."

"Yep." Beryl untied the picnic basket. To Rand, she said, "You want to get the blanket?"

They settled down, offered a prayer and began to eat, making quick work of the picnic and saving some in case they got hungry on the trip back to Esperanza.

On the road again, they headed toward town. Rand saw in the corner of his eye that Marybeth was twisting her hands nervously. He prayed she wouldn't be disappointed this time. Prayed that this mysterious Jimmy O'Brien had somehow made an impression on someone who would remember him all these years later.

He made a quick stop at the sheriff's office, mainly to let the lawman know he was in town, but also to tell him about Dathan Hardison and his threats. Hobart had been more than good to Rand after the shooting, refusing to charge him with a crime and insisting he take reward money that had been offered for Cole Lyndon, dead or alive. He'd also suggested it might be a good idea not to come back to Del Norte for a while. Rand wasn't sure three years was a long enough while, but for Marybeth's sake, it would have to do. Concerned that some unsavory sorts might be in the jail cells, he left the girls in the buggy and entered the office on Grand Avenue.

"Come on in, Rand." The sheriff seemed glad to see him, offering his hand and a warm pat on the shoulder. "I'm glad you came by. Have a seat." He waved Rand to a chair in front of his desk. After the usual polite inquiries about each other's families, the sheriff said, "I shouldn't have been in such a hurry to answer your letter the other day. After thinking on it, I do recall some redheaded cowpokes coming through town from time to time."

Rand felt a happy little kick in his chest, but he cautioned himself not to get too excited. Jimmy wasn't a cowpoke; he was a prospector. Marybeth had been adamant about that. "That's some memory you have there."

Hobart grimaced and scratched his head. "Not what it used to be. I don't think I can add anything. If a man doesn't have a distinctive scar or maybe an accent of some sort, it's hard to pin down a memory of him."

Rand nodded. "We thought we'd go over to the post office to see if Mrs. Sanchez remembers anything."

"Good idea." Hobart grimaced again. "I should have asked her myself and saved you a trip." He shuffled some Wanted posters on his desk. "Let me know what you find out."

"Yessir, I'll do that." Rand wouldn't tell him he was more than happy to have another full day with Marybeth. More than happy to help her search for her brother. "Say, while you're looking through those posters, do you have anything on a Dathan Hardison? He's a cousin of Cole Lyndon."

Frowning, the sheriff eyed him. "Cole's kin, eh?"

Rand nodded and gave him a brief account of Hardison's actions in Esperanza, including his threats and his so-called conversion, which even had the preacher suspicious.

The sheriff scanned the papers on his desk and then dug an envelope filled with more Wanted posters from his drawer. "These are new. Help me take a look." He gave half of the pile to Rand.

They sorted through the heavy paper sheets, some with photographs, others with drawings of men, most wanted dead or alive. Rand didn't recognize any of them as Hardison.

"Nope, nothing here." Hobart scratched his chin. "If

he committed a crime, he could have done it under a different name. Or he could have served his sentence."

"I suppose." Rand glanced out the window at the girls. Marybeth was making good use of her fan, so she was probably getting too hot. "Let me know if you hear anything, would you?"

"Sure thing." Hobart grunted. "I'll send out some queries and see what I can come up with."

"Much obliged." After taking his leave of the sheriff and setting aside his concerns about Hardison, Rand reported to the girls about Hobart's retrieved memories of red-haired cowboys. As he expected, Marybeth's pretty hazel eyes lit up with hope.

"Thank you, Rand." She clasped his arm as he drove the buggy farther down Grand Avenue to the general store, where the post office was located.

Despite the momentary hope he'd felt in the sheriff's office, as they drew closer to their destination, he had a sinking feeling this was all a waste of time.

Marybeth could barely contain her excitement. As hard as she tried to quiet her giddy emotions, she couldn't subdue her hopes. Even the bright, sunny day seemed to portend good news.

The streets were crowded with all sorts of people, both men and women, both decent community folks like those in Esperanza and some ruffians very similar to the worst she'd seen on Boston's waterfront. Rand explained that Del Norte was the stopping off place where prospectors on their way to the silver fields bought their gear. He said those men were pretty much harmless.

"On a Saturday, you can tell the difference between the cowboys and the prospectors." He nodded toward a rowdy group of men. “Those are the cowboys. They’re here to waste their hard-earned pay. That’s why they’re cleaned up and in their best clothes.” He snorted his disgust and shook his head. “Now that fellow over there, he’s a prospector.” He indicated a dusty traveler. “You can tell by his clothes and his sharp-eyed look. He’ll be buying his gold pans and picks over at the general store before heading farther west right past Del Norte Peak.” He pointed toward a mountain that rose above the town.

Marybeth studied the landmark, whose highest valleys still bore remnants of snow. Was Jimmy somewhere beyond that peak? Did he look like this shabbily dressed man so clearly determined to change his fortunes? If only her brother knew he held the key to enough treasure to take care of them both. That was, if he still had the locket.

“Here we are.” Rand reached out to hand her down from the buggy.

Back in Boston, buggy rides had been few and far between. Yet after only a few times out with Rand, Marybeth was becoming more adept at getting in and out of the conveyance without tripping on her skirts. She still needed to take his hand to step down, and his strong grasp sent a pleasant shiver up her arm. Only when he gently squeezed her fingers did she realize she was shaking. A quick look up into his gentle eyes calmed her and sent more agreeable feelings churning through her chest.

Oh, my. How will I ever keep hold of my heart when it seems to have a mind of its own? Yet how could she not respond to his kindness? His sacrifices for her sake? Mrs. Foster had told her how much work it took to run a ranch. With Rand neglecting his duties to help with her quest, she must at the very least be grateful. *Grateful enough to marry him?* She was far from ready to answer that question.

Beryl had jumped down from her perch and now waited on the boardwalk. Unlike Laurie, she didn't smirk or send teasing grins their way. Of course, she was a couple of years older than Laurie and thus more mature. Her restraint was both admirable and much appreciated.

"Shall we go in?" Rand offered an arm to both Marybeth and Beryl.

Beryl's face grew a bit pink beneath her freckles. Maybe she wasn't used to gentlemanly manners. Marybeth had learned how to receive such graces only two years ago at Fairfield Young Ladies' Academy, so she understood how the younger girl felt. If she could help Beryl and her sisters, including the irrepressible Maisie, learn about the finer customs of society, it might in some small way repay their kindnesses. After Marybeth inquired about Jimmy, she would offer to help Beryl shop for some feminine fripperies.

They entered the general store and Beryl's eyes lit up. Instead of perusing the aisles of fabric, laces and ladies' hats, however, she strode away toward the guns and saddles, the heels of her riding boots thumping on the wood flooring. Marybeth caught herself before laughing out loud at her own foolish thoughts about Beryl. Being a true cowgirl, maybe she didn't want to purchase fripperies or to learn social graces.

"The post office is that little room in the back." Rand indicated a sign above a small area similar to a teller's cage. "Looks like the postmistress is in." He gave a gentle tug on Marybeth's arm.

Her pulse quickened, especially when she saw the woman's gray-streaked hair. Surely she'd been around long enough to recall Jimmy.

"Howdy, Mrs. Sanchez." Rand gave her a charming grin, and her expression brightened.

"Señor Randall Northam, how good to see you." She leaned forward with her forearms on the counter. "The people of Del Norte, they still speak of your heroics in ridding our town of those evil men. You know how grateful we are, *sí*?"

Rand gave what seemed like an involuntary shudder. "Thank you, ma'am." He cleared his throat. "This is Miss Marybeth O'Brien from Boston."

The woman acknowledged Marybeth with a friendly smile. "I have met a certain Señor O'Brien. Perhaps you are related?"

Chapter Eight

Rand felt his jaw drop, while Marybeth yipped like an excited puppy.

"You've met Jimmy? You know my brother?" She looked about ready to jump through the bars separating her from the postmistress. "Oh, please tell me where he is."

From the way Mrs. Sanchez drew back, Rand was pretty sure it wouldn't be that simple. He put a bracing arm around Marybeth's shoulders. "Hold on, sweetheart." Oops. Better not let that slip out again until she really was his sweetheart. "Ma'am, was it recent when you met him or sometime in the past?"

The lady shook her head. "Oh, very long ago." She gave Marybeth a compassionate smile. "I have the excellent memory, but this one, he was easy not to forget by anybody. Hair the color of autumn sunsets, same color *la barba y bigote* just beginning, like he was trying to look older." She chuckled in her deep, throaty way. "James O'Brien. He came in the store many times wanting to mail his letter, but changing his mind. Finally he gave it to my late husband. It was to go to—" She gasped softly. "To Boston. Did you receive it?"

Marybeth swayed and Rand tightened his hold on her. "Yes," she said on a sob. She looked up at Rand, her eyes brimming. He guessed she couldn't speak, so he'd best do it for her.

"We appreciate your information, Mrs. Sanchez. By any chance, do you have any idea where Jimmy went after turning the letter over to you?"

"*Sí, naturalmente*. He go to the silver fields up there." She waved toward the west as if brushing away a pesky fly. "Carlos, my husband, God rest his soul, he tell the boy he should be the cowboy. Not like those." She batted a dismissive hand toward the front of the store just as some cowpokes walked by the display window. From their swaggering, staggering steps, Rand surmised they were already in the midst of their Saturday night celebration, even though it wasn't much past two o'clock in the afternoon. "Go to *el rancho del buen hombre*, the ranch of the good man like Colonel Northam or George Eberly. Work for him, Carlos tell him. It is good life." She shook her head, sadness emanating from her maternal eyes. "What can you do when the young ones refuse the wise advice? No, this one buy his mining supplies and go west. We see him no more."

"Well, then." Marybeth straightened, a smile brightening her face and making it even prettier. "I'll just have to go to Wagon Wheel Gap. Thank you, Mrs. Sanchez."

Her reaction to the news both surprised and worried Rand, but he gave her an encouraging nod anyway. For his own part, he couldn't be more pleased to find out for certain Jimmy O'Brien actually existed. Now he had to decide just how far to go in helping Marybeth find him.

Wagon Wheel Gap wasn't a place for a lady. If Nate agreed to it, maybe Rand and a couple of hands could go up there once the cattle came down from summer grazing in the mountains and the hay was in. He'd keep that to himself, though. No sense in putting ideas into Marybeth's head. No sense in stirring up hope too soon. Or stirring up any hope at all. After almost eight years, would O'Brien still be prospecting? Any sensible man would give up after all that time and take up a more realistic occupation.

On the way back to Esperanza, Marybeth found the day even brighter and the wild Colorado scenery even lovelier than when they'd traveled west that morning. Speaking with someone who actually knew Jimmy, knew where he'd gone, gave her hope beyond all her expectations. Although more than seven years had passed since Mrs. Sanchez had last seen him, Marybeth had no doubt her determined brother would still be searching for silver or gold or whatever valuable minerals the San Juan Mountains had to offer. If he'd already struck it rich, surely he would have contacted Mam, would have come to rescue her and Marybeth from Da.

The thought sobered her. Jimmy would be heartbroken when he learned Mam was dead. If he was still the loyal, caring person she remembered, he'd also grieve for Da, but more for his wasted life than his demise. Marybeth prayed he hadn't followed their father's habits, either the drinking or the everlasting search for quick riches. She thought, not for the first time, of prospecting as exactly that, a quick riches scheme. She added a prayer about the locket. If he'd sold it to buy his mining supplies, that would be the end of that. They'd both be working hard to survive for the rest of their lives. For her it wouldn't be quite so bad. She could marry Rand.

The thought shamed her. It wouldn't be fair to Rand if she married him just to get a husband to provide for her. Wouldn't be fair to her, either. At least Mam had loved Da, and Marybeth couldn't think of settling for anything else. That was, if she had to marry. Which she prayed would never happen.

"What's going through that pretty head of yours?" Rand gently elbowed her arm. "Are you pleased with what we found out?"

She looked up at him without answering for several seconds. Should she tell him what was in her heart? That she could not bear to postpone the trip to Wagon Wheel Gap? She would have to earn enough money for the stagecoach fare, food and lodging. It would take a while, even with the generous salary Mr. Means paid her. If she asked Rand, would he take her now? She couldn't bring herself to do it, not when she had no plans to marry him.

"Well, are you pleased?" Rand repeated.

"I'm sorry." She couldn't even tell him how sorry she was. She hadn't missed his slip in calling her "sweetheart" back at the post office. He wouldn't think she was so sweet or that she even possessed a heart if he knew how disloyal her thoughts were. "Yes, I'm more than pleased. Thank you so much for today."

"Glad to do it."

He gave her his cute, crooked grin, and her traitorous heart warmed dangerously in his favor. Oh, how she wanted to tell him everything. Well, not everything, but more about Jimmy. More about her growing-up years.

About Mam and Da. About why finding her brother was more important to her than marriage.

She couldn't very well discuss those things with Rand while Beryl sat at their shoulders. Maybe they could talk more once they delivered their chaperone to Maisie's house in town, where she would spend the night.

Marybeth glanced back to engage the girl in a more general conversation. But Beryl's head was propped on one arm against the top of the leather seatback, her wide-brimmed hat pulled low over her face and her newly purchased, pearl-handled six-shooter safely tucked in its wooden box and clutched close to her chest. Yet even with her steady breathing indicating she was asleep, Marybeth couldn't tell Rand about the things eating at her soul until they were completely alone.

They rolled into Esperanza just as the sun ducked behind the San Juan range and lengthening shadows spread darkness across the San Luis Valley like an ocean's rising tide swept over the seashore.

Rand turned off of Main Street onto Clark Avenue where the Henshaws lived. Beryl awoke just as they reached her sister's two-story house. Or so it seemed. Maybe she'd been awake the whole time. Or maybe that was Marybeth's own guilty conscience, which took for granted that everyone bent the truth in some way or another from time to time.

Leaving Beryl to explain the success of the day to Maisie and Doc, Rand and Marybeth made the two-block trip to Pike Street. As they traveled, Marybeth tried to summon the courage to tell Rand all that was in her heart, yet she found her moment for complete truthfulness had passed. Mrs. Foster met them at the door and insisted Rand must join them for a light supper.

Perhaps it was for the best. If she told Rand everything, she'd lose any semblance of control in the situation, and she might lose Rand's friendship. He certainly wouldn't keep helping her if she told him right out she didn't plan to marry him, maybe never had. At this point, she really couldn't say herself what she'd felt back in Boston. All she'd known then was that Colonel and Mrs. Northam had offered to pay her fare to Colorado. And not just any place in that new state, but the very area where Jimmy had gone. How could she not accept their offer? Yet now her guilty feelings diminished her joy over the day's revelations.

Despite her drooping spirits, she managed to smile and chat during supper, bringing Mrs. Foster into the circle of those celebrating her good news. Afterward, she saw Rand to the door. "Thank you for everything. I had a lovely time, and not just because of what Mrs. Sanchez told us." As she said the words she knew they were true. She'd become more than accustomed to his company; she honestly enjoyed it. If she did lose his friendship, the loss would be devastating.

"I had a good time, too." Even in the dim lantern light, his attractive smile stirred traitorous emotions in her heart. "I'll meet you at the church in the morning." He squeezed her hand. "We'll each choose a side of the church and see who can set out the hymnals faster."

Here he was again, making even the simplest task more fun. "I'll accept that challenge."

He bent forward but pulled back and questioned her with one raised eyebrow and a comical smirk.

She huffed out an indulgent sigh. "Yes, I suppose

you may kiss me." She couldn't contain a giggle over his silliness.

This time his lips made contact just a wee bit closer to hers rather than farther up her cheek, and once again her heart lilted. As he donned his hat, his knowing grin and waggle of his dark eyebrows suggested he knew how he'd affected her. If she truly was going to stay in control of her future, she really must stop reacting to him this way.

Satisfaction filled Rand over the events of the day, and he whistled as he drove home. He could tell Marybeth liked him, liked it when he kissed her on the cheek. One of these days he'd kiss those pretty, tempting lips and hope she liked it even more.

On second thought, he'd better postpone such plans until he found out what she was hiding from him. He could still see it in her eyes, the way she'd seem about to tell him something but then back off. Maybe she'd trust him more if he made that trip to Wagon Wheel Gap and located Jimmy. If he could reunite her with her brother, surely that would put an end to whatever was bothering her. Then he could court her in earnest.

He chuckled to himself. Remembering the fairy tale he'd read to Lizzy a few nights ago, he pictured himself as a knight courting a princess. To win her hand, he'd have to go on a quest to a distant location and bring back a particular treasure. What a fine story, one his friend Seamus would appreciate. But Seamus was up in the mountains with the cattle, and if Rand told his brothers, they'd never let him live it down.

After a lovely church service the next day, Marybeth visited with several people whom she'd met at the bank, including Mr. Hardison.

"How was your first week at the bank, Miss O'Brien?" His warm smile and courteous tone made her wonder again what Rand found so offensive in the man.

"Very enjoyable, thank you."

"Then you'll continue working there?"

"Why, I suppose so."

She started to add that she'd stay because Mr. Means was a pleasant employer, but across the churchyard, she saw the three Northam brothers coming their way. Rand's expression was nothing less than hostile. As before, she guessed he was jealous, yet this time she found no pleasure in it. Would he start an argument, a fight, right here in front of the church?

The three brothers were still a few yards away when Susanna hurried over and put an arm around Marybeth's waist. "You're coming out to the ranch for dinner, aren't you?"

"How do, Mrs. Northam?" As Mr. Hardison tipped his hat, he didn't seem to notice Susanna's warning glare sent toward her husband and his brothers. "A mighty fine sermon today, don't you think?"

"I would agree, sir. 'Blessed are the peacemakers' are words we all should heed." Her lilting accent carried the same Southern inflections as Reverend Thomas's. "Now, if you'll excuse us." She turned Marybeth away from the gentleman and urged her toward the grassy lawn where the smaller children were playing tag. "I spoke to Mrs. Foster and she doesn't mind sparing you for the afternoon. Do say you'll come."

Marybeth looked back to see whether Rand and his brothers had actually accosted Mr. Hardison, but the minister had beaten them to it. Reverend Thomas must have said something witty, because Mr. Hardison was laughing. With trouble averted, Marybeth gave her attention to her new friend. Her potential sister. The thought stirred a dormant longing within her. Having a sister meant having a confidante, another woman to share joys and secrets with, as Marybeth had had with Mam. As she'd just begun to with Rosamond back at the academy.

"I'd love to come." Yes, she did want to go, wanted to be with Rand and his lovely family, wanted to see this Four Stones Ranch he was so proud of. Putting aside questions about his dislike for Mr. Hardison, she joined the Northam entourage heading south from town.

The men rode horseback, following the ladies in the buggy. While Susanna drove, Marybeth found herself the center of Lizzy's attention. The child must have decided she was a worthy friend even without the bribe of a lemon stick, for she rested in Marybeth's arms as if she had always done so.

In return, her sweet scent and childish babble charmed Marybeth and stirred a longing to have her own child to pamper and cuddle. She imagined any child of Rand's would be a fine-looking boy or girl. If she didn't marry him, the privilege of bearing said child would belong to another woman. She found the thought more than a little annoying. Then she was annoyed at herself for being annoyed. She mustn't be a dog in a manger, not wanting the hay and not wanting another animal to have it, either. Yet the thought of stepping aside so another woman could have Rand's attentions grated inexplicably on her heart.

With the Northam cook off for the day, Susanna and Marybeth put together a simple but substantial dinner of sandwiches, potato salad and pickled vegetables. Afterward, Rand took Marybeth on a tour of the house. To her amazement, the roomy two-story abode had a ballroom on its north end where, Rand told her, the family enjoyed entertaining their neighbors for just about any special occasion they could come up with. With his parents back East, he'd been put in charge of the annual Christmas party.

"That's almost five months away, but Susanna's expecting about that time, so I'll need some help." He questioned her with a hopeful look.

"Of course." The words came out before Marybeth could stop them. But then, she would enjoy helping a friend throw a party. A little baking, planning a few games, handmade decorations, maybe a gift exchange. "I'd love to."

His grateful grin stirred agreeable feelings that were becoming all too familiar. Only by forcing her thoughts to Jimmy could she keep her mind in charge of her heart. More or less.

"Would you like to see the property?" His face exuded familial pride.

"Very much." She might as well look around at what she was giving up by not marrying him.

Rand took her by the hand and led her out the front door to the wide, covered porch. To the west, the San Juan Mountains stood out starkly against a rich blue sky on this bright, cloudless day. She could envision watching glorious sunsets from the nearby rocking chairs, a restful end to a hard day of work.

He took her down the front steps onto the neatly trimmed green lawn spreading beneath the shade of four elm trees. Everything seemed to be in full bloom, including the flower beds at every corner of the large house. Marybeth inhaled a deep breath, enjoying the clean, fresh scent of country living.

"It's so beautiful, Rand."

He beamed at her praise. "We like it."

Northam land stretched as far as the eye could see to the north, south and east. Beyond the fence bordering the house's front lawn lay a vast field of lush uncut green grass waving in the late summer breeze.

"I never imagined the place would be this big." Marybeth could scarcely take it all in. "What's growing in that field?"

"That's alfalfa hay." For a moment Rand studied the field with a critical eye. "When it's ready for harvest in another month, we'll winnow it into rows, fork it into wagons and store it in the barn. It'll feed Northam horses and cattle through the winter."

Rand explained that their drovers would herd the steers to market over the mountains, and the cattle left behind would be brood stock for the next year.

"Come autumn, this is a pretty busy place. While the men take care of the cattle and harvest the hay, the womenfolk harvest their kitchen gardens and preserve the produce. Everybody on the ranch has an important job to do."

"So much work." A sliver of understanding opened in Marybeth's mind as she recalled Da's complaints about how hard it had been back home in Ireland to bring sustenance out of the ground. He'd hated being a farmer.

"Yep." Rand's fond gaze, untouched by any such complaint, took in their surroundings. "But well worth it." His gaze remained unchanged as he turned to look at her. "It's a good life."

What did she sense in his look and tone? Pride, with

a hint of wistfulness, if that was even possible? Did he hope she would see his home and land with the same deep affection? At a moment like this she was all too close to saying she'd like to be a part of his family's "good life" here on Four Stones Ranch.

Forcing away words that would forever trap her, she considered her options. While she couldn't tell him the whole truth, she could strike a bargain with her conscience. Without telling him of her aversion to marriage, she would make sure he understood why she must postpone making plans for a shared future.

"I can't thank you enough for taking me to Del Norte yesterday." She looped an arm in his as they walked around the corner of the house toward the back, where an enormous barn dominated the scene. "It will take some time before I can earn enough money to make the trip to Wagon Wheel Gap, but I do have to go there and search for Jimmy." She offered him an apologetic smile. "Rand, please understand that I can't think of getting married until I find him." She swallowed hard as sudden tears threatened to undo her. "Or find out what happened to him."

"I do understand." He looked ahead, his face stoic, all smiles gone. "And I hope you understand my side of things. If there was any way I could take time off and go there now, I'd do it. But my brothers have been managing the ranch without my help for over a week now, and I've got to do my share."

"Yes, of course." Another rush of emotion surged up inside her, choking off the words she wanted to say. Lest he misunderstand her tears, she directed her gaze toward the great barn. "What a large structure. It's almost as big as Boston's Faneuil Hall." Not really, but still very large.

Rand's doubting frown, peppered with a healthy dose of humor, put an end to Marybeth's tears. "Faneuil Hall, eh? While that's a mighty complimentary comparison, I do think your memory is a bit off. Even after all these years, I remember how huge that place was. Three stories, isn't it?"

"Not to mention the attic and tower."

"Which, I notice, you *did* mention." His teasing chuckle dismissed the last of her sadness.

With him being so agreeable, why not just tell him everything? Confess it all and see how he took it. Before she could form the right words, four black-and-white dogs emerged from the barn, yapping and barking, and charged toward them. Terror gripped Marybeth and she grasped Rand's arm, thinking they would dash back to the house.

"Hey, there, you little scalawags." Instead of sharing her fear of the dog pack, he knelt and let them clamber all over him. They licked his face, nipped at his ears and vied for the best place in his attention.

Now she could see they weren't in the least bit dangerous like the dog packs in Boston, but merely half-grown puppies. While she couldn't fully share Rand's enthusiasm, she did pet one sweet-faced dog that insisted upon including her in the melee.

"Aren't you a cute one?" She had little experience with dogs, but this one seemed to like being scratched behind the ears, much like Mrs. Foster's cat. The puppy wagged its tail and licked her hand and turned around in a circle before coming back for more, tangling itself in her skirt.

"I think you've made a friend." Rand stood and beckoned to her. "Now that they've inspected us, I think they'll let us into their barn."

Inside were at least a half dozen cats, maybe more, but it was the dogs that garnered Rand's attention. "Would you like one of them? Maybe as a watchdog?"

She stifled a laugh when she saw his sober frown. "Why would I need a watchdog?"

"Might be nice to have one to bark a warning when somebody comes to call."

Somebody like Mr. Hardison? She wouldn't ask for fear it would stir up trouble. "Let me ask Mrs. Foster."

"Good idea." He picked up the hefty puppy that had been so friendly to her. It seemed a bit more aggressive than the others in demanding attention. "Maybe we'll just take this little gal with us when we go back to town. Once Mrs. Foster sees her, she'll say yes."

"You don't think that's presumptuous?" Marybeth copied the way Rand scratched the dog's head and received another friendly lick in return. What fun it would be to call it her own.

"Nope. In fact, I'm sure Mrs. Foster will like her." Rand ruffled the puppy's fur as he set her down. "She can always say no."

"Is the puppy old enough to leave her mother?"

"Oh, sure. They've been weaned for months. The mother is up in the hills with the cattle, along with her own mother. She and her brothers were our first litter and are old enough to be working dogs now. The men are trying to train them to help with herding." He shook his head and clicked his tongue. "One of my father's projects that didn't go as planned. The man he brought over from Europe to train the dogs found out about some gold strikes near Denver. He packed up and took off without a word." Rand huffed out a sigh of disgust. "Out here a man's word is everything. If there's anything I hate, it's when somebody backs out on an agreement, even when it's just a spoken promise. This man had actually signed a contract but broke it."

Marybeth managed to maintain an interested expression, but once again all the joy went out of her. Even though Rand didn't know it, she'd broken the agreement she'd made with his parents. Would he actually hate her when she told him the truth? It was no less than she deserved, but somehow she couldn't bear the thought of losing his friendship. To have those piercing green eyes filled with contempt for her rather than kind regard.

But was marriage the only way to keep his good opinion?

"Miss O'Brien, I am more than pleased with your work." Mr. Means stood beside Marybeth's desk reading a letter she'd just typewritten for him. As always, his countenance was a pleasant but professional mask. "I will sign it, and you can take it to Mrs. Winsted for posting when you go out for dinner." He turned away then back again, and she could not miss the warmth in his gaze. "I have been thinking… That is, I was wondering—" To her shock, he tugged at his collar and swallowed hard, almost like an awkward young boy. "May I take you to dinner at Williams's Café today?"

During her secretarial training, Marybeth had learned that some employers might attempt to take advantage of their secretaries. She could not think Mr. Means, a church deacon, would do such a thing. Still, as she and her fellow students had been taught, she kept in place a pleasant but professional facade. "Thank you, sir. I usually go home for dinner, and I should do so today so I can make sure Mrs. Foster is managing our new puppy without any difficulties." A simple ploy and not really necessary. Her landlady had been delighted with the puppy and together they'd named her Polly.

"Ah." Disappointment clouded his brown eyes. "Forgive me. I did not mean to—"

In an instant she knew her mistake. He hadn't meant to make an inappropriate offer at all. "Perhaps tomorrow?"

A smile lit his entire face. "Yes. Tomorrow." He strode away to his office with an almost jaunty gait.

Oh, dear. The last thing she needed to do was to incite the interest of another man. What would Rand say? Yet Mr. Means was her employer, and she mustn't offend him, either.

At noon, after posting his letter, she hurried out of Winsted's general store to go home for dinner. In her haste, she bumped smack into Mr. Hardison, sending him back a pace or two. He caught her upper arms in a powerful grip and righted her before she could fall to the boardwalk or even cry out.

"There now, Miss O'Brien." Courteous as always, he bowed and tipped his hat. "You must be in a hurry. May I be of assistance?"

"What? Oh, I mean, I don't believe so. Do forgive me for not watching where I was going." She inhaled deeply, taking in the scent of his expensive cologne, and started to move on. To her chagrin, he fell into step beside her.

"If it's not an intrusion, I beg the privilege of escorting you to whatever your destination might be."

"Please don't bother." She gave him a quick and, she hoped, dismissive smile.

"No bother at all, dear lady. Esperanza may be a quiet town, but one never knows when outlaws will ride through and stir up trouble."

"Very well. Thank you." She prayed Mrs. Foster would not invite him in for dinner. That would be more than she could expect Rand to tolerate, yet if it happened, she would have a hard time keeping it from him.

"Miss O'Brien, please don't think me impertinent, but I would be honored if you would accompany me on an outing this coming Saturday. We could take a picnic out to a scenic spot I've found in the foothills."

Had he been hiding in the bushes yesterday afternoon when Rand brought her home? He'd invited her to do the very same thing. "Thank you, sir, but I have unchangeable plans for Saturday." Despite his nice manners, she would *not* offer to go with him another day, as she had with Mr. Means. Juggling two gentlemen was already going to be a challenge she'd never expected or ever hoped to encounter.

At the house Polly lay in a furry ball on the front porch. She perked up as they approached and bounded down the stairs. Last night the little darling had slept on Marybeth's bed, and they'd already formed a sweet bond.

"May I see you to the door?" Mr. Hardison offered his arm just as Polly grabbed his trouser leg in her teeth. "Hey, you mangy mutt. Quit that."

Instead she tore at the cuff, growling and twisting as if she were tearing at some sort of prey. Just as Mr. Hardison reached down to strike her with a clenched fist, Marybeth snatched the puppy up, heavy as she was, and pretended to scold.

"Why, you silly little doggy. What's got into you? Don't bother the nice man." The nice man who now wore a dreadful scowl much like Da used to wear when he was in a temper. Marybeth took a deep breath. "Why, Mr. Hardison, she's just a puppy who needs a bit of training." Or so Rand had told her. "If she damaged your trousers, I will mend them."

His eyes narrowed and Marybeth stepped back with another deep breath. Would he strike her instead of Polly? Her terror must be obvious, for his expression quickly relaxed. "I'm sure my trousers will need no repair, Miss O'Brien. If they do, the Chinese laundry will mend them." Now his smile turned oily. "I wouldn't like to see those pretty hands engaged in such labors." With another tip of his hat, he bowed away. "You and I will have our outing at another time."

Was there an edge of a threat to his statement? Her throat closed in fear and no words emerged to contradict him. Right now she would like nothing more than to rush into Rand's strong arms for comfort.

Yet back at work, as the afternoon progressed, she convinced herself it wouldn't be wise to further prejudice him against Mr. Hardison. After all, Mr. Means's years of banking gave him more insight into people's characters than a rancher's years of chasing cattle. Her employer spoke of loaning Mr. Hardison the money to start a new business. Just because he had a temper, just because certain of his traits reminded her of Da, that didn't mean Marybeth should be afraid of him. Did it? After all, she had no plans to deepen her acquaintance with the man.

Only when she stepped out of the bank at the end of the day did she realize her folly in thinking she could hide her encounter with Mr. Hardison from Rand. As he had every day last week, he was leaning against the hitching post, waiting for her, and the stormy look in his eyes sent a shiver through her middle rivaling the worst fears she'd had growing up.

Chapter Nine

The instant Rand saw the startled look in Marybeth's eyes, he regretted his anger. After all, it wasn't her fault Hardison had accosted her. Still, he was just a bit miffed over her attitude toward the gunslinger. If Lucy from the diner hadn't told him about the encounter, would Marybeth have done so? He straightened and took a step toward her, offering a stiff smile, which was all he could muster at the moment.

"Afternoon, Marybeth. Did you have a good day?" He stepped up on the boardwalk and offered his arm.

She hesitated briefly before accepting it. "It had its good and not-so-good moments." As they began to walk, she looked straight ahead.

"Yeah, me, too." How would he get her to tell him about Hardison? Certainly not by being angry, so he forced a chuckle. "The other pups kept looking for the one you took. I tried to tell them she's found a better home, but since she's the alpha dog in the litter, they're sort of at loose ends." Thinking about the dogs helped to improve his mood. "Those crazy critters trailed me all over the ranch today while I was trying to get my chores done."

Marybeth's laugh sounded real. "Well, you be sure to tell them Polly's already made herself at home and doesn't miss them at all."

She glanced up at Rand with a sweet smile and something pleasant kicked inside his chest.

"Polly, eh? Not a very bold name for a watchdog."

"I wanted to call her Roly-Poly, but Mrs. Foster said she'd outgrow her puppy fat soon, so the name wouldn't make sense. We settled on Polly."

They shared a laugh over that but then Marybeth sobered and sighed. "In fact, she's taken over. You'll be fortunate if she lets you in the house."

Rand wanted to make a smart-alecky quip, but something in her voice cautioned him. "Care to explain that?" Lest he'd sounded too demanding, he added, "I mean, she was my dog until yesterday. If she misbehaved..." They'd reached the end of the boardwalk and he helped her step down onto the dusty street, where they continued their walk.

"Let's just say it was one of my not-so-good moments. When I went home for dinner, Mr. Hardison insisted upon accompanying me." She looked up, her gaze clearly questioning him.

"Humph" was all he could manage to say as relief crowded out the last of his ill feelings. For one crazy moment right after Lucy told him what had happened, he'd wondered if Marybeth and Hardison had been in cahoots all along. They'd arrived on the same train, so it was possible. Now his conscience questioned why he'd become so suspicious of her. And when would he get over thinking she was less than honest with him?

"Humph? That's all you have to say?" Marybeth removed her arm from his and stalked ahead. When he caught up and gently snagged her arm again, she shot an accusing glare his way. "He made me uncomfortable, Rand. I know Mr. Means is doing business with him, but… Oh, dear. That's confidential bank business. Please forget I said it."

"Already forgotten." Not by a long shot, but he wouldn't tell her. If Means didn't have any more discernment than to work with a man like Hardison, maybe Dad had better find another banker for Esperanza while he was back East. "Not the part about your feeling uncomfortable, of course. Did he do anything…eh, rude?"

"No. Well… No. He did ask me to go on a picnic on Saturday. I told him I had plans." She shot him another of those odd looks, like she was still hiding something. "He said we'd have our outing another day. I should have told him that was not likely to happen."

Rand felt her shudder, a vibration so small he wouldn't have noticed if they hadn't been arm in arm. "Something did happened, Marybeth. I can tell."

To his shock, she giggled in her cute girlie way. "Oh, yes, something happened. Polly came out to meet us and nearly tore the cuff right off of his trousers."

Rand burst out laughing. "Smart dog. Now aren't you glad I insisted that you take her?"

Marybeth rolled her eyes. "Yes, Rand. You were right. It's good to have a watchdog."

They'd reached Mrs. Foster's house all too soon and he didn't want to leave her. They had so much more to discuss and not just about Hardison. He sensed she was opening up to him little by little. Maybe it was time to ask her some deeper questions about her life so he could understand her hesitancy to marry him and at the same time answer his own concerns about what she was hiding.

He tried to stifle an idea that had occurred to him yesterday as he'd shown her around the ranch, but it was an honest concern for any rancher. Susanna and Rita would have a hard time getting the kitchen garden harvested all by themselves, and the food was necessary to get the family and hands through the winter. It sure would be nice if Marybeth could become a part of the family, live at the ranch and help the girls out. Yet it was hardly a reason for rushing either of them into a marriage that could end up being miserable for both of them.

As they walked toward the house, he saw Polly on the porch. The pup's ears shot up and she raced down the steps, practically falling all over herself. He knelt to gather her in his arms, but Polly had eyes only for Marybeth. Her new mistress squatted and cooed silly words, stirring an odd sort of jealousy in Rand. He wouldn't mind if Marybeth cooed silly words to him.

"Do you have to hurry in?" To emphasize his question, he climbed the steps, sat on the top one and patted the spot next to him. Through the open front window the aroma of beef and onions, probably a stew, set his mouth to watering. Mrs. Foster made the best stew and biscuits. Of course that was next to Miss Pam and maybe Rita's mother, Angela.

"Well…" Marybeth glanced at the door. "It's Mrs. Foster's turn to send supper over to Reverend Thomas, but she always gives me a few minutes to relax before I help in the kitchen. I suppose I can sit with you for a little while."

"Good, because lots of people pass by this time of day, and everybody can see I'm here, and you're with me."

She settled down on the step and gave him a teasing smirk. "As if everyone didn't already see you walk me home every day."

"That's right. Maybe I'd better ride into town and walk you to dinner, too, so certain people won't—" He'd started to say "try to horn in on my territory," but calling her his territory might offend her.

"Don't do that, Rand." She set one perfect, gloved hand on his sleeve and lightning shot up his arm clear to his neck. If she noticed the way he shivered with enjoyment, she was too much a lady to remark on it. "After seeing all the work you have to do at the ranch, I don't want to take any more of your time."

Her sweet smile and warm gaze only added to the pleasantness of the moment. Oh, to come home to that every day. Suddenly unable to talk, he coughed to clear his throat. Now if he could just clear his mind and come up with some way to open the discussion. Polly chose that moment to wiggle in between them and lay her head on Marybeth's lap.

"She sure has taken to you."

He reached out to scratch behind Polly's ears at the same moment Marybeth did. Their hands bumped and they shared a grin and then fell into a rhythm of petting the furry little rascal.

"Rand, I—"

"Marybeth, would you mind—"

They began at the same time. Both stopped.

"You go ahead." He encouraged her with a nod.

Maybe if she opened up on her own, he wouldn't have to ask questions she might find nosy.

"Thank you." Her warm response hinted at a growing trust. At least he hoped so.

She sat there for a bit, gazing out across the street toward a newly finished house, but seeming not to see it. In her gaze, her expression, he saw something familiar, but he couldn't quite capture the memory. Maybe she was becoming so much a part of his life that her features were burned into his thoughts. He certainly did dream about her every night; a welcome change from his nightmares about killing a man and being stalked by his cousin. He shoved aside thoughts of Dathan Hardison. If the gunslinger so much as looked at Marybeth in the wrong way, Rand would make sure he never did it again.

Lord, no. Not that blinding, killing anger. Please don't let me go back down that path.

Last night Marybeth had sorted out exactly how much she wanted to reveal to Rand. If he took her family history well, maybe he would understand when she told him she'd never wanted to marry and still didn't. Even if he didn't understand, she still had her job and could still save enough money to continue her search for Jimmy. The thought didn't please her as much as she'd hoped, but it was all she had. Forcing a sunny tone, she began.

"Back in Ireland, my father was a farmer, so I wasn't surprised to see how much work goes into ranching. Unlike you, Da hated working the land and raising sheep, probably because he wasn't very successful at it." She sighed, unable to maintain her false cheer. "So he sold the farm and brought us over here to Boston. Because he didn't have training in any other work, he had to take menial jobs. Mam worked as a housemaid, and Jimmy learned his way around the city at six years old so he could be a messenger boy. We rented a house in a poor neighborhood where a lot of other Irish folk live."

There. Now Rand knew her family had been poor. Yet his intense gaze held only interest, no censure. Encouraged, she went on to the worse details.

"Da had a couple of bad habits, which didn't do anything to help." She inhaled to gain courage to say words she'd never spoken to another living soul. "He drank and he gambled."

Rand winced slightly, maybe remembering his own gambling days. She hadn't meant to hurt him, so she hurried on.

"He was always trying to get money the easy way. I'm not sure, but I think he may have worked for some dishonest men. No matter whom he worked for, when he got paid, he would lose the money in a card game or buy whiskey until the money was all gone." She forced herself to say the next words, the very worst she could tell him about her childhood. "Drunk or sober, he beat all of us. He also took Mam's and Jimmy's earnings, even sold the furniture until there wasn't a stick that still belonged to us just so he could gamble." She'd intended to keep aloof from her sad tale, but she ended on a sob.

Rand set his hand on her back, right smack in the center where it felt so good, so comforting. "You don't have to go on."

Sniffing, she retrieved a handkerchief from her reticule and dabbed away tears. "Let me finish." At his nod, she braced herself with another deep breath.

"Do you remember when I told you Jimmy and I worked hard to get rid of our Irish brogue? We wanted to move up, to become respectable, so we could get better jobs. We decided to attend church and listen to the minister and try to talk like him." She grinned at the memory. "It was sort of a competition, and I think I did a little better than Jimmy. He always said it wore him out, made him have to think too hard. But really, he was pretty good at imitation." Rand was probably getting tired of the story, so she decided to cut it short.

"Anyway, after Da beat Jimmy one too many times, he left home to come out here. Mam died four years ago, and Da lasted until about three years ago when the whiskey finally took him. I found a job and kept going to church. I loved learning about God's fatherly love, because I sure hadn't received any from my da." She shook her head, determined not to dwell on that subject.

"The church ladies were very kind and two years ago offered to send me to Fairfield Young Ladies' Academy where I could learn proper manners and, if I wanted to, secretarial skills. When your parents brought Rosamond to the academy last January, she and I became friends, and for some peculiar reason, all three of them seemed to think you and I would suit each other. I can't imagine why." She bit her bottom lip before finishing. "I may have learned proper manners and got rid of my brogue, but that still doesn't change my rough upbringing, my family's poverty. It's a part of who I am and who I'll always be."

She gazed up at him to gauge his reaction, especially her last comment. Even through her tears, she could see compassion and kindness and maybe even a hint of affection in those green eyes.

He grasped her hand and gently squeezed it. "I disagree with you. You've worked hard to overcome a difficult upbringing. You've got spirit and a healthy dose of ambition." He shoved his hat back, leaned toward her and touched his forehead to hers in an endearing gesture that brought more tears to her eyes. "Overcoming hardship is the American way, so don't apologize for things that aren't your fault. You don't have anything to be ashamed of. Stand tall." He pulled back and gave her a teasing grin. "At least as tall as a little gal like you can."

She choked out a laugh and a sob at the same time. This wasn't at all what she'd expected. Why hadn't she trusted him sooner? Maybe she could finish it all right now and see what came of telling him the complete truth. Before she could speak, he stood and tugged her to her feet.

"Come on. Stand tall and be proud of all you've accomplished. There are so many paths you could have taken, but you chose a life of faith and following the Lord. My parents saw and admired that in you."

"So you don't think they'll ever regret arranging—" She couldn't bring herself to refer to their proposed marriage. "For me to come out here? I mean, once they learn the truth about my background?"

Rand gave her another one of those teasing grins that tickled her insides. "My father was a Union officer, and he knew every detail about the men who served under him. Not only that, but he grew up in Boston. I have no doubt he knew much more about you than you think."

Horror gripped her, but only briefly. She'd often been hungry, had even been forced to sleep in an alley sometimes, but she'd never fallen into such despair as to demean herself to survive. Early on, she'd seen what happened to such girls. Colonel Northam could ask anyone who'd known her and learn of her spotless reputation. In fact, as Rand said, he probably had. The thought both reassured and unnerved her at the same time.

"Hello, Rand." Mrs. Foster emerged from the house wiping her hands on a tea towel. "Will you stay for supper?"

"No, thank you, ma'am. I need to get back to the ranch." He brushed a kiss over Marybeth's cheek. "And I need to speak to the reverend on my way out of town. Why don't I deliver his supper to him?"

Disappointed to see their conversation end, Marybeth had no choice but to let him go. The rest of her story would have to wait for another day. Maybe. She'd never spoken so honestly with anyone before, and she wasn't sure she'd have the courage to take that last step of truthfulness and confess she'd never really planned to marry Rand. It was one piece of information Colonel Northam wouldn't have found out because she'd never told anyone. What would the Northams think of her then? What would Rand think of her?

After washing the supper dishes and cleaning up the kitchen, Marybeth sat at Mrs. Foster's piano and practiced a few of her favorite hymns. She also tried some new ones. Her landlady sat nearby in an overstuffed chair, busy with her knitting. On the top of the piano, Pepper, the black-and-white cat, lounged indifferently, his eyes occasionally straying in Polly's direction. From her spot on the floor by Mrs. Foster, Polly also eyed the cat. The moment the puppy had entered the house, she'd made it clear she expected to be in charge. Pepper, being a rather docile feline, had objected to the idea only briefly before realizing his ability to climb out of reach made him impervious to Polly's aggression. Marybeth thought for certain she saw a smirk on the cat's face.

After only a week and a few days of living here, she'd come to love this homey scene each evening. With the added amusement of the animals, she thought she could live this way forever. That was, after she found Jimmy. Of course she wouldn't mind visits from Rand, and the more the better. But she wouldn't keep him from courting other girls once she told him of her determination to remain unattached. The thought caused a stew in her stomach that had nothing to do with Mrs. Foster's fine cooking.

She turned the pages of the hymnal and found a song she didn't know so she could practice her sight reading. Before her fingers touched the keys, a knock sounded on the front door.

"I'll go." If it was Mr. Hardison, she'd simply have to tell him she would prefer not to receive him. If he truly was a gentleman, he would accept her decision.

Through the etched-glass window in the door, she made out the figure of Mr. Means. Even though the porch was deeply shadowed, Marybeth could see a bouquet of red roses in one hand, his hat in the other, and her heart sank. She had to let him in. How could she refuse to see him and still keep her job? Opening the door, she pasted on her most professional smile, though this clearly was not a business call.

"Good evening, Mr. Means. What a surprise." She stood back so he could enter. "Do come in."

"Thank you, Miss O'Brien." As he had earlier, he seemed a bit awkward, almost charmingly so. How could a wealthy, nice-looking young man be so unsure of himself? "I hope you will not mind my calling at this hour, but my gardener just cut these roses, and I thought of you."

"Oh, how nice. But you shouldn't have." Really, really shouldn't have. He knew she'd come to Esperanza as Rand's supposed bride. Had he seen her reticence to set a date and decided to court her himself?

Polly ambled over and sniffed Mr. Means's shoes and pant legs, causing Marybeth no end of concern. But the gentleman reached down and let her sniff his hand.

"Hey, there, little boy. What a fine little fellow you are." He ruffled her fur and patted her head.

Unfazed by his mistake regarding her gender, Polly licked his hand.

"Please join us in the parlor." Marybeth waved a hand in that direction. "I'll get us some tea. Or coffee, if you prefer."

"Tea, please." He hung his hat on the hall tree and followed her into the room.

Mrs. Foster bustled over to greet him, even as she questioned Marybeth with a look. "I'll get a vase and the tea. You youngsters sit down." She took the roses and disappeared through the dining room door.

Marybeth chose a chair rather than the settee, and Polly settled on the floor beside her. "It was very thoughtful of you to bring the roses. Their fragrance will fill the house."

"Yes, it will." He tugged at his collar and glanced around the room as if looking for something to talk about. "When did you get the dog?"

"Rand gave her to me yesterday."

"Rand. Of course. And it is a female. My mistake." He smiled at Polly and said no more.

Marybeth knew it was her place to keep the conversation going, but what on earth should she say to him? Mrs. Foster rescued them both by coming back with the tea tray.

"Now, dear," she said to Marybeth, "while you pour, I'll put the roses in a vase."

After she returned and placed the filled vase on the coffee table, she managed to coax some conversation from Mr. Means by telling him of Anna's improvement on the piano in her last lesson.

"Thank you." He shrugged in a self-conscious way. "We all know how important such accomplishments are for a young lady if she is ever to fit into society and make a suitable marriage. It is difficult enough to rear my sister out here in the West when the only examples she has are cowgirls such as the Eberly sisters." He grimaced as he glanced at Marybeth and Mrs. Foster, almost as though he expected them to voice their agreement to his obvious distaste. When they remained silent, he went on. "So of course when you arrived, Miss O'Brien, I saw immediately hope for Anna. Would I be too forward if I asked you to give her lessons in deportment? I shall pay you, of course, beyond what you earn at the bank."

"I, well..." Marybeth almost bit her tongue to keep from rejecting his request out of hand. No, indeed. This was entirely fortuitous. More pay meant her trip to Wagon Wheel Gap would happen sooner than she ever could have dreamed. And if this was the only reason for Mr. Means's visit tonight, his only reason for asking her to dinner earlier in the day, she had nothing to worry about. "I'd be delighted, sir. When would you like for me to begin?"

"I would be honored if you would come to our house for supper Saturday evening so you and Anna can get better acquainted." His broad smile and warm gaze seemed a tiny bit more familiar than before, though not inappropriately so.

"Of course. I would like that."

Only after she saw him out the door did she recall her plans to go on a Saturday picnic with Rand. Now what was she supposed to do?

Gripping a picnic basket in one hand, Rand held Marybeth's hand with the other as they inched across a fallen log over Cat Creek. The day couldn't be more beautiful. Except for a few little white clouds over the San Juan range, the sun shone with its usual brilliance, and just the right amount of breeze kept everybody cool. Of course it never got too hot here in the foothills, so he hoped she would be comfortable. At least physically comfortable.

She hadn't seemed relaxed with him since last Monday evening, even though he'd done his best to show her that a background in poverty was nothing to be ashamed of. Yet for the rest of the week when he walked her home, she'd been fidgety and didn't ask him to stay and chat. When he asked if Hardison had bothered her again, she assured him she hadn't seen the man other than when he came into the bank to speak to Mr. Means.

Not that he'd been too worried about the gunslinger. Reverend Thomas had promised to keep an eye on Marybeth as she walked to work in the mornings and during her dinner break travels. For a man of God, the preacher was no sissy, so that set Rand's mind at ease.

Once they'd crossed the creek, Rand glanced back

to be sure the rest of their party made it across. Tolley, three of the Eberly sisters and Reverend Thomas each took a turn balancing on the makeshift bridge without any problems. Maybe the preacher could figure out whether Rand was doing anything to annoy Marybeth, because he sure couldn't figure it out himself.

"What a beautiful view." A bit breathless, Marybeth gazed out across the San Luis Valley.

"You doing all right?" Rand set down the basket and studied her face.

"Very well, thank you." She inhaled deeply. "I'm still getting used to the altitude. I never understood what people meant when they said mountain air is thin. Now I know."

"Well, you just sit down." Rand hurried to lay out the blanket Beryl had brought. "We'll pass out the fixings." Maybe all this week she'd been reacting to the air, not to him. She'd just needed her rest after working all day.

"Do let me help." She resisted his attempt to seat her.

"Let her help, Rand." Grace, the second oldest of the Eberly sisters, set down her own basket. "She'll be fine. A little work never hurt anybody."

If anyone would know, it was these sisters, who'd done men's work all of their young lives. "All right, then."

"Say, when do we eat?" Tolley, always hungry, eyed the baskets with interest.

"Just hold your horses, cowboy." Laurie had carried three leather rifle sheaths from the buckboard. "Let's have our shooting competition first." She set the sheaths on a large flat rock, unsnapped them and pulled out the firearms. "Who's first?"

Rand had forgotten all about this part of their plans.

He shot a quick look at Marybeth and was relieved to see the interest in her eyes. While the others decided the order in which they'd shoot, she sidled up to him, and his pulse kicked into a gallop.

"I'd like to learn how to shoot." She blinked those pretty hazel eyes at him, and he found his own breathing a bit difficult.

"Since when, Miss City Gal?" He somehow managed to inject a note of teasing into the question.

"Since two weeks ago when we had an encounter with a rattlesnake." She answered in the same tone, which tickled him to no end.

While the Eberly sisters sent approving looks her way, Rand and the other men laughed. They quit laughing when she pulled a Remington double-barreled Derringer from her reticule.

"I bought this yesterday. Will you show me how to use it?"

"Yes, ma'am. I'd be happy to." Pride swelled in his chest over Marybeth's determination to fit into Western life. She'd make a mighty fine helpmeet if he could just win her heart. Of course he'd feel a little better about it if she'd sought his help in choosing the pocket pistol, but he'd have to let that pass. She was pretty independent and he didn't want to discourage that quality in her.

Using pinecones, rocks and empty tin cans they'd brought along, the party spent the next hour or so in competition. At the end of it all, Grace and Rand tied, with not a single miss, no matter what they shot at. Marybeth didn't join their contest, but Rand was pleased that she did learn to keep her eye on the target and not flinch when she pulled the trigger of her tiny firearm.

Later as they finished off their picnic with rhubarb

pie smothered in fresh cream, Rand pondered how to keep the party going. With Marybeth looking to him for her shooting lessons, maybe he could teach her his favorite game for winter evenings.

"How about we head back to the ranch and play checkers? We can have supper there."

For some reason, Marybeth gave a little start and bit her lower lip. Before he could ask why, Beryl piped up.

"Aw, you just want to show off, Rand. Everybody knows you can even beat the Colonel at checkers."

"I'd sure like to come, Rand," the preacher said, "but I still have a few things to do in preparation for church tomorrow."

"Sorry, Rand," said Grace. "We have chores to do. Maybe another time."

At that, Marybeth sighed with obvious relief.

Which gave Rand something more to ponder. Was she getting tired of his company? Or did she have other plans? Neither idea made him the least bit happy.

Marybeth had never faced such a dilemma. After a pleasant Saturday evening with Mr. Means and Anna, she felt obligated to sit with them in church the next morning. Yet while she and Rand passed out the hymnals, guilt caused a dull ache in her chest. She should tell him about the previous evening, but the words wouldn't come. Now, if her employer invited her to join him and his sister, what would Rand think? Would he still help her find Jimmy, or would he decide she was fickle and have no more to do with her? Above all, she didn't want the two men to see each other as rivals for her interest when she was trying very hard not to care too much for Rand.

As if she could see Marybeth's predicament, Susanna came to her rescue, just as she had last Sunday with Mr. Hardison. Accompanied by Lizzy, who flung herself into Marybeth's arms and insisted upon being picked up, Susanna put a hand on her waist and directed her to the pew near the front where Rand and his brothers were seated.

"You must come out to the ranch for dinner again today," Susanna whispered just as Reverend Thomas stood to speak.

With the entire service to decide how to answer, Marybeth settled on the excuse that Mrs. Foster could not do without her. In truth, the older lady had decided to make two more bedrooms available for boarders. With Marybeth gone the day before, this Sunday afternoon was the only time she could help her landlady. She would wait to tell Rand her Saturdays would also be taken from now on, for that was when Anna would have her lessons in deportment.

After the service ended Rand and Tolley hovered around her like mother birds, undoubtedly to keep Mr. Hardison away. They needn't have worried. The well-dressed businessman stood just beyond the churchyard chatting with Lucy from the diner. Marybeth found the pairing rather odd due to his well-spoken ways and Lucy's less-than-ladylike flirting. Surely there was no accounting for tastes.

When Marybeth told Rand about her plans for the day, he couldn't hide his disappointment. While it was admirable for her to help Mrs. Foster, he renewed his suspicion that she was hiding something. On the other hand, even if she was, he had a secret of his own, and fair was fair.

After the cattle came down from summer grazing and the steers taken to market, he and Tolley planned to head up to Wagon Wheel Gap to look for Jimmy O'Brien. If the weather turned bad and snow kept them from traveling over the mountain trails, they'd go first thing come spring. He understood Marybeth's eagerness to search for her brother, but Colorado weather could turn deadly in a very short time, killing horses and men. With all the dangers they'd face, he just couldn't let her go with them. She hadn't seen Jimmy in eight years, so a few more months shouldn't make that much difference.

He could just picture the way her sweet face would light up when she saw her brother again, and he sure did want to be the one who arranged that reunion. Then maybe she'd tell him all of her secrets. Then maybe she'd decide marrying him wasn't such a bad idea.

Waiting for spring would take a lot of patience, a trait to which he couldn't lay much claim. The last time he got impatient about his lot in life, he'd ended up killing a man. This time he wouldn't force the issue. But he would pray like crazy for the snow to hold off so he could bring Jimmy home to Marybeth before Christmas.

Chapter Ten

As she'd hoped, Mrs. Foster gained three additional boarders. Homer Bean, the new clerk from Mrs. Winsted's general store, took one room while he saved money to bring his wife and children from Missouri. In the other room resided the Chases, an elderly couple whose house up by Rock Creek had burned down. They needed a place to stay until their sons built a new one. None of the three could be expected to help with the household chores, so Marybeth and Mrs. Foster had extra cooking and cleaning.

After work each day Marybeth hurried home to help with supper, cutting short her time with Rand. Despite their usual banter, plus an occasional bit of jolly singing, not once did she feel as close to him as she had that Monday evening in August. With him being busy on the ranch and her being busy on Saturdays with Anna, their only other times together were Sunday mornings when they passed out hymnals. Marybeth missed him, missed being with his family, but with some effort, she was able to subdue such feelings by thinking of her quest to find Jimmy.

Due to Mr. Means's generosity, Marybeth's bank account had grown faster than she'd ever dreamed. By late September she had almost enough money to make the stagecoach trip to Wagon Wheel Gap. So far, she hadn't found the courage to tell Rand of her travel plans. From his comments about the volume of ranch work done in the autumn, she knew he wouldn't be able to go with her until after October. By then the stagecoach might not be running due to bad weather and deep snow. But she couldn't wait until spring, not when Jimmy might be so close.

Somehow she must summon the right words to tell Rand about her plans. While she was at it, she should probably tell him of her plans not to marry. Earning her own living had given her a self-confidence she'd never before experienced. How could she hand over the control of her life to a husband who would have the legal right to take her earnings, tell her what to do and even beat her if he felt the urge?

She reminded herself Rand wasn't like that, wasn't at all like Da. He never tried to tell her what to do. He never displayed a violent temper or threatened her. But after being married for any length of time, what husband wouldn't take charge? She doubted even Rand would let her continue to work, to have her own money with no one to answer to about how she spent it. No, marriage just wouldn't work for her. And she had one idea of how to show Rand she wouldn't make a good wife for a rancher.

With the church's annual Harvest Home only a few days away, she picked the last of the tart green apples growing on Mrs. Foster's tree. She made a pie with not enough sugar and a bottom crust so thick it would remain undercooked. She left the cinnamon out altogether. This would be her entry in the pie contest. Next, she would nominate Rand to be one of the judges. With all of his compliments to other ladies about their cooking, he'd made it clear he considered this an important issue. Once he tasted her entry, he'd think twice about wanting to marry her.

Fork in one hand, pencil and paper in the other, Rand stood in line with the two other judges as they moved down the table tasting each of the nine pies and writing down a score. Whoever nominated him to judge had no idea how much he disliked the idea of comparing one lady's cooking to someone else's. As a bachelor, he didn't want to hurt anybody's feelings, especially when each of the ladies had fed him at one time or another. Reverend Thomas seemed to have no such concerns. He enthusiastically moved from pie to pie, acting as though each one was the best he'd ever tasted before he wrote down a score.

Only one good thing might come out of the situation for Rand. The judges weren't supposed to know who baked each pie, but Marybeth had hinted that hers might just be resting on a blue-striped tea towel. He knew Mrs. Foster was a bit jealous of her kitchen, so Marybeth had been relegated to helping the older lady and hadn't had much chance to practice her own skills. Today he'd finally taste something she made. It would be a challenge to judge it impartially because he was sure she'd earn a perfect score.

Or so he thought. The instant he put a big forkful of the tart, undercooked apples and greasy, congealed crust into his mouth, he wondered how he'd even manage to swallow it. How had the preacher done it? Or Bert the blacksmith, the third judge? Yet both men had moved on to the next entry without any reaction.

Rand's eyes began to water as he chewed. Forcing the bite down his throat, he took a gulp of water from one of the cups the committee had provided for each judge to sip between entries. He blinked, and there before him stood Marybeth, a sweet, expectant smile on her pretty face. He answered with a nod and a shaky grin before writing down her score, a two on a scale of one to ten. Even that was generous.

Fortunately the next pie flooded his mouth with flavor, erasing the sour taste. He recognized Miss Pam's handiwork in the flaky crust, perfectly done apples, spicy cinnamon and just the right amount of sugar. He'd had her pies often enough to know she rated a score of ten on just about everything she cooked.

He couldn't fault Marybeth for her lack of cooking skills. She'd probably never had the opportunity to learn. Once they married, if they married, Susanna and Rita would teach her everything she needed to know.

Marybeth could hardly keep from laughing at poor Rand's expression as he bit into her pie. While the preacher and the blacksmith had taken small bites, probably saving room for the feast they would enjoy later in the day, Rand had forked up a huge mouthful. When he gave her a smile, weak as it was, guilt pinched her conscience. It was a mean trick to pull on him. On all of the judges. But if it accomplished her purpose, so be it.

Now that the judges had tasted all of the entries, other folks crowded around to finish off the pies, and Marybeth hurried to remove hers from the table. Unfortunately, Mr. Means reached for the pie tin just as she did.

"A little bird told me you baked this one." He served himself a large portion and took up his fork.

"Wait." How on earth would she stop him?

"Are you concerned I will ruin my dinner?" He chuckled. "We have two hours before it will be served." With that, he took a bite. His eyes widened and he grimaced. After swallowing, he chuckled again. "Well, Miss O'Brien, I admire you for entering the competition. My hope for Anna…and for you…is that you will always have someone to cook for you, as every well-bred lady should."

Such a charming, albeit two-edged comment. "Thank you, sir. I'll admit it would be a nice way to live." With that, she whisked the pie away and dumped it into a pail where all leftovers not fit for people were collected for pig food.

Rand promised himself he'd never judge another food contest again. Now how was he going to face Marybeth? Of course no one knew exactly what score each judge placed on each pie, only who won the first three places once the scores were tallied. The blue ribbon went to Miss Pam, with red going to Rita's mother, Angela. Mrs. Winsted took home the yellow and seemed more than pleased to receive it. But when Rand happened to see Marybeth's pie in the pigs' slop bucket, his heart ached for her, and he found a stick to stir the slimy mess until it was unrecognizable.

After a horserace, which Tolley easily won with his reckless riding, and a potato sack race, which the Barley twins won, dinner was served under the cottonwoods surrounding the church. Once Reverend Thomas said grace, Rand looked around for Marybeth and nearly bumped into her coming around the corner of the building.

"There you are." She gave him a sweet smile and nodded toward the folks lining up at the long makeshift tables where the food had been laid out. "Shall we join the crowd?"

His heart hitched up a notch at her use of "we" with its implication that she took for granted they'd eat together. So she wasn't avoiding him, something he'd worried about since she'd started spending her Saturdays with Anna Means. "Sure thing."

As they filled their plates, he considered whether or not to bring up the pie competition, at last deciding he should, but carefully. "I'm sorry your pie lost out to Miss Pam's. Year after year, nobody can beat her."

Instead of being upset, as some other contestants had been, she giggled in her cute way. "I always won the typewriting contests at the academy. I don't need to win everything."

All the tension Rand had felt for the past two hours dissolved. "Well, I can tell you another thing you've won."

They settled down on a blanket spread on the grassy lawn. "What's that?" The sweet look in her eyes gave him hope that today they could restore the closeness they'd enjoyed weeks ago.

"My—" He couldn't say she'd won his heart. It was too soon to say he loved her, especially when he still thought she was hiding something. "My utmost admiration, that's what."

"You're very kind, Rand." For some reason she grew

pensive, staring down at her plate and stirring her food yet not eating. She inhaled a deep breath and blew it out. “I have something to tell you.”

Her tone warned him this would be bad news, and his heart hitched in a completely different way. “Go on.”

“I’ve been saving my money, and I’ll have enough to go to Wagon Wheel Gap by the middle of October.”

Rand gaped at her. Nothing could have surprised him more. “You don’t mean you’re going by yourself.” He could hear the harshness in his own voice but couldn’t rein it in. “And you already know I can’t go with you until after we’ve taken the cattle to market.”

“Yes, I do mean I’m going by myself.”

Rand’s appetite vanished and he set down his plate as anger took over. “How do I know you’ll come back?” He hadn’t meant to blurt that out, and regret immediately filled him, especially when she leaned away from him with a gasp.

“Why would you ask that?” Her eyes widened as if she was afraid, and he wanted to kick himself. “Of course I’ll come back after I find Jimmy or find out what happened to him.”

He believed her, but he still couldn’t let her go. “Wagon Wheel Gap isn’t a safe place for decent ladies, especially traveling alone.”

She huffed out a sigh of impatience. “I traveled all the way across the country by myself. Decent people always look out for young ladies traveling alone.”

Rand also sighed. Deciding on a ploy he’d hoped never to use, he glared at her. “All right, you can go. That is, after you pay my family back for your train fare from Boston.”

Tears flooded her eyes and spilled down her cheeks,

and his heart ached for her. But he couldn't, mustn't, relent. Her expression hardened and then grew haughty. "Very well, Mr. Northam. I will repay you. Of course that means I won't have enough money to search for my brother right away, but you knew that."

She jumped to her feet. "I have no idea why you're being so unreasonable when I'm so close to having my dream come true. I thought you understood what finding Jimmy means to me. But since you don't and since you won't help me, I believe this sets a pattern for any woman who marries you." She huffed out a breath, stared off for a moment and then bent over him with her hands fisted at her waist. "Please do me the favor of not forcing your company on me again. Do not come to the bank to walk me home. Do not meet me at the church to pass out hymnals. Do not—"

"All right then." He stood, towering over her in a posture mimicking hers. "I'll leave you alone just as soon as you repay that train fare."

"Oh!" She stomped her foot. "You're being so unreasonable." She started to turn away, but he took hold of her arm. Finally after all this time, he figured out what her secret was, just as he'd suspected from the first.

"You never did plan to marry me, did you?"

Eyes filled with guilt and defiance were the only answer she gave him. He released her and she spun around and stalked away.

With every step she took away from him, Rand's heart shattered just a little more. He'd tried to protect her, but he'd said all the wrong things. Worst of all, at last he knew for certain what she'd been hiding all this time. Now he just had to figure out what else she'd kept from him and from the good people of Esperanza.

* * *

Marybeth knew she should stay and help the other ladies clean up after dinner, but she couldn't bear to run into Susanna and Lizzy or any other member of the Northam family. Once Rand told them about their conversation, they all would turn against her, just as he had. Nor had Marybeth missed the smirk on Lucy's face. The waitress had been sitting several yards away and obviously had heard the argument. Well, now she could flirt with Rand all she wanted, even though she was supposed to be sweethearts with Rand's friend Seamus. Or maybe Mr. Hardison was her beau now. Marybeth never bothered to keep up with gossip.

She found Mrs. Foster and told her landlady she wasn't feeling well, which wasn't a lie. As never before in her life, she was truly heartsick over ending her friendship with Rand. The three-block walk home seemed to take forever. With each step, the truth about how wrong her deception had been hammered deeper into her soul. Yet Rand wasn't without his faults. He might not be brutal like Da, but he was just as controlling. She would never be able to live with that. They were better off without each other.

At least he followed her order not to come early for church the next day. While Mrs. Foster practiced her hymns on the pump organ, Marybeth dusted the hymnals and placed them in the pews. Even though she knew her actions helped out, it wasn't as enjoyable as when she and Rand raced to finish first, each placing the books just so in each row as part of their merry competition.

The sanctuary began to fill and she saw him approaching through the front door. Before panic could set in, she saw Anna and Mr. Means move into a pew and asked if she could sit with them. Both seemed pleased with the arrangement. On the other hand, Rand's scowl, Susanna's concerned gaze and Lizzy's confusion were hard to ignore. Nor was she helped in the slightest by Reverend Thomas's sermon on the thirteenth chapter of First Corinthians. Love might suffer long and be kind, but look at what that kind of love had gotten Mam. A life of misery.

After church Marybeth declined her employer's invitation to Sunday dinner, explaining she needed to help Mrs. Foster. Although that was true, her aching head and heart were the real reasons she had no wish to spend the day with anyone except Rand. She told herself she'd simply grown used to him, even fond of him because of his kindnesses. Yet another thought would not let her be. Was it possible she loved him? She'd never been in love, never even dreamed of it because of her parents. Mam's unshakeable love for Da had kept her imprisoned in an unhappy marriage, something Marybeth vowed she'd never accept for her own life.

Another voice whispered to her that Susanna and Nate appeared happy, even blissful, after three years. Mrs. Foster often reminisced about her late husband's tender devotion to her, and her tear-filled eyes made it clear she still grieved for him. Maisie and Doc Henshaw, as different as two people could be in personality and upbringing, seemed wildly happy. Pam and Charlie Williams were like comfortable old shoes together, both wearing age lines that turned up in constant smiles. Was it possible Marybeth and Rand could find that same sort of happiness?

No, she just couldn't take the risk. Until she found

Jimmy, she would not place herself under the authority of someone as bossy as Rand Northam. Maybe not even then.

Despite all of her internal arguments against caring for him, she still felt the sting of disappointment when he wasn't waiting for her after work the next day. Annoyed with her own obvious contradiction, she stalked off down the boardwalk, the heels of her high-top shoes thumping against the wood in a most unladylike sound.

She stepped down onto the dusty street and came near to colliding with Mr. Hardison, who seemed to appear from nowhere.

"Say, young lady." He laughed softly as he gripped her arms and steadied her. "You and I keep bumping into each other."

"I'm so sorry, Mr. Hardison. I wasn't paying attention." She pulled free from his light grasp and continued her trek home.

He fell in beside her. "Where's Mr. Northam today?"

From his tone, one would think they were old friends. Maybe the animosity was only on one side. Still she wouldn't discuss Rand with a man he disliked.

"Lovely day, isn't it?" She gave him a bright smile to soften the rebuke of not answering his question.

He laughed again. "I understand. Yes, it is a lovely day when I have the privilege of escorting a beautiful young lady home."

The very idea! Heat raced up her neck and she stopped to face him. "Is that what you're doing, sir? Because I don't recall your asking or my granting permission for such a privilege." She never should have let him walk her home those weeks ago, for he seemed to think that gave him the right to do so anytime.

Hand on his chest, he blinked, frowned and tilted his head in a charming, clearly abashed manner. "Do forgive me, Miss O'Brien. I didn't mean to be presumptuous." He exhaled a wounded sigh. "Surely you know I've been admiring you from afar. If Mr. Northam doesn't realize what a prize you are, he's making a serious mistake. Someone is going to steal you away from him."

Marybeth huffed out a sigh of her own. She was not some sort of prize to be given to the highest bidder or stolen from someone who owned her, but she wouldn't contradict him again. He wasn't a bad man. In fact, from all she'd heard at the bank and at church, he was beginning to fit into the Esperanza community. According to Mr. Means, he was making plans to build a hotel or some such business.

"Yes, of course I forgive you." She resumed her walk. "And, yes, you may escort me home. Today." She hoped he understood this was not to be a standing arrangement.

"I'm truly honored." After a few moments of walking in silence he said, "Forgive me, but I couldn't help overhearing your, eh, discussion with Mr. Northam on Saturday. Something about you wanting to go to Wagon Wheel Gap and find someone named Jimmy? Mr. Northam seemed very much against your plans."

Marybeth's head ached from a long day at work and not eating enough dinner. What did it matter if the whole town knew about her missing brother? Somewhere in the back of her mind, she wasn't sure she'd seen Mr. Hardison sitting near enough at the picnic to hear her argue with Rand. And if he had been, hadn't he heard her order Rand not to come see her again?

No matter. It would feel good to talk about Jimmy. She gave Mr. Hardison a shortened version of her reason for coming to Colorado to search for her brother, taking care not to say she'd never intended to marry Rand. In any event, for the past two days, that idea had begun to sit sour in her stomach. But again, maybe Mr. Hardison didn't hear the part of the conversation that included Rand's accusation.

"Why, my dear, you should have told me about your brother sooner." He beamed as if she'd given him a gift. "Why don't you let me help you make that trip? Why, I'd even escort you there. What would you think of that?"

Hope sprang up inside her so fast that she couldn't speak for several moments. In that brief time, serious reservations crept in. Apart from Rand's dislike of this man, she had her own responsibilities to think of. She must honor Rand's wish and pay him back and then save more money for the trip.

Even beyond that, she could see God's hand in delaying her trip. Just today Mr. Means had explained more about banking during harvest time. With crops and herds sold, more people would be making deposits, even investments. For those whose crops had failed, loans could be granted to see them through the winter. Her employer needed her, and if she deserted him after all of his generosity, her integrity would be in shreds. He'd never rehire her and never give her a recommendation. Like Rand, he would lose all faith in her. Worse than that, she would be just like Da, who'd never even tried to be responsible.

"Well, what do you say?" Mr. Hardison jolted her from her thoughts. "Shall we make that trip before the snows block the roads?"

She cast a demure look his way. "You're very kind to offer, but I can't leave now. Mrs. Foster and Mr. Means both depend upon me."

"Maybe it's time you looked out for yourself, my dear."

Confiding in this man had been a mistake, as were her kinder thoughts toward him. He'd addressed her twice as "my dear" in an almost suggestive way. This time it grated on her nerves. Before she could comment, Reverend Thomas strode toward them from a side street. To Marybeth's shock, he wore a gun strapped to his leg. Even on their picnic to the foothills, he'd been unarmed.

"Hello, folks. How are you two on this fine day?"

Mr. Hardison answered with little enthusiasm, but Marybeth felt nothing short of relief at seeing the preacher.

"I'm well, Reverend." She soon found herself walking between the two men as they neared her home. "Are you coming to discuss next Sunday's hymns with Mrs. Foster?" She could think of no other reason for him to continue accompanying them, but she hoped he'd see her into the house.

"Ah, you've made an excellent guess." He laughed in a nonchalant way. "Do you suppose if I stick around long enough, she'll invite me to dinner?"

"If she doesn't, I will." Marybeth glanced up at Mr. Hardison. "How about you? Have you met Mrs. Foster's new boarders, Mr. Bean and the Chases? We have the nicest discussions around the supper table. The Chases have some exciting stories about settling here in the Valley right after the war."

His responding smile was more of a grimace. "Thank

you, my dear, but I already have plans. Perhaps another time?"

"As you wish." If he called her "my dear" one more time she would correct him in no uncertain terms.

He left them at the front gate, but Marybeth didn't relax until they entered the house and closed the door. "Oh, my. You came along at just the right time."

"Uh-huh. I couldn't get away as soon as I'd planned, but it worked out just fine. The Lord's will is never late."

"You planned?" Her voice rose a few notches above normal, so she quickly added, "How very thoughtful."

This sounded very much like some sort of collusion with Rand. Was he now trying to control her life through other people? Instead of anger, a feeling of being protected warmed Marybeth's heart. She hadn't resisted the help and protection of the church ladies back home in Boston. Why should she object to the decent people of this community looking out for her? If not for her desperate need to find Jimmy, she could easily sit back and enjoy that protection, as long as no one tried to control her.

As for Reverend Thomas's planning to walk her home, how could she fail to appreciate it? With men like Mr. Hardison roaming this town, she would do well to encourage him. Nothing in his demeanor suggested anything other than pastoral concern.

Everyone in town must have heard about her falling-out with Rand. The next day, several unattached men lingered at her desk or at the teller's cage when she took Mr. Brandt's place on his dinner hour. At the end of the day, as she donned her straw hat and white gloves, Mr. Means exited his office and approached her desk.

"Miss O'Brien, I have been sitting in my office this

past hour trying to think of a reason, an excuse, actually, for asking you a rather impertinent question." He cleared his throat and tugged at his collar. "I could think of nothing other than my wish to continue in your company. Therefore, if you would not find it disagreeable, may I have the honor of seeing you home?"

Was this more of Rand's collusion? No, he wouldn't ask her employer to watch over her, not when he'd exhibited a bit of jealousy toward the man on more than one occasion. Marybeth had never received so much attention in her entire life. While it should be flattering, she only felt uncomfortable. But Mr. Means's company was certainly preferable to Mr. Hardison's.

"I would enjoy that very much, Mr. Means."

"Nolan. Please call me Nolan outside of banking hours."

His eyebrows arched as if he was seeking her agreement, which gave her no choice but to say, "Yes, of course, Nolan. And you must call me Marybeth."

As they walked, a cool autumn wind cut through her light shawl and threatened to blow off her straw hat, and grit sprayed over them, preventing conversation. Halfway home, they passed the preacher, who tipped his hat and kept walking in the other direction.

Appreciation and understanding swept through Marybeth, and the tears stinging her eyes had nothing to do with the sand blowing into them. God's servant, Reverend Thomas, was indeed keeping an eye on her, just like the angels mentioned in the book of Hebrews who ministered to Christians and kept them safe. When he didn't join Mr. Means and her in their walk toward Mrs. Foster's, she assumed he approved of Mr. Means… Nolan. Which was a good thing, wasn't it?

* * *

In late October, Rand watched as his drovers herded the last of the steers off the property and up the trail toward La Veta Pass. Maybe next year he and Nate could convince Dad to send the steers in boxcars to the Denver market so they'd be more likely to make it over the Pass before the first snows hit. They'd argued it was a much safer, easier mode of transport than driving the critters through the long, dangerous mountain passes. In previous years they'd lost too many steers, whose market value surpassed by a long shot the cost of sending the herd by train. But Dad held out for the old ways, still not entirely trusting trains for such a valuable cargo. So now the drovers faced countless nights sleeping on the cold ground and always having to watch out for wolves and grizzly bears on the lookout for an easy meal.

Their best cowhand, Seamus O'Reilly, told Rand and Nate he planned to stay in Denver for a while. Seems he'd come down from summer grazing to find Lucy sporting with another man, so he needed some time away to heal. He'd heard about a camp meeting to be held in the city by some preacher from back East, so after the cattle were delivered, he planned to herd the cowhands in that direction to keep them out of trouble. He promised to be back at the ranch by Christmas. After a summer in the mountains, he deserved the time off.

Rand understood how Seamus felt, but he hadn't wanted to burden his friend with his own woman troubles in the middle of sorting out the cattle. Nor did he tell him about Hardison. Knowing the Irishman, he'd want to take care of the gunslinger before he left town. As much as Rand needed to confide in someone, he figured he and his friend would have time to talk on the way to Denver. Being out under the stars had a way of making men open up to each other.

Rand had just begun to pack his gear when Nate announced he'd be taking the trip instead.

"Sorry, brother," Nate had said over dinner a few nights earlier. "I just got a letter from Dad today. I'm going to Denver. You stay here and see the church addition gets started."

After losing Marybeth, Rand had felt like he'd been kicked for a second time. Since that fatal card game three years ago, he'd been trying to live a perfect life, trying to do everything in his power to make his family proud of him. Did his father think he couldn't be trusted to get the money from the cattle sale safely home? Did Dad think he'd gamble it away, as he used to gamble away his own pay? Or maybe get into a gunfight in Denver, where countless cowboys would be congregating in the worst areas of town?

He wouldn't argue with Nate or try to usurp his authority, but watching that last steer being driven off the property without him sure did stick in his craw. His commiseration with Seamus would have to wait.

After his long morning of work, he ambled over to Williams's Café for some pie. Maybe Marybeth would be fetching coffee for that pompous banker. The last he'd heard from her, she'd sent Tolley home with a deposit slip and a cryptic note stating she had transferred the cost of her train fare into the Northam account. Nothing else. No mention of missing him or wanting to see him. Of course he didn't blame her. After his harsh accusation, why would she want anything to do with him?

That didn't stop his chest from aching every time he

saw her, especially when she was with Nolan, the man who walked her home every day, the man who sat next to her in church and who probably had her over to his fine house for dinner all the time. All the things Rand wanted to do. He couldn't even bring her flowers because none grew on the ranch in this cold weather. Yet Nolan's gardener managed to keep hothouse flowers on the pulpit most Sundays, so the banker probably gave some to Marybeth, too.

Reverend Thomas had told him about her uncomfortable encounter with Hardison back in September. Apparently the gunslinger had gotten the message she didn't want his company, but that still didn't mean she was entirely safe from him. On the other hand, now that Nolan was courting her—Rand couldn't think of it any other way—he doubted Hardison would make a move on her. Not when the gunslinger was so busy trying to convince the good people of Esperanza he was an upstanding businessman. He had some nefarious plans up his sleeve like the extra ace his cousin Cole used to cheat with, but Rand hadn't seen him do a single thing to indicate what those plans might be.

He hung his hat on a peg in the café and eyed the pies in the new glass pie safe sitting on the sideboard. Miss Pam sure was making her restaurant nice with such fancy touches. Settling in the back corner, he hoped no one would spot him and put to words the questions their faces asked every time he was in town. Everybody knew Marybeth had come out here to marry him. Now that she'd won all of their hearts, they probably wondered what terrible thing he'd done to lose her to Nolan.

"What'll it be, Rand?" Miss Pam greeted him with a sweet smile that held no such censure. "I just baked apple and peach pies this morning, and I still have a slice of elderberry left over from yesterday."

"Let me finish off that elderberry. I'll take home a slice of peach pie for Susanna."

"It's real nice of you to take care of her while Nate goes shopping for furniture." Miss Pam blinked, as if her own words surprised her. "Oh, dear. Now don't you go telling her what I said. Nate made me promise to keep it a secret."

As she hurried off to get his pie, Rand leaned back with a grin. So it wasn't a lack of trust in him that sent Nate to Denver in his place. Dad probably hadn't even sent a letter, at least not one concerning who was to deal with the cattle buyers. Nate would do a fine job, as always. Plus he and Susanna did need more furniture for when they moved back into their own house after Mother and Dad returned from Boston.

When Miss Pam brought the pie, he noticed extra whipped cream topped it, and he chuckled. "With that bribe, you can be sure I'll keep your secret." Not that he would ruin Nate's surprise. In fact, he'd do everything he could to keep his sweet sister-in-law occupied until Nate came home.

That evening over supper, he quizzed her about her Southern upbringing, her favorite recipes and several other subjects on which he already knew her thoughts. While he searched his mind to come up with something else, Susanna laughed in her musical way.

"Rand, you can quit beating around the chokecherry bush. If you want my advice on how to win Marybeth's heart, just ask me."

"Hold on." Tolley scooted his chair back and picked up his dishes. "If you're going to talk about mushy stuff, that's my cue to go do evening chores." He shuddered comically and made his way toward the kitchen.

Susanna laughed again. "One day that boy's going to discover girls, then Katie bar the door." She leveled a gaze on Rand that was decidedly maternal, although he was a year older than she. "Now let's talk about you, brother dear. We've all been busy with harvest and getting the cows off to sell, but don't think I've failed to notice you're not courting anymore."

Rand looked down at his empty plate, over Susanna's head and then at the kitchen door Tolley had just exited. "After three years of being in this family, you should know it's not the cows we sell, but the steers."

"Don't change the subject." Susanna pasted on what seemed like an attempt to look stern, but her sweet face just looked prettier. Nate was one blessed man to have her. "What happened between you and Marybeth?"

The warm concern in her voice soothed something deep inside him. Maybe he didn't need Seamus, after all.

He told her the whole story, including his early suspicions about Marybeth and how, when they'd argued, she hadn't denied his accusation of never planning to marry him.

"Trouble is, now that she's told me she doesn't want to see me anymore, I realize how much better I could have handled the situation. And I don't have any way to fix what I broke."

"So you do want to fix it?"

He choked out a mirthless laugh. "Sure do. This is killing me."

"Well, sometimes love feels that way."

"Love?" He shook his head. Then nodded. "I guess I

do love her. We have some things to work out, but after sorting through it all these past few weeks, I don't see why we can't."

"Neither do I. That girl's only fooling herself if she claims not to love you. You just have to get together and talk about it." Susanna's blue eyes twinkled like they did when she had a surprise for Lizzy. "Now pay attention. Two weeks from this Saturday, we're holding the meeting about the church addition. The ladies are going to make it a box social to raise money. With crops in and cows—*cattle*—sold, we're hoping everyone will feel generous and make big contributions."

Rand scratched his chin. "Sis, did you just change the subject, or does this somehow pertain to Marybeth and me?"

"Silly boy, of course it pertains to the two of you. You can buy Marybeth's box, and she'll be required to sit with you. It's the perfect opportunity for you to apologize and get all of this nonsense straightened out."

"Right. Apologize." Rand took a deep gulp from his coffee cup. Did he care enough about Marybeth to eat her awful cooking? The question had no more formed in his mind than his heart leaped up and slapped him broadside on the head. Of course he could, along with the crow he'd need to eat as he apologized.

After the sting of realizing she'd never planned to marry him had worn off, he'd admitted to himself she had plenty of reasons to remain single. If he could just tell her how much he admired her for her loyalty to her brother, how much he'd like to build a loving family like his in which that sort of familial love made everyone feel secure and appreciated, maybe he could change her mind.

But only if he won her basket. Bidding against the banker, who could afford to employ four servants, a gardener and a groom for his horses might cost Rand his entire share of the income from this year's cattle sale. Could he do that and still look Dad in the eye and claim to be reformed and responsible? What if his parents found out about how she'd deceived them and decided she wasn't worthy to be a member of the family?

It was a chance he'd just have to take.

Chapter Eleven

He lost! Just when he thought his eight-dollar bid would win Marybeth's box, Nolan jumped to the new ten-dollar limit set by the committee this year. They'd cited last year's sad event when one love-struck cowboy sold his saddle to buy his girl's box, only to have her marry someone else the following week. Nobody could say the people of Esperanza were insensitive to the limited funds of cowhands…or to their broken hearts.

To hide his disappointment, Rand tipped his hat to the banker. It wouldn't do for a Northam to show poor sportsmanship. Then, waiting to bid on the next box, he hunched down in his thick woolen coat to ward off the cold November wind blowing through the churchyard.

They could have held the proceedings in the sanctuary, but some folks thought that would be as irreverent as the moneychangers whom Jesus threw out of the temple in Jerusalem. Even though the fund-raiser was for the church, out of respect for those views, Reverend Thomas said they'd set up the tables outside on the brown lawn. But these folks were a hardy lot, used to Colorado winters, so there were few complaints.

The four unattached Eberly girls had each prepared dinners sure to hold some mighty fine cooking, so he'd bid on Grace's box. As nice-looking as her sisters, she'd grown tall and awkward and had no beau, so he'd do the neighborly thing and have dinner with her. But the preacher beat him to it, so Rand moved on to the next sister. Beryl's and Laurie's boxes were also snatched up by eager bidders. Rand ended up with twelve-year-old Georgia, named for her father when it became apparent no son would be born to George and Mabel.

So much for Susanna's plan for him to make up with Marybeth. Instead he was stuck with a child who was more interested in talking to another girl than to him. So he ate by himself and stared across the churchyard at Marybeth and Nolan chatting up a storm. Didn't those two talk to each other enough at work?

He wanted to think this was all a part of God's plan. Maybe the Lord didn't intend for him to win Marybeth's heart. After killing a man, maybe he wasn't fit to have a sweet, pretty wife. But if she married Nolan, it would be mighty hard for Rand to stay in the same community and watch her have a happy family life with someone else.

When Rand had actually bid on her box, Marybeth's heart had skipped with hope, and she'd prayed he would win it. She'd missed him so much and longed for a chance to beg his forgiveness for taking advantage of his family. But after their bitter parting at the Harvest Home, she'd assumed he'd never want to see her again. He certainly hadn't tried to, had certainly minded her orders to stay away. Maybe his attempt to win her box was a sort of peace offering, one she gladly would have accepted.

Nolan's bid of ten dollars brought a gasp from the crowd then applause. Of course a wealthy banker would think nothing of contributing that amount to the church building fund. No doubt he would donate a great deal more over time, as would the Northams.

Yet as they sat there in the cold, she couldn't think of a single thing to say. With Nolan walking her home from work each day, they didn't have much left to talk about other than the weather. The topic turned out to be his favorite as he waxed eloquent about how different the moist cold of New York was from the dry cold of Colorado. She could only smile and nod and wish her employer would cease courting her. Yet if she rejected him, he might dismiss her, and then where would she be? On the other hand, encouraging him was no less a lie than failing to tell Rand the truth about not wanting to marry.

How foolish she'd been to accept Colonel and Mrs. Northam's offer to pay for her train fare in exchange for her marrying their son. In addition to being dishonest, it proved she wasn't trusting the Lord to help her find Jimmy.

But here she was, and she no longer owed the Northams any money. Now, if she could just keep her employer from taking his courtship as far as a proposal, maybe she could find a way to encourage Rand to resume their relationship. He'd taken the first step by bidding on her box. She would pray for an opportunity to return the favor. This very evening, she would write him a bread-and-butter note thanking him for his bid. If he didn't take the bait, she'd understand.

After Nolan escorted her and Mrs. Foster home, however, her landlady suffered a bad chill and took to her bed. Marybeth made chicken soup and bread and fed the boarders before taking a tray upstairs to Mrs. Foster. The dear lady's cough rattled in her chest, just as Mam's had in her final illness. Terrified, Marybeth sent Homer Bean to fetch Doc Henshaw, and indeed the diagnosis was pneumonia.

"Keep out as much of the cold air as you can," Doc said as he applied the mustard plaster he'd concocted in the kitchen to the older lady's chest. "Keep her sitting up as much as possible, and set a teakettle to boiling in the fireplace. The steam will put moisture in the air, which should help her breathe." The young doctor gave her an encouraging smile. "Can you do that?"

"Yes, of course." Marybeth had done all of these things for Mam, yet they hadn't saved her. After Doc left, she tended to each detail and then knelt beside her landlady's bed and prayed she wouldn't die.

In that moment something shifted inside her, and God's immediate path for her became clear. Instead of being so desperate to find Jimmy right away, when he might not wish to be found at all, she would turn her attention to this dear woman who'd opened her heart and home, becoming like a mother to Marybeth. In effect, her family. How could she do any less than stay by her side and see to her needs, whatever they might be? If it meant giving up her job, so be it. As far as Jimmy was concerned, she would go to Wagon Wheel Gap as soon as the snows melted in the spring.

Rising from her prayer, she felt an odd pinch of irritation toward her brother. Why hadn't he contacted her all these years? Why hadn't he sent another letter or even come home to Boston to see how the family had fared in his absence? If he'd done his duty by them, she never would have had to come searching for him.

What a silly thought. She was glad to be here in Esperanza. Glad to be taking care of Mrs. Foster. As to her deceiving the Northam family, well, the Lord would have to straighten that out in His time.

She stuffed rags around the rattling windows and closed the green-velvet drapes for an added layer of protection against the icy night wind. The upstairs hearth didn't have a cooking arm, so she found a small cast-iron grate to set the teakettle on close to the fire. She brought her bedding to Mrs. Foster's room and slept on the chaise longue to be near the invalid and to keep the fire going.

Sometime during the course of a long night, she remembered the note she'd planned to write to Rand. That would have to wait. Maybe if the other boarders pitched in to help, she could write to him tomorrow. As far as attending church was concerned, she trusted the Lord would understand that she couldn't leave Mrs. Foster alone.

In the morning, to her dismay, the Chases announced they would leave after church to stay with one of their sons, despite cramped accommodations that must be shared with seven grandchildren. Marybeth's next disappointment came from Homer Bean. After filling the wood box in the kitchen, he told her he would find other lodgings so she wouldn't have to cook for him. He did promise to keep the wood box filled and to bring anything they needed from the general store. She supposed she should be grateful for whatever assistance he could give, but she couldn't help but feel a bit stranded. Whom would she send in case of an emergency?

With the other boarders gone, Marybeth scrambled to think of ways she could help her landlady. As far as she knew, Mrs. Foster's income would now depend solely on the piano lessons, so Marybeth would teach the students. If she could find someone to sit with Mrs. Foster during the day, she could still work at the bank and use her salary to make the house payments. If the monthly amount exceeded what she made, surely Mr. Means would grant an extension. Perhaps Mrs. Foster, being a Union army officer's widow, received a pension from the government. Marybeth wouldn't ask because discussing money might distress the dear lady. She knew only one thing. Whatever it took, she was determined to lift every burden from this woman who had been so kind to her.

Even though Marybeth hadn't withdrawn her orders for him not to visit her, Rand decided to speak to her after church. If she agreed to let him visit, he would remind her of her promise to help with the Northam family Christmas party. He'd remind her that Susanna would have her baby in another month, so she wouldn't be able to perform the hostess duties. If he could persuade Marybeth to help, maybe that would open the door to more conversation and even a restoration of their friendship. Maybe even courtship. He would try real hard not to rush that last part.

In a jolly, hopeful mood, he arrived at church early to renew their competition in passing out the hymnals. Reverend Thomas had just completed that chore and gave him the sobering news that Mrs. Foster was gravely ill.

"When I visited a short while ago, she looked mighty poorly." The preacher frowned and shook his head. "Doc's more than a little concerned, but thank the Lord, Marybeth's doing her best to take care of her."

Rand's heart sank. "Do they need help?" He cast around in his mind to think of what could be done. Susanna couldn't even make it to church these days, and of course in her condition, she had no business nursing a sick person. Surely other church ladies could help, such as elderly but spry Mrs. Chase, who was right there in the house. "Maybe I should go over there and check."

"You could, but why not wait until after the service. I'd like for us all to pray for Mrs. Foster."

As anxious as he was to see how Marybeth was coping, Rand couldn't disagree. He managed to sit through the service, thankful for Laurie Eberly's somewhat competent organ playing. The girl had only played piano before, so her efforts on the double keyboard were greatly appreciated. The preacher delivered a short sermon and then the entire congregation joined in prayer for the dear lady.

Afterward, Rand told his brothers he'd follow them home later. He made his way to Mrs. Foster's just in time to see Mr. and Mrs. Chase leaving the house, valises in hand.

"Can't stay and be a burden on that poor lady." Mr. Chase's wide-eyed look bespoke more fear than concern.

Rand couldn't fault them. They'd suffered a lot when their house burned down. That sort of loss could shake a man's soul and make him fear more tragedies.

Rand had been to the house so often it seemed like a second home, so he didn't bother to knock. Marybeth must have heard him because she emerged from the kitchen and came down the center hallway. For a moment he thought she was going to rush into his arms. He'd have gladly let her. Instead she drew back.

"Rand." She brushed loose strands of hair from her face with the back of flour-covered hands. "What can I do for you?" No smile accompanied her words. Did she prefer not to see him? Or was she just worried about Mrs. Foster?

"What can I do for *you*, Marybeth? Name it and it's done."

Now a hint of a smile touched those smooth, plump lips he'd so often wanted to kiss.

"Please make sure everyone knows Mrs. Foster's illness isn't catching, so her students can come for after-school piano lessons beginning at four-fifteen each weekday and all day Saturday. As soon as I'm home from work, I'll be teaching them until she's back on her feet."

He could tell she'd already made a plan, probably during a long, sleepless night, if the tiny dark smudges under her eyes were any indication. How would she manage to work at the bank and teach piano lessons in addition to caring for Mrs. Foster? He wouldn't question her, though.

"I'll spread the word. Anything else?"

A tiny sigh escaped her. "If there's a lady who can sit with her while I'm at work, that would be…wonderful." She breathed out that last word on another sigh, and he longed to take her in his arms. Instead he crossed them to keep the temptation from overpowering him.

"Maisie Henshaw, of course." He should have thought of her before. Maisie and her sisters were in the thick of things no matter what was happening in the community.

Marybeth laughed softly, wearily. "Of course."

"I'll go right over there and ask her, but I've no doubt she's already planning to come by today with Doc."

With those details taken care of, he stood gazing into those shadowed hazel eyes. Right then and there, he knew he loved her with all his heart. She could have moved out like the others. Could have done a lot of things to ensure her own ease and interests. But she'd stayed to help an old widow who couldn't do a thing for herself. That bespoke a deeper character than he'd given her credit for after realizing she'd never planned to marry him. He'd forgive her and forget all of that. The Lord knew well and good how many times Rand had needed forgiveness in his life.

This wasn't the time to talk about it, though. Nor was it the time to ask if she would still help with the Christmas party. In fact, if Nate and Susanna agreed, he'd cancel the whole thing because he sure couldn't do it all by himself. An event like that took a lot of planning and work, and he'd never paid attention to how Mother and Rosamond did it all.

He sure hoped his parents wouldn't be disappointed in him for failing to continue a family tradition, their annual gift to the town they'd founded. The children in the community would especially miss it, and so would their parents. He was disappointed enough in himself. This was just another failure to add to his list. How could he even think of courting Marybeth if he kept on letting people down? What kind of husband would he make?

* * *

He came to offer help. Until that moment Marybeth hadn't realized how utterly bereft she'd felt after the other boarders moved out. Through a sheen of tears, she watched Rand leave, enjoying the view of his manly form as he strode out the front gate, leaped into the saddle on his brown-and-white horse and rode away at a gallop.

Other than being grateful for his help, she wasn't quite sure what all had happened just now, but clearly Rand no longer hated her for her deception, if he ever had. No, his eyes had held more tenderness, more admiration, than she'd ever seen in them before. Maybe in time they could patch up their friendship, if nothing more. She had to admit that when he'd entered the house and walked down the hall toward the kitchen, she'd experienced a jolt of happiness. How would it be to have him come home to her every day? Maybe marriage—to the right man, of course—wouldn't be such a bad thing.

She had little time to ponder such ideas because she must finish kneading the small batch of bread she'd started and set some stew meat and onions to browning. Even if Mrs. Foster couldn't eat anything besides a little broth, it was always important to have food prepared in the larder.

Maybe Rand would come back to help later today and she could serve him some of her stew. She could imagine him hesitating to take a bite, but not wanting to be rude, he'd give it a try. That would take care of any memories of under-baked apple pie he might still have.

There she was, thinking of him again. As if he'd ever been far from her thoughts. Funny how those few minutes as they'd stood in the hallway could banish her exhaustion and give her strength to carry on.

Mrs. Foster needed almost constant care, and Marybeth could only catch a few short intervals of sleep. Maisie and Doc came later in the afternoon for a short while. Then, after a second long night with little rest, Marybeth welcomed Maisie back as she prepared for work.

"Don't you worry about a thing." The lively redhead, Marybeth's first acquaintance here in the San Luis Valley, plopped down in a chair beside Mrs. Foster's bed and pulled her knitting out of a tapestry bag. "I'll be right here, and Doc will come by a couple of times today."

Glad to have something besides sickness to focus on, Marybeth touched the tiny white wool garment coming into shape on Maisie's needles.

"Oh, Maisie, are you—"

A hint of sorrow flickered briefly in the other girl's eyes. "No, no. Not me. This is for Susanna's baby."

"Well, I know she's going to love it." Marybeth's heart went out to Maisie, married nearly a year and still no blessed event loomed on her horizon. How difficult it must be to watch her husband deliver babies all over the area and yet not be able to give him one of his own.

Would Marybeth fare any better once she and Rand…*if* she and Rand married? Although she'd postpone her search for her brother to take care of Mrs. Foster, she still couldn't bring herself to marry anybody until she knew what had happened to Jimmy.

She bundled up in her brown woolen coat and plowed into a headwind all the way to work. By the time she arrived at the bank, her face stung and her toes had no feeling at all. As she entered the building, Mr. Brandt called a greeting from the teller's cage as he counted the ready cash into the drawer. Returning a smile, Marybeth warmed herself for a moment beside the potbellied stove in the center of the lobby.

Mr. Means emerged from his office and hurried over to help her take off her coat.

"I didn't expect you in today, Marybeth, eh, Miss O'Brien." He hung the coat on the coatrack beside her desk.

"Thank you." She removed her gloves and unpinned her hat and placed it above her wrap.

"How is Mrs. Foster?"

"Doing poorly, but Maisie's with her today." She looked at her desk. "Do you have any letters for me to typewrite?"

"Actually, since you're here, I do. Let's go in my office and I'll give them to you."

She followed him into the well-appointed office and waited while he shuffled papers on his desk.

"I must tell you, Marybeth, I am not pleased to see you staying at Mrs. Foster's while she is ill. You could fall ill yourself, and I could not bear to see that."

Marybeth felt a flush of heat creep up her neck, dispelling the last of the chill she'd gotten on the way across town. How could he, a church deacon, be so heartless in regard to a dear elderly lady—the church organist who gave them all so much joy with her music? His sister's piano teacher!

Marybeth sent up a quick prayer not to answer her employer harshly and then spoke in her most matter-of-fact voice. "Thank you for your concern, Mr. Means. Doc says it's unlikely anyone will catch it. In fact, I'm going to continue giving piano lessons for her, so you can send Anna over on her usual day."

"Ah. I see." He had the grace to look abashed. "I suppose by Friday we will know whether that is an acceptable idea."

Marybeth softened her inward criticism. She couldn't blame him for being cautious. Like her, he and Anna had lost their parents to illness, maybe even pneumonia. She hadn't asked for details when he'd told her they'd died. Yet she certainly understood his devotion to his little sister, for she would do anything to protect Jimmy…if she just knew where he was.

On the other hand, she believed with all her heart that people had a responsibility to others in the community who weren't part of their family.

With Mrs. Foster so needy, she just hoped the citizens of Esperanza felt the same way.

Chapter Twelve

On Thursday, Rand hurried his mare into the livery stable, dismounted and shut the doors. If today's wind was any indication, this would be a bitter winter. Not unusual for Colorado, of course, but still unwelcome. Eager to get his business taken care of, he glanced around the large building.

"Ben, you here?"

"Coming." Ben emerged from the side room that served as his office and sleeping quarters. "Just finishing up with another customer." He tilted his head toward the man behind him.

Hardison! Rand's hand twitched, as it always did when he saw the gunslinger. The man hadn't caused any trouble during the months he'd been in Esperanza, but he'd never failed to shoot a sly grin in Rand's direction when no one else was looking. That was enough to make Rand practice his draw every chance he got, praying the whole time he'd never have to use it.

"Rand Northam." Hardison reached out as though they were old friends. With Ben looking on, Rand had no choice but to shake hands with him.

"Hardison." Rand gave him a brief nod and then turned to Ben.

"Haven't seen you for a while," Hardison said. "How's that pretty little gal of yours? Last time I was over at the bank, she seemed to be real happy working there." The leer on his face was unmistakable, as was the threat inherent in his tone.

Rand swallowed a sharp retort. Returning threat for threat wouldn't protect Marybeth. Best to divert him, make Hardison think she didn't mean too much to him. "Didn't you hear? Miss O'Brien and I called it quits at the church fund-raiser." He snorted out a phony laugh, even as his stomach tightened. "We were so loud, I would have thought everybody heard us." He handed his reins over to Ben, who led his mare to a stall. "That's the way it goes sometimes."

"Well, then." Hardison's eyes narrowed and his grin widened, giving him the look of a weasel. "You won't mind if I step in and court the little lady myself."

Rand forced a shrug. "Can't think she'd be interested in your sort." He walked toward the door. "Ben, I'll be back in an hour or so."

"Hold up." Hardison followed him out into the wind. Once the door was shut behind them, he set a hand on Rand's shoulder, again as if they were friends. "Y'know, Northam, folks around here are real nice. They've taken to me just fine and respect me as an upstanding citizen. It'll be a shame to let them all down by killing you. Of course, when you draw first, what's a man to do? He's got to defend himself."

Rand jerked away from the gunslinger's hand. If he didn't have important business at the bank, he'd have done with Hardison right now. *Lord, help me. I can't bear to kill another man.* "Don't hold your breath. I don't plan to draw first on anybody. Never have, never will."

Hardison said something more, but his words were lost in the wind. Rand had already turned away and begun his trek toward the bank. He couldn't let anything stand in the way of today's errand. Last night he and Tolley had decided to pay off Mrs. Foster's house, something they knew Dad would approve of. Captain Foster had taken a bullet for Dad during the war and never really recovered from the injury. In spite of that, he'd come out to Colorado to help Dad build this town, and his death last year had grieved everybody in Esperanza.

In the center of the bank lobby, a fire roared in the new potbellied stove, offering warmth to customers and workers alike. Marybeth sat at her typewriting machine copying a letter on the desk beside her. He hadn't seen her since Sunday and was glad to see she appeared rested. She looked up and gave him a quizzical smile. Rand thought his heart might melt on the spot.

"Mr. Northam, how nice to see you."

Mr. Northam? When had she decided to stop calling him Rand? Maybe that was best, though, considering what he'd said to Hardison.

"Same to you, Miss O'Brien." He held back a familiar smile. Maybe it was best to start backing away from her now.

"Rand." Nolan came out of his office with his hand extended. Here was someone Rand didn't mind shaking hands with, even if he was a bit pompous. Even if he obviously had an interest in Marybeth. "What can I do for you today?"

"Just a little bit of business." He nodded toward the other man's office.

"Sure. Come on in." Once inside the room Nolan stepped behind his desk and waved toward a chair. "Have a seat. Would you like some coffee?" He indicated a steaming pot on the small, square woodstove in the corner.

"No, thanks." Rand waved away the offer but liked what he saw. Now Marybeth wouldn't have to fetch coffee from Miss Pam's café on days like this. "We want to pay off Mrs. Foster's house loan."

Nolan's jaw dropped, and he blinked. After a moment he seemed to recover. "That is very generous of you. Are you sure your father would approve?"

A blast of hot anger shot up Rand's neck, but he pulled in a calming breath. "In the Colonel's absence, my brothers and I are in charge of ranch business, including finances." He referenced his father's title for effect, and it worked. Nolan sat up a bit taller.

"Ah, well, then. Never let it be said this banker turned down money." His laugh was a bit strangled, and he chewed on the edge of his lip. "I am certain you have the say-so, but just to protect the two of us, I would like to have one of your brothers sign the transfer of funds with you."

"That's reasonable." Not really, but he wouldn't argue. "Tolley and I are working fence the rest of this week. Nate's in Denver, but he'll be back any day now. Two of us can come back in next Monday."

"Now that we have it settled, I have a question." At Rand's nod, Nolan continued. "Would I be stepping on anyone's toes, namely any Northam toes, if I hosted a Christmas social at my house?" While he chuckled,

Rand's heart sank. "I know your family hosts a large event each year but—"

"Go ahead." Rand jumped to his feet. Just what he needed. In spite of what Nolan had said about stepping on toes, the pompous city boy was muscling in on Northam territory. Dad had warned him about that. Said if a banker became the town's social leader, the poorer folks would be left out. "Just remember to invite the whole community. Especially the children."

"Children?" Nolan tilted his head, clearly puzzled. "You cannot be in earnest. I really cannot have children running around in my house. We have too many delicate vases and figurines and works of art. Why—"

"Do what you think is best." Rand clapped his hat on his head and stalked out of the room. Somehow he would find a way to give the children a party. Maybe he and his cowhands could finish the addition to the church by Christmas in spite of the weather.

With a brief nod to Marybeth, he stepped out onto the street. Over in front of Mrs. Winsted's general store, Hardison stood watching him. A shudder coursed through Rand that had nothing to do with the biting wind, and a sad truth sank into his chest. Even if he never had a showdown with Hardison, there would always be someone after him who would use Marybeth to goad him. She would always be in danger. If he truly loved her, and he did, he would stay far away from her and let her marry the priggish banker. The thought made him sick to his stomach.

"Is there anything else I can do for you?" Marybeth lifted the supper tray from Mrs. Foster's lap and set it on the bedside table.

Sitting up in bed for the first time in almost a week, the elderly lady wheezed out a cough before answering. "No, dear. Not right now. Do you think Anna will come for her lesson?"

"Yes, she will. Mr. Means said he would bring her over at five, which is—" she checked the watch pinned to her shirtwaist "—in five minutes."

"Oh, dear. You'd best hurry down." Despite her words of dismissal, she grasped Marybeth's hand with fragile fingers. "I can't tell you how much I appreciate all you're doing. What would I have done without you?"

To hide an unexpected burst of emotion, Marybeth leaned down and placed a kiss on one pale, wrinkled cheek. "I'm just happy to see you feeling better. Now, before I go, shall I hand you a book or help you lie down?"

"I think I'm up to reading my Bible." She nodded toward the holy book on the table.

"Very good." Marybeth placed it in her hands, adjusted the lamplight and carried the tray downstairs.

Just as she emerged from the kitchen, shadowy figures appeared beyond the window in the front door. She hurried to greet Anna and Nolan.

"How is Mrs. Foster?" Nolan still looked skeptical about being in the house.

"Much improved, as I told you this morning." She gave Anna an encouraging smile. "Are you ready for today's lesson?"

Something akin to a pout appeared on the girl's face, but she quickly replaced it with a smile. Marybeth had taught her that a lady was always gracious, even when she was displeased. Apparently her lessons in deportment were being taken to heart. "I suppose."

"Go warm up your fingers, Anna." Nolan gave his sister a gentle nudge toward the parlor. "I would like to speak to Miss O'Brien."

As the girl left them, Marybeth gave him an encouraging smile. "Let me assure you that while my methods are a little different from Mrs. Foster's, I don't think I'll completely spoil her playing."

"That does not concern me." He gave her a shy smile and rolled his bowler hat in a nervous gesture. "I thought I should tell you…that is, would you please inform Mrs. Foster that her house loan will be paid in full? After Monday, she will not owe the bank another penny."

Marybeth stepped back as tears welled up. "Oh, Nolan, that's wonderful." She moved closer and gripped his arm. "She's been so worried about her bills, and now, thanks to you, she can set her mind at ease. This is sure to help in her healing."

"But I—"

Unable to stop herself, Marybeth reached up and placed a quick kiss on his cheek. "Oh, my. I'm so sorry. Please excuse me."

Color flooded his face, and he put a hand on the spot her lips had touched. "I cannot permit you to give me the credit, not even for a moment." He shuffled his feet, ever the schoolboy around her. "The Northam family is responsible for this charitable act. That is why Rand came to the bank last Monday. He will return this coming Monday to complete the transaction, so Monday morning I will have you typewrite the papers for him to sign."

Rand did this! What a good, kind, generous man. Hope sprang up in her heart. If he would do that for Mrs.

Foster, he surely would keep his promise to Marybeth and help her find Jimmy. And once that was done, she would be a hundred kinds of foolish if she didn't marry him. Strangely, that thought no longer dismayed her, nor did it feel like an obligation. In fact, she felt her heart lighten at the prospect for the first time since she'd met his parents in Boston.

On Sunday morning, Mrs. Foster felt well enough to be left alone so Marybeth could attend church. Just as Marybeth expected, the dear old lady's health had improved significantly after she learned of the Northams' generosity. Marybeth couldn't wait to tell Rand the results of his remarkable gift and to thank him on behalf of her landlady.

To her surprise and disappointment, he didn't come early to help her distribute the hymnbooks. After their chat last Sunday, she thought they'd begun to heal their friendship. She managed to complete the task before practicing on the little pump organ, so different from the massive pipe organ at her home church in Boston.

After she'd played the opening and offertory hymns, she sat in a chair beside the organ rather than having to choose between Rand and Nolan. If Rand noticed, his face betrayed no emotion. Nolan gave her a fond smile that almost seemed proprietary. She resolved not to make eye contact with him again during the service.

With the weather being colder and most of the cattle gone to market, more cowhands attended church, so the sanctuary was filled almost to overflowing. Some of the men had to stand against the back wall. At first Marybeth thought Reverend Thomas's sermon would be addressed to them, for he once again spoke on the passage in Psalm 119:9. "'Wherewithal shall a young man cleanse his way? By taking heed thereto according to Thy word.'" The preacher went on to urge the congregation to study and memorize the Scriptures. "For only when we hide God's word in our hearts do we have the spiritual resources to know His will and to keep from sinning against Him."

His words pricked Marybeth's conscience. Surely the Lord meant this sermon for her. How long had it been since she'd memorized a Bible verse? Before guilt could consume her for her neglect and for her sinful deception of Rand's parents—her sin that was ever before her—the minister went on.

"But when in our human weakness we do fail to keep His Word, 1 John 1:9 tells us, 'if we confess our sins, He is faithful and just to forgive us our sins, and to cleanse us from all unrighteousness.' If you find yourself in the midst of a sinful way of life…" He paused and looked around the room to take in every congregant. "Stop now. Confess your sins. And let our Lord Jesus Christ cleanse your heart and fill you with His peace."

As always, he invited anyone who wished to come to the Lord to leave their seats and come forward for prayer. Or, if they preferred, he would be happy to meet with them in private.

Marybeth played the final hymn, watching in the corner of her eye as Rand and Tolley left the sanctuary. Once again disappointment struck. Was he ignoring her? What had happened since that sweet moment the previous Sunday when he'd come to ask how he could help her care for Mrs. Foster? In fact, he'd been a little brusque last Monday when he'd come to the bank. Maybe he'd decided she wasn't worth waiting for. If so, he might not keep his promise to help her find Jimmy. After all of his kindnesses to others, that would be the cruelest cut of all.

Due to a light snowfall that threatened to get worse, Rand and his brothers spent most of Monday making sure the cattle had enough shelter and hay, especially the expectant cows who would deliver their calves come January. By midafternoon, Rand was as restless as a cat at milking time. Finally he and Tolley were able to saddle up and head to town. He could postpone signing the papers to pay off Mrs. Foster's house loan, yet for some reason he felt the need to show Nolan his word was good.

"I don't want to forget the peppercorns Rita asked us to get." Tolley nodded toward the general store. "Can't have her fixin' steak without fresh ground pepper. Can we do that first?"

"Fine with me." Now that they were in town, Rand relaxed a little. The bank wouldn't close for another hour.

They found Grace and Beryl Eberly inside the store doing a bit of shopping, too. They traded the usual information about their cattle and their families and the threatening snows, even though they'd chatted about the same things yesterday before church. Once Tolley had the peppercorns tucked in his pocket, Rand stepped toward the door.

As he reached for the glass doorknob, Laurie burst in, bringing with her a hail of powdery snow. "Grace, Beryl, come quick. The bank door's locked and something's going on in there."

Rand's heart seemed to stop. "Marybeth."

Tolley and the girls gave him a brief look before they drew out their guns and headed for the door.

"Hold on." Rand's heart now hammered in fear, just as it had three years ago when he knew Cole Lyndon had meant to kill him. "You can't just go over there waving your guns. If the bank's being robbed, we have to be careful or somebody's going to get shot."

"Come on, Rand." Tolley shoved his gun back in his holster. "You know who it is. Tell 'em." He jerked his head toward the girls and Mrs. Winsted, who'd grabbed her own rifle from behind the counter. The clerk, Homer Bean, watched the proceedings wide-eyed.

In that moment Rand could see how foolish it had been to keep this a secret from the townsfolk. How could he have made the mistake of thinking Hardison was only after him? The man was a criminal, just like his cousin. A killer and a thief. He'd aim to hurt as many people as possible.

"Dathan Hardison's been threatening me since he arrived in town. His cousin Cole Lyndon is the man I killed..." After all this time, he still nearly choked as he said it. "He wants revenge."

Grace Eberly snorted. "I had a feeling he was no good."

"Too much of a charmer." Mrs. Winsted checked her Winchester to be sure it was fully loaded. "Always trying to sweet talk me like I was some green girl."

"All this yammering doesn't solve the problem." Tolley headed for the door again.

"Hey." Grace caught his arm. "I've got a plan."

Rand's own mind was spinning with wild imaginings about what the gunslinger would do to Marybeth, and it would be his fault. At twenty years old, Grace had a good head on her shoulders, so he gave her a curt nod. "Let's hear it."

Marybeth watched the light snowfall through the bank window. In another hour she could go home and prepare supper for Mrs. Foster. This had been a quiet day of work. Other than typewriting the contract for the Northams, she'd had little to do. Perhaps the weather was keeping people at home.

Mrs. Foster would be so pleased to know she now officially owned her house as of today. That was, if Rand and one of his brothers arrived before closing time. She had to admit to herself that her heart had skipped a beat each time the door opened, only to dip with disappointment as the person entering wasn't Rand.

In spite of all that, she had another delightful bit of news to give her landlady. This morning Doc had sent a boy to fetch Mr. Brandt because Mrs. Brandt had safely delivered a baby girl. Nolan had generously given the new father the rest of the day off, so Marybeth had taken his place behind the bars of the teller's cage.

"I wonder where those Northam boys are." Nolan emerged from his office reading the time on his pocket watch. "They must be held up by the weather."

Bristling at his reference to the Northam men as "boys," she inwardly scoffed at the idea that a little snow would prevent Rand from keeping his word. Well, at least for Mrs. Foster. If he wasn't even speaking to Marybeth, she doubted he would still want to search for Jimmy, snow or no snow.

The door opened with a jangle of the bells above it, and her foolish heart once again suffered disappointment. Instead of Rand, Mr. Hardison and another man entered, and she didn't like the look in either man's eyes. When the newcomer locked the door and pulled a gun from his holster, a wave of dizziness swept over her. They'd come to rob the bank.

Just outside her cage, Nolan stiffened. "Gentlemen, what can I do for you?" His voice was tight, but she sensed no fear in him.

Mr. Hardison had the nerve to laugh in a malicious way. "Did you hear that, Deke? Mr. Means wants to know what he can do for us."

The other man, dressed in shabbier clothes and sporting a ragged beard and long, greasy hair, laughed in a coarse way that sent a sick feeling through Marybeth's stomach. "Jest tell 'em we came to make a withdrawal."

Mr. Hardison snickered. "That's right. Now, Mr. Means, if you'll just unlock the door to the money room, we'll get along just fine."

"As you wish." Nolan took the duplicate key from his pocket. Instead of unlocking the cage door, he tossed it through the bars to Marybeth. "No matter what happens, do not let them in there. Remember your training."

"Yes, sir."

If he could be brave, so could she. As he'd taught her, she scooped up the cash in the drawer and hurried over to the safe. Before she could close and lock it, or even put the money inside, a shot rang out, startling her so badly, she tossed the cash into the air. The flutter of bills and the sound of coins clinking on the marble floor would have been comical in any other circumstance. As it was, all she could do was stare at the open safe, frozen in fear.

With the sound of the gunshot still reverberating

throughout the lobby, she slowly turned, terrified at what she would see. She choked out a breath of relief that Nolan had not been shot. Instead Mr. Hardison held him around the neck and pressed his gun against the captive's temple. A red welt caused by the just-fired weapon's barrel had already spread around the point of contact. Even so, Nolan simply stared at her, his eyes soft with care, his jaw clenched.

"Now, missy, you just open that door before anybody gets hurt."

"No," Nolan choked out, only to receive a tighter tug on his throat.

Trembling as she never had in anticipation of Da's worst beatings, she gazed sadly at her brave employer. "I can't let him murder you."

Nolan's eyes reddened, and he gave her as much of a nod as he could.

Her hands shook so badly she could barely get the key into the lock. Once she turned it, the man named Deke shoved the door open and thrust her out. She spun around to catch her balance on something, anything, but failed and crashed to the floor, her head striking a hard object as she went down. Pain roared through her and spots swam before her eyes. For a moment her world went black. She'd been in this position before, and as before, a primal craving for survival gripped her.

She forced herself into awareness. *Lie still. Force yourself to relax. Pretend to be unconscious. If he thinks you're dead, he'll leave you alone.* Mam had taught her this lesson well. Now her mind reached for something more.

Her face was turned away from the shuffle of feet and grunts of a struggle. Was Nolan trying to fight off the robbers? She prayed he would simply let them take the money. She slowly opened her eyes just a slit and saw the coatrack had been overturned. Her reticule and the loaded Derringer within it lay too far away, but her hat, along with its long, sharp hatpin, was inches from her right hand.

"Get the money bag." Mr. Hardison's voice. "Fill it." He must be talking to Nolan.

More scuffles. More grunts. She moved her hand a half inch. When no one stopped her, she reached for the pin, wrapped her fingers around it and drew it into concealment against her wrist. Now there was nothing left to do but lie here and pray for an opportunity to thwart the robbers. For all the lessons Mam had taught her, fighting back was one she'd failed to impart.

Rand knew he should just go to the bank, break down the door and have it out with Hardison. But that would double the risk to Marybeth. If she died because of him, he would never forgive himself. Against his better judgment, he must participate in Grace's crazy scheme.

Being the second oldest after Maisie, Grace had outgrown her whole family, even George. At maybe five feet, ten inches tall, taller in her high-heeled riding boots, she often walked with stooped shoulders as though she was trying to hide from the world. Today, however, she threw those shoulders back, held her head high and marched across the street to the bank, while Beryl and Laurie trailed behind through the deepening snow, talking and laughing as if they were out for a summer stroll.

More guilt plagued Rand over letting these girls lead this rescue, for he had no doubt both Nolan and Marybeth needed to be rescued. But the Eberly girls had been raised to face anything the Wild West threw at them. They'd been deeply offended when Rand had tried to talk them out of helping and argued that their family's money was in that bank, too.

In case Hardison was watching, Rand and Tolley walked in opposite directions and then each circled back to creep close to either side of the bank's double front doors. With Mrs. Winsted and Homer Bean sounding the alert to other townsfolk, he could count on more help coming soon. Rand prayed as he never had before that no one would be killed today. And if someone had to be, he asked the Lord to let him be the one.

Once he and Tolley were in place, Grace banged on the door. "Hey, Nolan, open up. We need to make a deposit."

Beside her, Laurie and Beryl continued to chatter and giggle, something as far from their natural behavior as a cow jumping over the moon. So far, the act was going just as planned.

Through the fog in her mind, Marybeth heard someone banging on the bank's front door. "Hey, Nolan, open up. We need to make a deposit."

Grace Eberly's voice! *Lord, no. Please don't let anyone else get involved.*

"Let her in." Mr. Hardison spoke, probably to that horrid Deke person.

"No." Nolan's voice sounded hoarse. Did Mr. Hardison still have an arm around his neck?

"Shut up." Mr. Hardison added a curse Marybeth hadn't heard since her father died.

Slowly she turned her head just in time to see Mr.

Hardison approach to yank her to her feet. "Now you listen and listen good, missy. If you don't want your friends shot dead, you act like there's nothing wrong." He turned to Nolan. "You got that?"

Nolan nodded and Marybeth did the same.

A loud click indicated the lock had been turned. "Come on in, ladies."

Deke's weasel-like invitation sickened Marybeth, but the odd way the sisters were acting sent a strange little thread of hope through her. None of them ever giggled or minced around like silly girls trying to catch a man's attention. Why were they doing it now?

"Gracious me," Grace said. "Who's this?" She gave Deke a wide grin and gave Mr. Hardison an expectant look. "You gonna introduce us?"

Marybeth could hardly hold back a laugh at the harried expression on the man's face. "Uh, sure. Deke, the Misses Eberly. Ladies, Deke." His expression grew grim. "Now, about that deposit. Deke, hold out the bag."

"What!" Grace glanced at her sisters and spoke with exaggerated horror. "Why, they're robbing the bank. Who'd have ever guessed that such a nice gentleman as Dathan Hardison would rob a bank?"

"And with such a greasy, slimy partner," Laurie quipped.

"Now, see here, you little brat, I'll—" Deke stepped toward Laurie with one hand raised, but before he reached her, she ducked away.

In that moment Rand and Tolley burst through the front door, guns drawn. At the same time the Eberly girls drew theirs.

"Watch out!" Nolan cried.

Already holding his gun, Mr. Hardison fired at the

girls. Someone screamed in pain. The gunman aimed at Rand. Without a thought, with all her might, Marybeth swung her right hand back and stabbed the hatpin into the gunman's upper arm, which was all she could reach. With a howl of pain worthy of a banshee, he dropped the gun and flung her down on the floor. Another gunshot. More screams. Then utter chaos as the bank filled with townspeople, all armed and ready to put an end to the robbery.

Within seconds Mr. Hardison and his cohort were tied up with rope provided by Mrs. Winsted. Deke howled in pain over a gunshot wound to his leg. Mr. Hardison held his injured arm and glared at Marybeth with murder in his eyes.

Nolan gently helped her to her feet. "Are you all right?" He brushed a hand over her temple and showed her the blood on his fingers. "You're hurt."

"I can't even feel it." She let him pull her into a comforting embrace, though his arms were not the ones she longed for. Not ten feet away, Rand gazed at her, frowning. He turned away, clearly with no mind to do that comforting himself. "Oh, Nolan, it was so horrible. Thank the Lord you're all right." Thank the Lord that Rand and Tolley and the Eberly sisters were all right, too.

"You were very brave. I am very proud of you." He breathed out a laugh of relief. "Everything is all right now. Everyone is all right."

All right. All right. She heard the phrase echo throughout the room as everyone confirmed their friends' well-being. Yet sobs from the other side of the lobby proved them all wrong. Marybeth and Nolan made their way through the cluster of people to where

Grace and Laurie knelt on the marble floor weeping. Across Grace's lap lay Beryl, her eyes closed, her face white as a sheet and a dark red stream of blood staining the front of her blue plaid shirt.

Chapter Thirteen

Wavering between fear and rage, Rand paced the hallway outside Doc Henshaw's surgery. He stopped from time to time to give Laurie and Grace an encouraging hug. Beyond the surgery door, Maisie helped her husband as he tried to save Beryl's life.

Tolley had gone out to the Eberly ranch to tell her folks what had happened. They would arrive soon, if their buggy could make it through the snow. Mabel no longer rode horseback, but she'd probably make the effort for one of her daughters.

Charlie Williams had tended the wounds on Deke's leg and Hardison's arm. Now the two outlaws were trussed up like Christmas turkeys and stuffed like baggage into the cargo room at the train station under the watchful care of Charlie, Mrs. Winsted and two upstanding cowboys.

Rand couldn't have been prouder of the way the courageous townsfolk had come together to stop the robbery. Nolan's courage had surprised him most, but he supposed bankers lived with the possibility that they could be robbed. No wonder he'd wanted to hire a sheriff. Too bad he hadn't seen through Hardison sooner.

Once Dad heard about the robbery attempt, he'd no doubt say it was indeed time to hire a lawman for the town and build a jail, too. Until then, the closest law was Sheriff Hobart over in Del Norte. The townsfolk all agreed they needed to escort the prisoners into Hobart's care until the circuit judge came to the area. They'd elected Rand to lead the posse, but he refused to go until he knew whether Beryl would survive. If she didn't, Hardison and Deke would get their due. A long jail term for attempted robbery would be nothing compared to being hanged for murder.

Despite the successful thwarting of the robbery, Rand couldn't help the flash of annoyance sweeping through him. He'd prayed that if someone had to get hurt, it should be him. The preacher would no doubt tell him God was still in control, but Rand would have to think on that for a while. The Eberly girls weren't the dainty sort of female, but they still deserved respect and protection, as all women did. He'd gladly take a bullet for any one of them.

The face of one dainty girl who'd been just as brave as the sisters came to mind. Rand had been sick with fear when he saw Marybeth in Hardison's clutches. Yet she'd struck the man with her hatpin just as he was about to shoot Rand. Brave girl. She'd saved his life. But when everything got sorted out, it was Nolan's arms she'd sought. Or maybe Nolan had just reached out to her before Rand could. He'd probably never know.

Though it grieved him, this was probably for the best. Even with Hardison in custody, someday somebody else would come gunning for Rand and would try to make a reputation for himself. He couldn't risk Marybeth's life again, not when she'd come so close to being killed. Best to let her go so she could marry someone like Nolan and live in a nice house in town with servants to do all the work. He reluctantly dismissed his fond images of her living on the ranch because there she'd be doing chores as even well-off ranch women did. Like Mother and Rosamond. Like the Eberly girls, who were too much like sisters to interest him in a romantic way.

The door to the surgery opened, and Maisie emerged, her bloodstained white apron a frightening symbol of her sister's tragedy. She rushed to gather her other sisters in her arms.

"She's hurt bad, but she's gonna make it." While the three of them wept together for joy, Doc came out looking tired but pleased.

"Hardy stock, these girls." He emitted a broken laugh. Or maybe it was a sob of relief.

Rand couldn't speak over the emotion welling up inside his own chest. *Thank You, Lord.*

Until that moment he hadn't realized how much he'd wanted to kill both Hardison and his partner for their evil deed. He didn't know whose bullet had hit Beryl because both of them had fired several shots. And both of them had had murder in their hearts or they wouldn't have fired in the first place. With all the bullets flying around, only the grace of God kept more of them from finding a target. God truly was in control, just as the preacher always said.

Until Marybeth sat beside Mrs. Foster's bed to tell her about the robbery, she'd managed to hold on to her emotions. After the amazing people of Esperanza had come together to imprison the two crooks, Nolan had asked Marybeth to visit Anna and explain why he would be late coming home for supper. Anna had taken the news with remarkable stoicism for a twelve-year-old. It was the Meanses' housekeeper who'd struggled to maintain her composure. Marybeth had felt the need to sit with both of them until the older lady calmed down. Once they'd received word Beryl would survive, she'd made her way home along the snow-covered streets.

Now in the presence of her landlady, she felt her own self-control slipping. After relating the afternoon's events as gently as she could, she laid her head on her friend's lap and let the tears flow. Mrs. Foster caressed her hair and murmured comforting words. Soon a soft rumbling in Marybeth's ear alerted her to her duty. She sat up and dried her damp cheeks.

"Well, now that that's all done, I'll go fix us some supper." She forced a brightness she didn't feel into her tone. "We have some of last night's shepherd's pie left over. Does that sound good?"

"It sounds very fine indeed." Sympathy and understanding shone from Mrs. Foster's eyes. "And if you want to talk some more, I would be happy to listen."

Their supper warmed, Marybeth brought it to the bedside so they could eat together. Mrs. Foster consumed a few bites before putting down her fork and regarding Marybeth with a searching gaze.

"My dear girl, when are you going to marry Rand Northam?"

Marybeth gulped down her bite and took another. At last she put aside her tray. "Rand no longer wants to marry me."

"What nonsense." Mrs. Foster barked out a harsh

cough, but the deathly rattle no longer reverberated through her chest. "I've seen that boy's eyes when he looks at you. He loves you. And when a Northam falls in love, it's forever."

Marybeth shook her head. "After he realized I came out here with no intention of marrying him, I think he decided I didn't deserve his love. He's been ignoring me these past few days, and I don't blame him."

"He may be trying to guard his heart. That's understandable. But if you ask for his forgiveness, I have no doubt he'll give it."

Hope flickered briefly inside her but then died. Even before they'd all discovered Beryl had been shot, Rand hadn't tried to comfort her after her ordeal. He'd left her to Nolan, which had cut her deeply, not to mention how much it complicated matters. By accepting Nolan's calming embrace, she may have given both men the wrong impression about where her affections lay. But how could a person control an emotional reaction in the aftermath of chaos?

She would do as Mrs. Foster suggested. She'd go to Rand and ask forgiveness. Yet even if he gave it, even if he proposed to her, she simply could not marry him until she learned what had happened to Jimmy. Too much of her life, too much of her heart, had been invested in finding her brother. She couldn't give up until she looked on his face…or his grave.

On Tuesday, after the six men in the posse had packed warm clothes and provisions for a trip of uncertain length, Rand fetched the outlaws' horses from the livery stable, paying their bill with money from Hardison's pocket. Nolan, ever the gentleman, informed

Hardison that his deposit would be safe in the bank until he needed it. Charlie Williams suggested they should make sure it wasn't stolen before giving it back to the outlaw.

In high spirits, and ignoring the complaints of their wounded prisoners, the group rode out of Esperanza, some hoping, others praying, they would be back by the end of the day, or at least by Wednesday. Although the snow had stopped and the sun had steamed off a goodly portion of it, a surly bank of dark clouds hovered above the mountains at the north end of the Valley. None of the men wanted to be stuck in another town due to the snow because it might be weeks before they could return home.

Heading west on the rolling trail, they were slowed by deep drifts the sun couldn't reach, so it was late afternoon before they arrived in Del Norte. They found Sheriff Hobart in a sad state, coughing and wheezing and unable to lift his head off the pillow on the cot beside his desk. Fortunately he had no prisoners at the time.

"My deputy quit last week," he said when he could catch his breath. "A couple of you men will have to stay and keep watch over these scalawags until the judge comes."

Rand groaned inwardly but straightened his shoulders. "This is my responsibility. I'll stay." He couldn't wait to see the last of Dathan Hardison, but wait he must. "Sheriff, you'd best go home so your wife can take care of you." He didn't like the old man's gray pallor and prayed he could whip this sickness.

Between coughs, the sheriff wheezed out, "I need to deputize some of you men first."

They'd decided Frank Stone and Andy Ransom, both unmarried cowboys, would stay to help Rand. The sheriff managed to say all the right words, receive their pledges to uphold the law, and pass out three silver badges before collapsing back on his cot.

While Rand and two others kept an eye on the prisoners, now locked safely behind the iron bars of the jail cells, the other three men helped Hobart get home. When they returned, they brought a fresh loaf of bread and a steaming kettle of stew to go along with the ever-present coffeepot on the jailhouse's potbellied stove.

On Wednesday, those who were leaving got an early start in hope of beating the storm now moving south across the Valley. As the day darkened and snow began to fall, Rand's spirits sank. His family would be all right. Beryl was on her way to recovery. But in all the chaos, he and Tolley hadn't managed to sign the papers to pay off Mrs. Foster's house. Worse still, in his absence, Nolan could court Marybeth all he wanted to.

Rand hadn't had much chance to think about his decision not to court her anymore, but here in this desolate jailhouse over the next few days he began to think he'd made a mistake. In front of him was a stack of Wanted posters bearing the faces of men who'd made the wrong choices in life, just like Dathan Hardison and Cole Lyndon. Just like Deke Smith, whose simpleminded countenance belied his evil soul.

Rand didn't want to reach the end of his own life with any more regrets added to his grief over killing a man. As the days wore on, he realized he would always regret not trying to win Marybeth's heart. He'd be honest with her about the risk of being married to a man whom other gunslingers might want to outdraw and then let her decide whether or not to take that risk. For his part, he'd be downright foolish not to find out whether she would prefer him over Nolan.

Risk was a part of life. After the war Rand's parents had risked their future to come out to an untamed territory and start building a new life far from the safety of Boston's upper class into which they'd both been born. George and Mabel Eberly and Captain and Mrs. Foster had done the same. In Del Norte he saw many people risking everything, including their lives, as they set off for the mountains to look for silver and gold. In Rand's view, Marybeth was worth far more than any material wealth. And she'd risked everything to come West in search of her one remaining family member.

Love and admiration for her flooded his heart, his mind. How he wished he could go right now and find Jimmy O'Brien and bring him home to her for Christmas. Then maybe she would feel free to marry him. And, oh, how he wanted to marry her. But responsibility demanded that he stay to see this matter to an end. Even if Nolan won her heart in his absence.

In the meantime he regretted not having made arrangements with Mrs. Winsted to purchase some Christmas presents for the children of Esperanza. Before he could even send up a prayer that Nolan would change his mind and let the children attend the party, he noticed Andy Ransom seated across the jailhouse whittling on a piece of wood. As it took on the shape of a wooden soldier, Rand's burden eased. This was the Lord's answer even before he prayed. They would carve wooden toys, soldiers for the boys and tiny baby dolls for the girls. That would be just the thing to keep his mind off of Marybeth.

Who was he trying to convince? She would always be at the forefront of his thoughts. If she married Nolan in his absence, Rand would never be able to stay in the San Luis Valley.

For the rest of the week after the robbery, Marybeth didn't have to report to work until midmorning because Nolan shortened business hours due to the snowstorm. By Friday, the early December sunshine brightened the landscape and even gave a suggestion of warmth for most of the shorter daylight hours. Marybeth was grateful when Nolan dismissed her at three o'clock so she could purchase some provisions at Mrs. Winsted's general store on the way home.

As Nolan helped her put on her coat, his hands lingered on her forearms for a few seconds. "May I bring Anna for her usual piano lesson this afternoon?"

"Of course." She stepped away from him, trying not to give offense for the abrupt movement by picking up her hat and pinning it in place. While she doubted she'd ever have to use that long hatpin as a weapon again, it certainly had come in handy the previous Monday.

"After that, if you do not mind, may I speak with you?" He dipped his head in his shy way. "Since you've assured me Mrs. Foster is much better now, perhaps Anna can visit with her."

Marybeth secured her dark blue woolen scarf around her neck and then tugged on the matching mittens her landlady had knitted for her during her convalescence. As much as she wanted to deny Nolan's request, perhaps it was time to settle this matter. Even if the man she loved never spoke to her again, she certainly wouldn't play with the affections of her employer. "Yes, of course." Manners required her to add, "Perhaps you could stay for supper."

Mild alarm flitted across his pleasant face. "Well, um—"

Her confusion was brief, followed by amusement. He'd eaten a bite of her pie at the fund-raiser and probably shared Rand's concerns about the quality of her cooking. She would not correct him. "Of course, if you have other plans for the evening, I understand."

With the matter settled, she made quick work of her shopping and hurried home to prepare supper. Even if Nolan didn't wish to eat her cooking, Mrs. Foster always praised whatever she prepared.

Perhaps affected by the attempted robbery and the mortal danger her brother had faced, Anna had practiced diligently all week, as proved by her competent if not brilliant playing. She made her way through Brahms' "Lullaby" and Luther's "A Mighty Fortress is our God" with very few mistakes. Still, as she gathered her music at the end of the lesson, she whispered to Marybeth, "Did Grace Eberly really shoot the bank robber?" The wonder and admiration in her eyes revealed that her longing to be a cowgirl had not lessened.

Marybeth gave her a solemn nod. After all the details had been sorted out, Grace received the credit for taking Deke down, shattering one of his legs. The man would be fortunate if he ever walked normally again.

Marybeth didn't want to think about the damage she herself had done to Mr. Hardison. She shuddered at the memory of how her hatpin had dug deep into his upper arm and then raked downward after he'd knocked her to the floor. According to Charlie Williams, she'd managed to stab his upper arm in just the right spot to render the entire appendage useless. The thought had sickened her until several people commented that the now former gunslinger would never be able to draw a gun on anybody again. Although she cringed at the thought of hurting anyone so badly, perhaps the Lord had allowed it to stop the killer. After all, the Bible related the story of how a shepherd boy named David had killed the evil giant Goliath.

With Anna upstairs, Marybeth sat in the parlor sipping tea with Nolan, who seemed to forget why he'd lingered. He chatted about his gardener, who always managed to keep the hothouse warm enough so his flowers continued to bloom. "It is remarkable to have fresh flowers year-round in such a cold climate." He went on to describe additions he'd planned for his house and asked if she had any suggestions for improving his property. Then he thanked Marybeth for calming his housekeeper after the robbery. "Mrs. Browder could not say enough about how poised you are." He took a sip of tea and eyed her over his cup. "That is a very high compliment coming from an Englishwoman."

Marybeth could only smile and nod and wonder where this all was leading.

Nolan set down his cup and saucer and inched closer to her on the settee. "Marybeth, it cannot have escaped your notice how much I admire you. I fully understand that you came to Esperanza to marry Randall Northam, but it appears to me…and to others…that your plans have changed." His eyes glowed with fondness and he chewed his lower lip briefly. "If that is true, I hope you will not find this question inappropriate."

Marybeth's heart dropped. Surely he would not propose. Before she could stop him, he went on.

"As you may have heard, the Northam family usually holds a Christmas party for the community. In the absence of Colonel and Mrs. Northam, and with the Northam family's blessing, of course, I will be hosting a formal dinner and social at my house on Saturday evening, December 17. You may have already noticed Christmas Eve is the following Saturday, and I thought some people may want to stay home the night before Christmas. Hence my choice of that date. You are invited, of course. And in addition, would you do me a great favor and teach Anna about her duties as a hostess?"

So he didn't plan to propose. Marybeth withheld a sigh of relief. "Yes, of course." Rand's party was to be on Christmas Eve, so there would be no conflict. That was, if he returned from Del Norte in time. "I would be happy to help Anna and you with the party."

He seemed relieved, as well. Had he doubted she would help? "I plan to invite the leaders of our entire community." Now he took on his shy look. "I have not had the chance to tell you of my plans for the future, but perhaps you will find them interesting. It is clear to me that Esperanza requires more leadership, and at the party I will propose that we have an election right away. Further, I will put myself forward as a candidate for mayor."

She supposed every town needed a mayor, but why was he telling her of his ambitions?

"Of course, in that position, I will need a wife, a helpmeet, as the scriptures say, to stand by my side as a leader among the fair ladies of our town." He coughed softly. "I can think of no one but you who would fill that office to perfection."

For a moment she could only stare at him. Then an idea came to mind. "I'm honored, Mr. Means." She must step back from the familiarity of using his Christian name. "However, I believe you deserve a wife who has moved in higher social circles than I have. You should know that I come from very humble beginnings. My parents were poor immigrants and died in poverty." She would not reveal Da's drunkenness or gambling unless Nolan became persistent. Besides, Rand knew all of these things and had made it clear none of it mattered to him.

Nolan chuckled. "Poor beginnings do not mean anything in America. My father was also an immigrant. He simply managed to build a fortune where some could not." He leaned over and grasped Marybeth's hand. "Due to your finishing school training, you have all the grace and dignity of the most elegant society ladies I knew in New York. Any man of intelligence would be proud to have you by his side. Would you do me the honor of becoming my wife?"

There it was, the unwanted proposal. Yet in no part of this discussion had he spoken of love, for which she was glad. It made turning him down much easier. She pulled her hand free from his grasp.

"Mr. Means—"

"Nolan, please."

She sighed. "Nolan. I admire you, too, but that's not enough for me. I want...*need* to be in love with the man I marry."

"But that can come in time, as it did in my parents' marriage."

"It's too late." She injected as much firmness as she dared into her words. "I'm already in love with someone else." Now if she could only confess her feelings to the object of that love.

Nolan's shoulders slumped. "Yes. Of course. Randall Northam."

"Yes."

He chewed his lip again. "I hesitate to ask this, but will you still help Anna with our Christmas social?"

"Of course I will." How interesting, even comical, that he took her rejection so easily. Whom would he pursue now? One of the uncultured Eberly girls? Another comical thought.

The circuit-riding judge rode into Del Norte on December 14. Within two days he pulled a drunken lawyer away from his gambling over at the saloon, summoned a jury of upright citizens—all of whom remembered Cole Lyndon—conducted a trial and received the verdict. Dathan Hardison and Deke Smith were found guilty of attempted robbery and attempted murder. As soon as the north pass cleared in the spring, they would be escorted to the prison in Canon City, where they would spend the next thirty years. In the meantime, Frank and Andy agreed to stay on as deputies so Rand could return home.

As he carefully packed the carved toys and his few belongings into his saddlebags, Hardison taunted him from his cell. "I'll get out, Northam, and when I do, I'll be gunning for you. You just keep looking over your shoulder. And I've got plans for that little gal of yours, too. She owes me for what she did to my arm."

Eyeing the limp appendage hanging at the man's side, Rand considered several responses before deciding on the best one. He stepped closer to the cell and leveled a hard stare on Hardison. "Word is a lot of men die in prisons. Sickness. Murder. So-called accidents. You need to be planning what you're going to say to the Almighty when you leave this earth. Did you ever listen to a word Reverend Thomas preached while you were sitting there pretending to believe in Jesus Christ? I hope so. You need to be thinking about Him and what He did for you."

Hardison's curses followed Rand out the door, along with poor, stupid Deke's cackling laugh. These past few weeks had reminded him of the kind of men he used to gamble with, and he couldn't get away from these two fast enough.

The weather smiled on his travels on Saturday, December 17, and he arrived in Esperanza just after the sun ducked behind the San Juan Mountains. He rode directly to Mrs. Foster's house, determined not to let another day pass without proposing to Marybeth or at least getting her permission to court her. To his disappointment, no one was home, so he rode over to Main Street. With Esperanza having no night life, only a few people walked the streets. Lucy was just emerging from Miss Pam's café. After she closed and locked the door and turned toward her home, he reined his horse in her direction.

"Hey, Rand." The usually talkative girl didn't seem too eager to chat, but continued on her way. No doubt she was still ashamed of throwing over a good man like Seamus and taking up with a scoundrel like Hardison.

"Hey, Lucy." He dismounted and fell into step with her. "Where is everybody? The town's even quieter than usual of an evening."

She shrugged. "Most of 'em are probably over at

the banker's mansion." Pulling her thin shawl tighter around her, she cast a wistful look in that direction, though the house was several blocks away and not visible from where they were. "He's having a party."

"Ah. Right. The Christmas party." Rand had forgotten this was the day Nolan had picked for the event. That's where Marybeth and Mrs. Foster were. His heart dropped into his stomach like a rock as he realized what this meant. Marybeth had chosen Nolan, and that was that.

Lucy seemed as depressed as Rand. He'd known her all her life and couldn't just ride away with her about to cry. "Why aren't you there?"

"Me?" She burst out with a bitter laugh. "Mr. Banker man only entertains Esperanza's *elite* citizens. He didn't even invite my ma, and she's as good as anybody in this town."

Not invite the town's best seamstress, a dedicated member of the church? What was the matter with Nolan? In the gray illumination of twilight, Rand could see tears glistening on Lucy's cheeks. He wanted to encourage her but had to be careful so she wouldn't misunderstand his intentions.

"Well, don't feel bad. As the preacher might say, we're all elite in the Lord's eyes. Scripture says when we belong to Him, we're chosen and accepted."

She gave him a soft smile not at all like her usual flirting ones. "Thanks, Rand. Good night." With a wave over her shoulder, she turned down her street.

Now his own words came back on him. Chosen and accepted. Maybe not by Marybeth, but by the Creator of the Universe, the Savior of whosoever believed in Him. Rand couldn't lightly dismiss the ache in his heart, yet he would seek the comfort of the One who offered the peace that passed understanding. He would also pray that Mother and Dad would come home soon so he could explain to them in person why he'd be leaving the San Luis Valley forever.

Out at the ranch, Nate welcomed him home and gave him the news that he and Tolley had taken care of paying off Mrs. Foster's home. Susanna added that Tolley had gone to Nolan's party tonight to represent the family. That was fine with Rand. His younger brother needed a healthy social life. Right after the shooting, right after seeing Beryl nearly die, he'd admitted to Rand that he'd lost his interest in gaining a reputation as a gunslinger. That had eased some of the guilt Rand still felt over killing Cole Lyndon.

"Say, I almost forgot." Nate shoved back from the kitchen table where they'd just finished supper. "You have a letter from Wagon Wheel Gap. I'll get it." He picked up a burning kerosene lamp and moved toward the door.

Pulse pounding in his ears, Rand followed his brother down the hallway to Dad's office. "Did you read it?"

Nate glowered at him briefly. "I don't read other people's mail." He shrugged. "Besides, if it's bad news, I knew I wouldn't be able to hide it from Susanna, and she wouldn't be able to keep it from Marybeth. With the baby due any day now, she's a bit emotional." He grinned, clearly not bothered by his wife's changing moods.

Rand grunted. "Right." He sat at Dad's desk and slit open the envelope, pulling out the folded page. At the first words, sorrow gripped him for Marybeth's sake.

Dear Mr. Northam,

Have located grave marker for one Jimmy O'Brien. Date of death, September 14, 1876. Wish I could give you better news.

Yours sincerely,
Archie Doolittle, Sheriff
Wagon Wheel Gap, Colorado

Rand handed the letter to Nate then folded his arms across the desk and rested his forehead on them. How could he tell Marybeth? How could he bear to see her heart break?

"Lord, have mercy. He's been dead for over five years." Nate gripped his shoulder. "What are you going to do?"

"I don't know." Rand raised his head and scrubbed his hands over his eyes. "I was looking forward to going to church tomorrow." In spite of his dread at the idea of seeing her with Nolan, he longed for the comfort of an hour of worship with fellow believers. "But how can I look her in the face? She'll know something's wrong right away. What do you think—?"

Urgent knocking on the door interrupted him. "Señor Nate, come quick. Señora Susanna, she needs you."

Nate bolted out the door, with Rand right behind him. In the kitchen Susanna leaned back in a chair, her hands pressed against her protruding belly.

"Nate, honey, it's time."

Nate knelt beside her. "Let's get you upstairs, darlin'." He shot an expectant look at Rand, his eyes asking the question he didn't voice.

"I'll go for Doc." Tired as Rand was, he would do anything for his sweet sister-in-law.

While Nate tended Susanna and Rita took care of little Lizzy, Rand retrieved his tan oilcloth duster from the closed-in back porch and then headed to the barn to saddle a fresh horse.

He had no doubt Doc and Maisie would be at Nolan's party. Would it be possible to get their attention without seeing Marybeth? If he did see her, what would he say? Just a week before Christmas, how could he destroy all of her hopes of ever reuniting with her brother? The best thing would be to completely avoid her, no matter how much he wanted to talk to her.

Chapter Fourteen

Marybeth guided Anna around the spacious drawing room to greet each guest, giving hints as to what the girl should say to each one from the ideas they'd rehearsed. As they moved away from their short chat with Doc and Maisie, Anna sighed…again.

"I know everybody here. I know what they did today and what they think of the weather. Why do I have to ask these silly questions?" The now-thirteen-year-old crossed her arms and huffed out a sigh.

"Because Nolan wants you to learn how to be a gracious hostess." Marybeth had worked hard to absorb the lessons at Fairfield Young Ladies' Academy. Teaching them to Anna reinforced them in her own mind. "You must practice so it's second nature. You can appreciate that, can't you? You never want to be caught not knowing what to do or say."

Another sigh. "I suppose not." Anna's face brightened. "There's Tolley Northam. What should I say to him?" She giggled. "Can I tell him how much I like the way those big green eyes of his light up when he wears that gray shirt?"

Just like Rand's. Marybeth stifled a smile. One day soon she'd be able to tell him she admired more than his eyes. "Only if you want to make him uncomfortable."

"That'll be half the fun." Anna took a step in Tolley's direction. "All the girls like to torment him just to see his face turn red."

Marybeth caught her arm as gently as she could. "Save that for another day and—"

A small commotion at the drawing-room door cut her short. "Come, Anna. It's your responsibility to learn what's going on so you can smooth over any unpleasantness."

They approached a cluster of people gathered around…Rand! Marybeth's heart leaped into her throat. He must have returned home in the past couple of hours, because Tolley had told her earlier his brother was still in Del Norte. She left Anna and shoved through the crowd, for the moment dispensing with the manners she'd worked so hard to learn. She did manage not to cast herself into his arms, but her whole body trembled with wanting to do just that.

"Is Doc here?" Rand appeared exhausted and a bit unkempt. Dark whiskers on his handsome face suggested he hadn't shaved for several days, yet he looked wonderful to Marybeth.

Doc and Maisie approached from the other direction, already donning their wraps.

"Is it Susanna?" Maisie pulled on her leather gloves while Doc retrieved his black bag from a nearby table.

"Yes." Rand's gaze lighted on Marybeth and he gave her a brief nod.

Her heart jumped again but then sank when he didn't offer a smile or other greeting. Maybe it was time to be a little more like Maisie and Anna. She stepped over to him.

"Hello, Rand. It's good to see you back."

Maisie and Doc swept past him, and he started to follow them. "Good night, folks."

"Rand—" She couldn't let him go without asking him to come see her. That was, if he still cared for her.

He turned back just as Nolan stepped up beside her and snaked his arm around her waist. "Good evening, Rand. We are glad to see you back. When it is convenient, Marybeth and I would like to hear all the news about Hardison."

Glaring at Nolan, Rand plopped his hat on his head. "Sure thing." He disappeared into the hallway. Seconds later the front door slammed.

Marybeth spun around to face Nolan. "Why did you do that?"

"My dear, you cannot blame me for trying to discourage the competition." He put on his shy face and for the first time she could see it was all an act. Further, his "my dear" sounded entirely too much like Dathan Hardison.

Mindful of several people watching, especially Anna, she smiled, leaned close to his ear and whispered in her sweetest tone. "But, *dear* sir, as I thought I'd made quite clear to you, there is no competition. There is no *we.* And since you refuse to hear me, I will be going home now."

His possessive smile drooped slightly. "May I at least have one dance before you leave? Please do not embarrass me in front of my company."

Every instinct shouted "no." Every lesson she'd

learned at Fairfield Academy insisted she must comply. "Very well."

Yet as they twirled around the drawing room to Mrs. Foster's slightly rusty Strauss waltz, Marybeth chanced to glance out the front window. There stood Rand in the light streaming through the glass, his hands shoved into the pockets of his long coat, his shoulders hunched, his eyes on her. Before she could lift a hand to hail him, he turned and strode away.

The wind slicing around the edges of Rand's oilcloth duster wasn't nearly as sharp as the pain in his heart. He spun away from the mansion and nailed shut the door of hope he'd briefly opened when he knew he'd see Marybeth this evening, after all. Maybe the Lord planned it this way so he'd finally get it through his head that she wasn't for him. With all of her fancy training back East, no wonder she preferred to marry a banker. He tried to console himself that a ranch wife should know how to cook, but his heart answered that he would eat anything she prepared and love it because it came from her hands.

Back home for the second time this evening, he set aside his troubles and kept Nate company in the ballroom, the farthest spot in the house from poor Susanna's cries. She was a brave little gal, but even a cow sometimes bawled when dropping a calf.

To keep Nate's mind off of his wife's suffering, Rand showed him the toys he'd brought home. "Frank and I carved the rough shapes, and Andy finished up the details. He's got a real talent."

"Those are really something." Nate turned a four-inch toy soldier over in his hands and then picked up one of the smaller doll babies. "I know Lizzy will love to have one of these. Maybe Susanna can sew little blankets for them when she's up and about." He gazed around the ballroom he'd built just over three years ago for their parents' twenty-fifth wedding anniversary. "You know, being in here makes me want to give the Christmas party, after all. We could do it next Saturday, this one just for the children. If all goes well…" He glanced up toward the other wing of the house as though trying to see Susanna through the ceiling and walls.

Rand patted his brother on the shoulder and sent up another prayer for the little mother and her coming baby. A party was a good idea. Maybe it would be just the thing to help him forget Marybeth. Mother always said doing for those less fortunate helped a person get over his own troubles. He'd speak to the preacher about the party after tomorrow's church service.

Around three in the morning Maisie came downstairs and invited them to come see the newest member of the Northam family, a healthy baby boy with a head full of the signature dark brown hair. Susanna was already sitting up, looking tired, happy and every bit as healthy as her son. Nate wiped away tears of relief and happiness before embracing the two of them.

A bit emotional himself, Rand let the happy event soothe away some of his sorrow over losing Marybeth. He fell into bed for a long, deep sleep, only to wake up around noon on Sunday and realize he'd missed church. He offered an apology to the Lord, but he figured the Almighty had mercifully let him sleep so he wouldn't have to see Marybeth sitting with Nolan. After all, a man could only take so much heartbreak.

* * *

Worn out from the previous night, Mrs. Foster stayed home from church to recuperate. Although several other ladies could have taken her place at the organ, they'd all urged Marybeth to play the hymns. They didn't have to ask twice. Now she wouldn't have to sit with Nolan, nor would she have to explain to Anna why she wouldn't be sitting with them anymore. She would, however, smile at Rand to let him know she would welcome a chance to talk with him. If he didn't approach her after the service, she would chase him down before he could mount his horse and ride away.

To her disappointment Tolley was the only member of the Northam family present at church. During announcement time, he revealed the good news of Nathaniel Junior's birth. He also said that since the church addition wasn't quite finished, his family would be holding a Christmas party for the children of the community the next Saturday, Christmas Eve. Several ladies volunteered to bring food and help through the week, as well as with the event itself.

Marybeth loved the idea of the party. This would be the perfect opportunity to show Rand how well she could cook. If that didn't restore his interest in her, nothing would. The thought of failing to win him sobered her, yet she couldn't be entirely depressed about helping out. At least she'd get a chance to see Lizzy and the new baby.

After the service, the ladies gathered at the back of the church to decide when each would take a meal out to Four Stones since Rita would be too busy helping Susanna with the children to do all the cooking. Marybeth volunteered to go on Saturday. That would give her time to plan and prepare her best recipes. It would also give her time to come up with Christmas gifts for the Northam family. She knew exactly what she would give to Rand.

On Friday afternoon Seamus and most of the cowhands returned home from Denver, all of them better off after their extended stay at the camp meeting. Seamus's faith in the Lord had already been as solid as the Rock it was founded upon. Now his entire countenance, bearded though it was, glowed with an inner peace and joy. Some of the other hands had seen the Light and been converted. Of the fifteen drovers who'd taken the herd north, only three decided the seedy section of Denver was more to their liking than being preached to. Sorry to hear about the reprobates, Rand and Nate agreed the three had never been happy in a town with no saloon and no liquor.

After the men cleaned up from their travels, the trail cook fed them supper in the bunkhouse, during which Rand told them all about Hardison's attempted bank robbery. Later Rand took Seamus to the ballroom to show him the decorations for the next night's party.

"If you're not too worn out, maybe you could help me finish trimming the tree in the morning."

"I'm your man." Seamus plopped down on a sturdy settee and laid his head back against the antimacassar protecting the green velvet upholstery from just such actions. In his absence he'd let that beard grow out, the long, bright red whiskers contrasting sharply with his shoulder-length dark auburn hair. "I don't suppose you've seen Lucy while I've been gone."

Rand sat in a nearby chair, pleased for a chance to

finally talk with his friend. "I saw her last Saturday. She looked pretty miserable." He explained about the party at the Meanses' house.

"It's a shame he treats folks that way." Seamus got a faraway look in his eyes. "Y'know, Rand, a while ago when you told us about what happened with that scoundrel she took up with, instead of being angry, I felt sorry for her. I believe with all my soul the Lord's forgiven us for that shooting over in Del Norte. He's forgiven me for a whole lot more I've never told you about. I'd be a hypocrite if I didn't forgive her for misjudging Hardison. From what you said, I guess he put on a pretty good show that could turn any girl's head. What would you say if I rode into town tomorrow and invited her to the party?"

Rand thought for a moment as more of his own guilt sloughed away. "I'd say you're right about forgiving others as we've been forgiven. Go ahead and invite her."

"Now, tell me about your little gal. You never did tell me her name." Seamus seemed to have lost some of his Irish brogue, but the accent had always come and gone depending on the situation. Tonight he sounded more like a regular cowboy, probably from hanging around with the other men for so long. "When are you two getting hitched?"

Rand blew out a long sigh. "She's not my girl anymore. She took that job at the bank and Nolan Means started courting her. While I was in Del Norte guarding Hardison, he won her over." And just as Seamus forgave Lucy, he needed to forgive her for breaking his heart.

Seamus sat up and reached over to grip Rand's shoulder. "I'm sorry to hear that."

"Thanks." Annoyance cut into his self-pity. "Let's

talk about something else. Can we count on you to stick around and work for us another year, or do you plan to become a circuit-riding preacher?"

Seamus chuckled. "Nope. No preaching for me. But during the camp meeting, the Lord convicted me about some things I've done. I have some business to attend to back in Boston before I make any promises here."

"Boston? I thought you were from Philadelphia."

Seamus hung his head. "I guess I should come clean about a few things in my past."

"You don't need to do that." Rand gave his friend's arm a little shove. "It's all forgiven, remember?"

"Yes, but I still need to reconcile with my family, at least Mam and my sister, Marybeth. Even my da, if he's still alive…and sober."

Rand nearly passed out on the wave of shivers running through him. "Jimmy O'Brien."

Seamus jumped to his feet. "How did you know my real name?"

Rand could only stare at his friend, unable to speak. Now he didn't have to tell Marybeth her brother was dead. It might be too late to win her heart, but at least he could give her the Christmas present he'd so desperately wanted to.

After making certain Mrs. Foster was as well as she claimed, Marybeth slid her perfectly baked apple pie from the oven and placed it in a towel-lined basket. The cast-iron pot full of Irish stew sat in a wooden crate by the front door beside one sturdy leather case and a canvas bag full of presents, all ready to be carried out when Doc and Maisie came to fetch her.

Excitement and nervousness vied for control of her

emotions, with excitement winning the moment the Henshaws arrived in the late afternoon. In the backseat of their surrey sat the three young daughters of the Chinese couple who operated the laundry at the edge of Esperanza. The girls' coal-black eyes were round with wonder, as though they thought perhaps a mistake had been made in their inclusion in today's festivities. Having grown up Irish in Boston, Marybeth knew all too well about such doubts. She gave the girls a warm smile as she climbed into the back and took a seat beside them. Soon they were on their way south toward Four Stones Ranch, singing Christmas carols as they went.

Several other wagons traveled in the same direction. Mrs. Winsted drove her supply wagon filled with children and young people who joined in the singing once they were in earshot. Among the passengers, Marybeth saw Lucy, whose contrite demeanor for the past month had gone a long way to restoring her reputation. Marybeth decided she would make friends with the girl this very evening. After all, they'd both been taken in by Mr. Hardison's charming ways. Marybeth had just seen through his façade.

The singing made the trip seem faster and soon the buggies and wagons turned down Four Stones Lane. At the house Marybeth helped unload the smaller children. With many hands available to take the food and presents inside, she carried only one item in her hands, the leather case holding the gift she'd bought for Rand at Mrs. Winsted's general store.

The presents had cost all of her savings, yet she'd enjoyed buying them. Over the past few days an abiding sense of peace had overcome her in regard to Jimmy. Winning Rand's love was more important to her now, especially since her brother might not still be in Wagon Wheel Gap or even Colorado. Besides, as long as Nolan didn't dismiss her for refusing his courtship, she could save more money for the trip. If he did discharge her, the Lord would show her what to do next.

Now, looking up at the lovely two-story house where Rand had grown up, she could no longer doubt this was where she was supposed to be. Love for her cowboy welled up inside her as she climbed the steps onto the wide front porch. But would he even want to see her after Nolan's possessive behavior last Saturday? Maybe not, because it was Nate and Tolley who welcomed the guests at the front door and sent them through the parlor to the ballroom. Rand wasn't there, either. Disappointed, Marybeth set the round leather case near the Christmas tree.

Across the room Susanna sat in an overstuffed brocade chair holding her new son. Marybeth joined the other ladies cooing over the beautiful baby boy. What a fine head of dark hair he had, just like his da. Just like his uncle Rand. Amidst the hubbub, she couldn't help but wonder how she would react when she saw him. More important, how would he react when he saw her?

"Now, you don't want to give her apoplexy." Rand had been worried since last night trying to figure out the best way to reunite Seamus and Marybeth. "Maybe you should stay here until I can talk with her and slowly introduce the idea that we may have found you."

Seamus, usually a calm man, paced the dining-room floor, stopping from time to time to grab a bite of beef or chicken or a cookie from the food-laden table. "This morning I had a hard time not telling Lucy about all of this. A harder time not riding over to Mrs. Foster's to find Marybeth. But I didn't want to spoil your surprise." He chuckled and his hazel eyes shone brightly in the light from the crystal chandelier hanging in the center of the ceiling. "I sure hope the girls will be friends 'cause they're gonna be sisters." He stroked his long red beard thoughtfully.

Rand's emotions slowed considerably at the thought of his friend's upcoming marriage. Just this morning, Seamus and Lucy had mended their fences. He had no such chance with Marybeth. He tried without success to summon up some of the joy he'd felt over being able to reunite her with her brother. Yet all he could think about was watching her dance with Nolan last week.

"Well, go on." Seamus gave him a little shove. "See if she's in that last group of folks who just came in."

Rand's knees shook as he approached the ballroom. There across the wide space Marybeth knelt beside Susanna, her face filled with sweet admiration for Junior. It sure would be nice to have her look at him that way. He squashed the dream. It would never happen.

He stepped down into the room just as she turned his way. To his surprise, that sweet smile broadened and she hurried through the crowd to meet him.

"Hello, Rand." She sounded a bit breathless, exactly the way he felt. Her hazel eyes twinkled brightly. Why hadn't he ever noticed how they resembled Seamus's?

"Hello, Marybeth." His pulse pounded in his ears. She seemed mighty glad to see him. That could only be good. Did he dare to revive his dreams about her?

"Before you say anything, I have something for you." She grabbed his hand and tugged him toward the Christmas tree. Lifting up a leather case with a red bow on it, she shoved it into his hands. "This is a concertina. I can teach you how to play it, and I'll play piano. We can sing together like we did that first Saturday after I arrived. That is, if you want to."

As he took the shiny new music box from its case and examined it, understanding swept through him. This was her way of saying she wasn't engaged to Nolan. That the two of them had a chance. "A concertina? Wow." How had she known he'd always wanted to play one but just hadn't had the time to learn? "These are pretty expensive." Maybe as much as ten dollars with the leather case, a lot for a young lady of limited means to spend.

She shrugged. "I had some money saved up."

"Sure. For your trip to Wagon Wheel Gap." Yet she'd spent it on him. That made the gift all the more priceless.

Again she shrugged. "I'll save some more while we wait for spring."

Stunned, Rand could only gaze at her for several moments. She'd postponed her most precious dream so she could give him a present. Nothing in the world could proclaim her feelings for him any better than that. Now he must give that precious dream back to her. He carefully put the concertina in its case and set it back under the tree. "What would you say if I told you there's no need to go up there?"

Her happy expression dimmed a little. "I have to go, Rand, just to find out for myself whether Jimmy's up there." She put a hand on his arm. "You can understand, can't you?"

"I can." He couldn't keep his news any longer. "I've found your brother."

Just as he'd feared, she swayed toward him, her face pale. He caught her before she went down and steadied her.

"Don't worry, darlin'. He's alive and well." Rand chuckled nervously. By now everyone in the room was watching them. "'Scuse us, folks." He put an arm around Marybeth's waist and propelled her out to the parlor through the front hallway and into the dining room. "Marybeth, this is Seamus O'Reilly, once known as Jimmy O'Brien."

She stared in disbelief. "But—"

"Mary, me sister dear." Seamus put on his brogue and held out his arms. "Come give your brother a welcome kiss."

"It is you! It is! Oh, Jimmy!" She dashed across the room and threw herself at him, bursting into choking sobs. Seamus shed a few happy tears, too.

As much as he wanted to comfort her, Rand stood back and let them have their reunion. Grateful she'd never have to see the sheriff's letter about the grave bearing her brother's name, he would let Seamus tell her what he'd been up to all these years.

"So after those miners put a price on my head, I gave all my poker winnings to the undertaker to help me fake me own death. We even put up a wooden grave marker. After that, I hightailed it out of town, took the name Seamus O'Reilly and became a cowboy." Jimmy gave Marybeth a rueful grin, his eyes filled with shame. "You'd think after watching Da gamble away all of his money, I'd have better sense. But it took that shoot-out in Del Norte to complete the job."

Marybeth had just about cried out all of her tears, but

emotion still churned within her. "If only Mam could see you now. So tall and handsome. And with dark hair. I guess all the red sank down to that impressive beard."

He chuckled. "It's a good thing I changed over these past few years. None of the miners ever recognize me when we happen to cross paths. O'course, not many of 'em venture this far from the mining fields. They're all so wild to strike gold or silver, I suppose Jimmy O'Brien is long forgotten."

"But never forgotten by me. Never." Marybeth couldn't stop a fresh flood of tears. Finally regaining her self-control, she needed to settle one last thing in her mind. "Do you still have Mam's locket?"

"I do." Jimmy tugged at a silver chain around his neck and produced the beloved piece of jewelry. "It's been a great comfort to me over the years, making me think of Mam as it did, God rest her sweet soul." He blinked away a tear. The news of her death had devastated him. "You can have it now. Maybe it'll do the same for you." He managed to tangle the chain in his beard, but with her help, he undid the clasp and put the inch-and-a-half oval locket in her hands.

She turned it over and over, studying the finely etched floral design. She looked at Rand, sitting by so quietly, so patiently, through their long conversation. If she opened the locket and found the key to the treasure Mam had promised, how would it affect their relationship? Did she still wish to be wealthy and independent? To never have to marry or be under a husband's rule?

Somehow those dreams no longer mattered. Rand had proved himself to be far different from Da. Far different from every man she'd ever met. Her heart welled up with love for him and she had her answer. Randal

Northam was treasure enough for her. That was, if he would still have her.

She placed the locket back in Jimmy's hand. "Mam put it in your care. You keep it."

Jimmy blinked in surprise. "But don't you want to look inside? To see the wee picture of the four of us in happier times?"

"I do." Rand took the locket from him. "I want to see *wee* little Marybeth before she grew up to be so sassy." He unclasped the lock and folded out the two sides. There in a tiny framed picture sat Mam, Da, Jimmy and herself, just as they'd looked fresh off the boat from Ireland. "Aw, such a pretty baby." He sent her a teasing grin that made her heart jump. "You've grown up to look just like your beautiful mother. Or should I say your mam?"

"And here's the best part." Jimmy retrieved the trinket and revealed a second opening behind the picture. "Mam always said this was the key to a great treasure. After all I've been through, I know 'tis true." He placed the locket back in Marybeth's hands.

Inside the second frame, written in delicate script, were the words "What time I am afraid, I will trust in Thee. Psalm 56:3."

Wonderment filled Marybeth such as she'd never known. Now at last she understood what real treasure was. Not gold. Not independence. Not even Rand's love. But rather, faith in God, her heavenly Father. Mam had trusted in Him through all the miseries, all the beatings, all the fears. And these many years, Marybeth had been just like Da, gambling on obtaining material wealth to make her happy. Despite her belief in God, she hadn't fully trusted Him for her future. Yet He had been preparing the happiest of *earthly* treasures for her: Rand.

"Jimmy, I want you to have this." She gave the jewelry back to him. "When you find your true love, you can give it to her." She blinked. "Oh, dear. You're this Seamus person Rand's been telling me about, so *Lucy* is your—" It was one thing to be friendly to Lucy, but could she stand to see Mam's precious locket hanging around the girl's neck? Well, if her brother loved Lucy, she supposed she could, too.

"That, she is." Jimmy beamed and his eyes twinkled. "And I'd best be getting over to the ballroom so she and I can visit before this party's over." He stood and pulled Marybeth up into his arms, placing a kiss on top of her head. My, he'd grown so tall and strong, no longer the slight boy Da had so cruelly abused. "Rand, if I leave my sister to your care, will you behave yourself in a proper manner?"

"You can count on me." Rand rose and shuffled his feet in a charmingly shy way, so different from Nolan's deceitful attempts at the same.

Jimmy opened the dining-room door and the sounds of laughter and singing wafted in from the ballroom. He gave Marybeth a wink before leaving her alone with Rand.

"Marybeth, would you—?" Rand began.

"Rand, I wonder—"

They both stopped. For her part, Marybeth's entire being tingled with emotion and anticipation.

"You first." She must give him a chance to say the words his bright green eyes were already speaking.

"Ladies first." His grin sent her heart spinning. "I insist."

"Oh, all right. But just know I'm not going to be one of those mousy little wives who always gives way to her husband." That didn't come out right. Of course she would honor and obey her husband. So she added, "At least not without some discussion."

"Well, now, Miss Sassy, exactly whose wife are you planning to be?" He stood tall, crossed his arms and gave her a long look, as though trying to appear severe. He didn't succeed.

Subduing the giggle trying to escape her, she ambled over to the side table where the desserts were laid out. "I thought maybe yours. But you have to pass a test."

His puckered his lips as though smothering a grin. "And that is?"

She took a small plate from the provided stack and dug a triangular server into her apple pie. "You have to prove your love for me by eating an entire slice of the pie I baked."

His smothered smile became a grimace, which he tried to hide with a cough. "Sure thing, darlin'." He slowly, reluctantly, closed the space between them and accepted the offered plate. With a sigh and an apologetic shrug, he took a bite she could only call dainty. His eyebrows arched. His eyes widened. He blinked.

"My, my. This is the most delicious apple pie I've ever eaten, bar none." He ate another, larger bite. When he'd practically gulped down the entire piece, understanding spread across his handsome face. "Back at Harvest Home, you knew exactly what you were doing, didn't you?"

"Sure did." She sampled the pie. Should have put in a bit more cinnamon, but this wasn't at all bad. "Just wait until you taste my Irish stew."

"I hope I don't have to wait much longer." Rand set down his plate and grabbed her around the waist. He lifted her from the floor and spun her around. She squealed with delight, throwing her arms around his neck and wishing he'd never let go. When at last he set her down, he cupped her face in his hands. "Miss Marybeth O'Brien, may I kiss you?" His husky voice overflowed with emotion.

Joy bubbled up inside her, making it just as hard for her to speak. "Mr. Randall Northam, I do wish you would."

"But I mean may I really, truly, kiss you?"

Now she understood. Not a brotherly peck on the cheek. Not a sweet kiss on her forehead. But a kiss smack on her lips promising her all the good things to come. "Oh, yes, Rand, me love, you may."

And so he did.

Chapter Fifteen

After Christmas the men of Esperanza took advantage of every sunny day to complete the church addition. With winter slowing down many ranch duties, Rand had time to supervise the building project, which would benefit the entire community. As nice as it was to have the ballroom at the Northam house, folks in town needed a place to gather so they didn't have to travel so far for special events.

Rand enjoyed working with his hands. Seeing the structure take shape gave him a sense of satisfaction as nothing else he'd ever done. Every board he sawed, every nail he hammered, meant the church would soon have rooms for Sunday school. And none too soon.

At the Christmas Eve party, Nate had read the Christmas story from the Bible. With Susanna seated nearby, baby Nathaniel in her lap, Lizzy standing beside them, Nate had then talked about how special every baby was. Yet as much as he loved his son and daughter, he reminded everyone that the most special baby ever born was baby Jesus, the Son of God, because He had come to save His people from their sins. The children listened quietly, their eyes full of wonder, partly because Nate had a gift for storytelling, partly because some of the children were hearing the story for the first time.

Yep, they sure did need Sunday school, and Nate would make a very good teacher. Funny how a man who could make his drovers quake in their boots could speak so gently to the little ones, yet still capture their attention, just like Dad.

Rand would gladly take on the job of teaching the older boys. He'd make sure they knew all about his careless attitude toward life at their age and how it had caused him nothing but grief. Maybe he could keep them from following in his footsteps. As always, that thought reminded Rand of Tolley and his turnaround after the shooting. It was the one good thing to come out of the bank robbery.

As the days passed, Rand's former feelings of failure and inadequacy faded away. Like Tolley, instead of admiring him for killing a dangerous outlaw, his neighbors now followed his leadership in building the church addition. He didn't ever expect to completely be free of the guilt over killing Cole Lyndon, but he'd come to a place of peace with the Lord about it. It was time to move on and take his place in the community, with his beloved Marybeth at his side.

So Rand set a fast but careful pace for the men, urging them to give as much time as possible to the completion of the addition. For his part, he was there every day. It didn't hurt that the first social event to take place after the building's dedication would be his own wedding reception.

On a Saturday in late January 1882, Marybeth and Lucy stood in the cloakroom at the back of the sanctuary, both dressed in white. Lucy wore Susanna's three-year-old wedding dress, let down a few inches to accommodate her greater height. Marybeth wore the satin gown her future mother-in-law had bought for her last spring in Boston.

Although Marybeth would have been pleased to have Colonel and Mrs. Northam at the wedding, she couldn't wait for spring to become Mrs. Randall Northam. All fences had been mended, including her relationship with Lucy. Even Nolan wished her well and admitted his affection for her was no match for Rand's obvious devotion. He proved the truth of his sentiments by providing white roses from his hothouse for the bridal bouquets.

Attending Marybeth and Lucy were Laurie and Beryl Eberly, each dressed in a new blue gown made by Lucy's mother. Beryl had survived the gunshot wound, and her color, while still a bit pale, promised full recovery.

Also recovered was Mrs. Foster, who now played Richard Wagner's "Bridal Chorus," signaling the time had come for the brides to make their grand entrance. Nate offered an arm to each girl, and they proceeded down the aisle toward Rand and Seamus. Tolley stood up with his brother, and Wes, another longtime Northam cowhand, stood beside Seamus. Marybeth thought her red-bearded brother presented a very fine picture, but surely no groom had ever been as handsome as clean-shaven Rand in his new black frock coat, white shirt and black string tie.

Her heart overflowing with love and joy, tears clouding her vision, Marybeth traded a look with her soon-to-be sister. Lucy's blue eyes shone bright in the morning sunlight streaming through the east windows.

Did any bride ever remember saying her actual wedding vows? Before Marybeth knew it, Reverend Thomas had pronounced the two couples men and wives, and Rand was kissing her right in front of the whole congregation. Everyone burst into applause, something she'd never witnessed in her more formal Boston church. Her Fairfield Young Ladies' Academy training notwithstanding, she much preferred the relaxed and homey feel of Esperanza Community Church. Here no one looked down on her for being Irish.

The reception hall in the new church addition was festooned with evergreen garlands. Two tables laden with presents, each with a three-tiered cake baked by Miss Pam in the center, awaited the bridal couples. In the corner, a trellised arbor decorated with white silk roses provided the perfect spot for wedding pictures.

Lucy and Seamus posed first for the traveling photographer, whose large black camera served as a source of great interest to the children. The young man promised to take a picture of them all together if they would just stand safely away while he worked. He ducked under the black cloth and held up the lighting pan. As the magnesium powder flashed, the children shrieked with delight. Next, Rand took his seat beneath the arbor, and Marybeth stood just behind him, her lace-gloved hand on his shoulder. Again the powder flashed and again the children shrieked. Marybeth had to blink several times to clear her vision.

By late afternoon the reception dinner had been served by the ladies of the church, the presents opened and the cakes cut and eaten. Now Marybeth longed to be alone with her beloved. Standing behind the table that held their gifts, she stood on tiptoes to whisper in his ear. "Can we slip away without anyone seeing us?"

He cast a furtive glance around the room. "I did hear mention of a shivaree, but that would be later on this evening." He chuckled. "Funny how I was annoyed with Nate for skipping out after his wedding so we couldn't do the honors for him and Susanna. Now I'm hoping we can escape it." He tugged her to his side and gazed down at her, love shining in his eyes. "You ready to go?"

"Oh, yes. More than ready." She noticed a few ranch hands huddled together in another corner and occasionally glancing her way. Nothing terrified her more than the idea of being carried away from Rand now or ever. "How are we going to get away without being noticed?"

"Slip out into the hallway and hide in the second room on the right. I'll enlist Tolley's help. He owes me." He placed a quick kiss beneath her ear that sent delightful shivers down her neck.

In the Sunday school room, she found her woolen shawl among the other coats and wraps and flung it around her shoulders. She waited by the window until Rand came around with his horse. Why hadn't he brought a buggy? He knew she'd never ridden. Yet once he helped her out through the window, placed her in the saddle and then swung up behind her, she felt safe and secure in his arms. Circling around the church, they rode south of town. The sun was near setting by the time they passed Four Stones Lane and continued south.

"Where are we going?" Marybeth called over her shoulder.

"Nate and Susanna said we could stay at their house until Mother and Dad return. After that, they'll move back in. I plan to start building our own place right away."

With its columned front porch and numerous windows, the pretty one-story white house looked homey and inviting. Rand shoved open the front door and carried her inside. He set her down in the center of the charming little parlor, lit a kerosene lamp and started a fire in the stone fireplace.

"Susanna promised to send over some provisions from the big house." He led Marybeth to the well-stocked kitchen. "Looks like we could hole up here for weeks without anybody knowing where we are." He checked the cast-iron cookstove. "Needs wood, but there's a pile by the back door."

Lamp held high, he showed her the rest of the house, including three bedrooms. Baby Nathaniel's nursery was equipped with brand-new mahogany furniture Nate had bought in Denver after the cattle drive. Lizzy's room had dainty feminine furnishings. Marybeth could hardly wait to decorate such rooms for her own little ones.

Next, Rand took her to the master bedroom, a spacious and well-appointed chamber. He set the lamp on an oak chest of drawers, from where it cast a warm light on the bright quilt covering the four-poster. Heat rushed to Marybeth's cheeks as she considered the implication of standing in this room with her new husband.

"Now that you've had the tour, did you get any ideas for our house?" Rand tucked his thumbs through his belt loops and leaned back against the door jamb. "I'll build whatever you like."

"Well, right at the moment, I wasn't exactly thinking about our house." She gave him a saucy grin.

He blinked those big green eyes in mock astonishment. "Why, Mrs. Northam, are you thinking what I think you're thinking?"

"Why, I don't know, Mr. Northam." She giggled. "What do you think I'm thinking?"

Instead of answering he gathered her in his arms and leaned down to deliver another one of those heart-stopping kisses. She did her best to answer in kind.

Then he froze. "Do you hear that?"

"Rand, don't tease." She tried to capture his lips again.

"Wait. Shh. Listen."

Sure enough, discordant sounds reached her ears from afar, growing closer by the second.

"Oh, no."

"Quick. Put out the lamp. I'll douse the fire." He hurried away from her toward the parlor.

After turning down the lamp wick, she followed close on his heels through the darkened house. He raced from window to window, locking them and closing draperies. Outside the noise had grown to a loud cacophony of rattles, bangs, gunfire, whooping and who knew what else.

Marybeth grabbed her new husband's arm. "Oh, Rand, don't let them take me away from you. Please."

"Take you away?" Even in the dim room, she could see his tender expression. He pulled her into a secure embrace. "They won't do that, darlin'."

"They won't force their way in?"

He chuckled. "No. We don't do it that way around here. They'll just keep us awake all night. Unless they decide we're not here."

Relief swept through her and she leaned into his chest. "I hope they didn't see the smoke from the fireplace."

"Maybe they missed it in the dark."

From the noise still resounding through the walls, she was fairly sure they hadn't.

"Even so," he said, "they'll smell the smoke."

Marybeth chewed her lip for a moment. "Do you suppose if we feed them, they'll go away? I could make some soup."

"It's an idea."

She spied his concertina beside the settee. "And we could sing to them."

His broad shoulders slumped. "I've been too busy to practice."

Now she giggled. "With a little warm-up, I think my fingers will remember a couple of songs."

He laughed with her; a deep, throaty chuckle that tickled her insides. "Shall I invite them in?"

"Why not? I'll fix some coffee to warm them up and then start the soup."

Within a few minutes the Eberly sisters, the Northam brothers, the other newlyweds Seamus and Lucy, and numerous cowboys and townspeople had crowded into the parlor and kitchen. Lamps were lit, fires were stoked in the hearth and kitchen stove and soup bubbled in a cast-iron pot.

As the laughter and merriment swirled around her, Marybeth couldn't regret this interruption of her wedding night. After all, she was now a part of a wonderful community. All of these people accepted her, loved her. Like Rand's love for her, this was a treasure greater than any she'd ever dreamed about.

And she could live with that.

* * * * *

Dear Reader,

Thank you for choosing *Cowboy Seeks a Bride*, the second book in my Four Stones Ranch series. I hope you enjoyed the adventures of my heroine, Marybeth O'Brien, and my hero, Randall Northam. For many years I have wanted to write a series of stories set in the beautiful San Luis Valley of Colorado, and now I'm doing just that.

I moved to the Valley as a teenager, graduated from Alamosa High School and attended Adams State College. Later my husband and I settled in Monte Vista, where my parents owned and operated a photography business, Stanger Studios. Three of our children were born in Monte Vista, and one was born in Alamosa. Even though we moved to Florida in 1980, my heart remained attached to my former home in Colorado. Writing this book has been a sweet, nostalgic trip for me.

Those familiar with the history of this area of Colorado may recognize a little bit of Monte Vista in my fictional town, Esperanza. I could have used the real town, but then I would have shortchanged the true pioneers of Monte Vista, who deserve accolades for their courage and foresight in building such a fine community. In addition, I wanted the freedom of artistic license necessary to create an interesting story without offending the residents of my former home. Other than Pam and Charlie Williams, my dear friends who granted me permission to use their names for two of my fictional characters, any resemblance between my other characters and those who actually settled in this area is strictly coincidental.

If you enjoyed Marybeth and Rand's story, I hope you'll look for Book Three in my series. Rosamond Northam was raised on a Colorado ranch along with her three brothers, but three years in a Boston finishing school may have transformed this Wild West cowgirl. Has she changed enough to win the heart of a proper English aristocrat?

I love to hear from my readers, so if you have a comment, please contact me through my web site: http://blog.Louisemgouge.com.

Blessings,

Louise M. Gouge

Questions for Discussion

1. Marybeth's love for her brother is commendable, but why does she hesitate to be truthful with Rand? What is her deepest secret? Is she justified in keeping her secret from Rand? Would their relationship have grown or faltered if she had told him from the first about her fears and reservations about marriage?

2. Rand is filled with guilt over killing a man three years before, yet everyone else considers him a hero. How do you feel about that fatal shooting? Do you think he's a hero? What is your definition of a hero?

3. Despite being abused, Marybeth's mother left a strong legacy for her children. How was the locket a symbol of this legacy? In the end, Marybeth decides she doesn't want the treasure hidden in the locket. How does she feel once she knows what the actual treasure is?

4. Throughout the story, what does Rand do to show his understanding of Marybeth's need to find her brother? What does this reveal about his character? Even before Marybeth is reunited with her brother, she decides to spend the money she's saved on gifts for Rand and his family. What does this sacrifice say about her character?

5. The overarching theme of this story is forgiving oneself and others. How did Marybeth and Rand

work through their own issues? Could each one of them have taken an easier path to resolving their issues? How so?

Newly returned Duke Caldwell is the son of her family's enemy—and everyone knows a Caldwell can't be trusted. But when Duke is thrown from his horse, Rose Bell must put her misgivings aside to help care for the handsome rancher.

Read on for a sneak peek of
BIG SKY HOMECOMING
by Linda Ford

"You must find it hard to do this."

"Do what?" His voice settled her wandering mind.

"Coddle me."

"Am I doing that?" Her words came out soft and sweet, from a place within her she normally saved for family. "Seems to me all I'm doing is helping a neighbor in need."

"It's nice we can now be friendly neighbors."

This was not the time to point out that friendly neighbors did not open gates and let animals out.

Duke lowered his gaze, freeing her from its silent hold. He sipped the tea. "You're right. This is just what I needed. I'm feeling better already." He indicated he wanted to put the cup and saucer on the stool at his knees. "I haven't thanked you for rescuing me. Thank you." He smiled.

She noticed his eyes looked clearer. He was feeling better. The tea had been a good idea.

"You're welcome." She could barely pull away from his gaze. Why did he have this power over her? It had to be the brightness of those blue eyes…

What was she doing? She had to stop this. She resolved to not be trapped by his look.

Who was he? Truly? A manipulator who said the feud was over when it obviously wasn't? A hero who'd almost drowned rescuing someone weaker than him in every way?

He was a curious mixture of strength and vulnerability. Could he be both at the same time? What was she to believe?

Was he a feuding neighbor, the arrogant son of the rich rancher?

Or a kind, noble man?

She tried to dismiss the questions. What difference did it make to her? She had only come because he'd been injured and Ma had taught all the girls to never refuse to help a sick or injured person.

Apart from that, she was Rose Bell and he, Duke Caldwell. That was all she needed to know about him.

But her fierce admonitions did not stop the churning of her thoughts.

LIHEXP0115